W.P.B. BOTHA was b[...]
Afrikaner working class [...]
stepfather's employers – [...]
became the first member of his family to go to university. He left South
Africa in 1975 after graduating as a teacher, and has taught in Papua
New Guinea, the Transkei and Northern Ireland. His first novel, *The
Reluctant Playwright*, was published by Heinemann in 1993.

Crossroads School Library
500 DeBaliviere Ave
St Louis MO 63112

W.P.B. BOTHA

WANTOK
(ONE TALK)

Heinemann

Heinemann Educational Publishers
A Division of Heinemann Publishers (Oxford) Ltd
Halley Court, Jordan Hill, Oxford OX2 8EJ

Heinemann: A Division of Reed Publishing (USA) Inc.
361 Hanover Street, Portsmouth, NH 03801–3912, USA

Heinemann Educational Books (Nigeria) Ltd
PMB 5205, Ibadan

Heinemann Educational Boleswa
PO Box 10103, Village Post Office, Gaborone, Botswana

FLORENCE PRAGUE PARIS MADRID
ATHENS MELBOURNE JOHANNESBURG
AUCKLAND SINGAPORE TOKYO
CHICAGO SAO PAULO

© W.P.B. Botha 1995

First published by Heinemann Educational Publishers in 1995

The right of W.P.B. Botha to be identified as the author of this work
has been asserted by him in accordance with the Copyright, Designs and
Patents Act 1988.

British Library Cataloguing in Publication Data
A catalogue record for this book is available from the British Library.

AFRICAN WRITERS SERIES and CARIBBEAN WRITERS SERIES and
their accompanying logos are trademarks in the United States of America
of Heinemann: A Division of Reed Publishing (USA) Inc.

Edited by Victoria Ramsay
Cover design by Touchpaper
Cover illustration by Cathy Morely

Phototypeset by
Wilmaset Ltd, Birkenhead, Wirral
Printed and bound in Great Britain
by Cox & Wyman Ltd, Reading, Berkshire

The quotation from *Memories, Dreams, Reflections* is reproduced by permission of
Pantheon Books/HarperCollins Publishers

ISBN 0 435 909 69 X

95 96 97 98 99 8 7 6 5 4 3 2 1

For Laura

'When I look back upon it all today and consider what happened to me during the period of my work on the fantasies, it seems as though a message had come to me with overwhelming force. There were things in the images which concerned not only myself but others also. It was then that I ceased to belong to myself alone, ceased to have the right to do so. From then on my life belonged to the generality . . .

'I was never able to agree with Freud that the dream is a "façade" behind which its meaning lies hidden – a meaning already known but maliciously, so to speak, withheld from consciousness. To me dreams are a part of nature, which harbours no intention to deceive but expresses something as best it can. These forms of life too have no wish to deceive our eyes, but we may deceive ourselves because our eyes are short-sighted.'

C.G. Jung, *Memories, Dreams, Reflections*

PART ONE

1

A lion soaked in the blood of its kill – that's what he looks like, she thought, as he sauntered out on to the balcony – a heavily-gorged lion, with eyes glazed. That, or someone who's just been clubbed in the mouth.

Leaning over the rail, Richard Green sprayed the giant tree fern in front of the house with a mouthful of betel-juice. As the blood-red mucus spattered the leaves a cloud of miniature blue butterflies floated into the air, escaping the sticky threads that stretched and broke before plunging to the ground, staining the rich volcanic soil.

Brushing his lips on the sleeve of his shirt, he turned, dragged a chair over, so that he could continue to spit over the edge and settled into the rough wedges of uncovered foam. The harshness of his once broken nose was softened by the vague look in his eyes. It was a vagueness that prompted his partner, Rachel Tormey, to extract a handful of letters from her satchel and drop them into his lap.

'You did promise when we left England you'd keep in touch. You're all she's got, Richard.'

'*All she's* . . . ?' He tried to swallow but it was too late. A bubble of crimson betel-juice burst over his lips, spilling down his chin.

Handing him a pen and a blue airmail pad along with her handkerchief, Rachel returned to the book she'd been reading.

Richard stared at the empty pad, and then as even the shrill sawing of cicadas failed to break the uneasy silence between them he started to write . . .

> Dear Janice,
>
> Your letters, far from 'piling up outside the Elysian gate', appear to be getting through with remarkable ease, considering their tortuous route via London, Sydney, Fairfax and Biyufa, finally arriving under the plucky flag of Kumul Air who, once a fortnight, weather permitting, dispatch one of their single-

engine Cesnas over the cloud-capped mountains into the Keramuti.

The Ruatok are the highest mountains in Melanesia. Like muscles rippling through the earth's flesh, they soar up out of dense, tropical rainforest. Their sides are scarred with rockfalls and muddied landing strips from which the light aircraft, after depositing their cargo of government mail, food, medicines and spare generator parts, dart up into the sky like grasshoppers – not your average grasshopper, mind, but *grasop bilong Jesus* – the local pidgin managing to evoke a sense of the miraculous.

It's less than forty years since Malachy Davis first crossed the mountains into the Keramuti. He was the Australian war veteran who ran a vital listening post near Biyufa that enabled the Allies to monitor Japanese movements on the island. But he was driven out by the local villagers. Today the Malachy Davis Highway, linking the Keramuti with Biyufa and the coast, cuts a swathe through the forest, with its main opposition no longer coming from the villagers but from numerous anthropologists who liken the road to the needle of a clumsy back-street abortionist. A view not shared by the area's Chief Education Officer, Tony Meredith: 'Bugger the anthropods! Whadda they know? *Pikininis* crapping all over the place. Bout time some-a these concubines were sterilised.'

Already the 'concubines' have spawned a multitude of languages – a legacy of the wildness of the mountains, which has left them isolated and wary, each follow their own *pasin bilong ol tumbana*, or ancestral customs; preserving their own myths, legends, and of course, *ples tok*. It is this widespread use of *ples tok* which is seen by some to be the chief obstacle to island unity. However, the Education Minister's directive that pupils use English rather than pidgin or their native tongue while they are at school shows the government is determined its people should learn to *bung wun taim*.

Sadly, a shortage of English teachers means progress on this front has been rather slow. This is especially true of the Highlands, where few people from the coast are willing to venture, fearful that the locals, whom they refer to as *kanakas*, might suddenly leap out of the forest and attack them. Meredith's desperation, therefore, was all too plain when, upon hearing that Rachel and I were bound for the Keramuti, he enquired whether we 'fancied a go at some exotic chalk-bashing, tax-free salary, use of a Government Land Cruiser, also a week at the Flight Deck Hotel while you make up your minds.'

Needless to say it did not take long, although as Rachel pointed out, neither of us had had any experience. In addition, I'd already signed a contract with the Department of Industry and Agriculture to set up a regionally based co-operative – a job I have since managed to combine with teaching as classes finish by midday. This gives me plenty of time to visit the surrounding villages, to impress upon the people the importance of their investing in the co-operative. After all they will be investing in the long-term future of the region, thereby helping it to catch up with the rest of the island – already carving out a small but significant role for itself on the edge of the Pacific Basin.

In spite of Rachel's initial misgivings – as you know she had also hoped to start writing a book on that fellow, Jung – the experience has turned out to be hugely enjoyable. It's not been the slightest bit like . . . what is it seventeen years at Kingsleigh had led you to call it . . . 'a cattle drive'? It seems to me teaching is rather more like fishing – a matter of choosing the correct bait. In some places one may not need any bait at all. Indeed in the Keramuti the most important thing is to avoid being dragged overboard by the eagerness of one's catch. For there really is quite an extraordinary enthusiasm among the pupils for learning. Which is why as I stand on the balcony before school each morning watching them pour over their notes even as they perform their ablutions, I feel such an immense thrill of excitement; I can't wait to get started. It's an eagerness I won't allow to be choked off by the past, Janice. Not now that I'm beginning to find a new part of myself emerging, beginning to reach forward into the future. This is the future, my own brave new world if you like, here in the mountains, among the people of the Keramuti; here, where my life is no longer my own; my pulse regulated by the roar of the river, my breath a part of the enchanting mist . . .

Propably the result, I hear you laugh, of my chewing all that betel-nut! The truth is one has only to watch the steady progress of the women as they climb the steep mountain paths with large *bilums* of *kaukau* slung across their backs, to know that they too draw strength from the harmony which exists between themselves and their surroundings. How else could so arduous a procession assume such grace? In this respect the mountains, though we are surrounded by them, do not dominate. They are a part of us as we are a part of them. Just as a solitary truck rattling across the bridge below fails to intrude, so the chugging of the station generator is swallowed up by the babble of the river, itself interwoven with the chorusing of insects. Rain is preceded by heat, the heat by the freshness of the morning . . .

The only intruder, Janice, is . . . well, the mail, which is about to be unloaded from the plane that's just landed – a signal for Rachel to hurry down to the landing strip as the *grashop bilong Jesus* is engulfed by villagers, all jubilantly waving their bows.

I can see her plaited hair and white shoulders standing out against the dark green of the forest. Her stride is a little tense, but dignified. Her eyes, fixed on the path ahead, no doubt betray the self-consciousness of someone who knows she is being stared at. As she always is, even in class. The villagers, fascinated by her red hair, invariably gather to peer in through the windows.

It's true she sometimes feels a little put out by it all, but then it would seem churlish to complain. She is, after all, delighted to be helping. We both are. For we have both found a new purpose to our lives. If we have a complaint it's no more than that the Keramuti lacks that concept of time which we are used to. It doesn't inculcate the same sense of uniqueness or individuality among its people, with the result that we are beginning to adopt perspectives without perspectives; to find ourselves members of a community where individuals or individual experiences fail to dominate, so that we merge and flow, everything together, everything in one smooth . . .

Yes, perhaps it is the betel-nut talking. I'd better stop. My throat feels dry. I can see the clouds building up at the far end of the valley. Everything is still. Beyond the darkening mountains swells the past, threatening to break through. I must plug the dyke.

2

Their paper-white faces floated over the playing field, over the half-way line and goal line, over the makeshift boundaries they had drawn up with their burgundy striped blazers that blew this way and that in the wind, like corpses rolling in the surf.

He could discern no pattern in their play, detect no prospect of either victory or defeat. Wherever a ball emerged out of the deadening fog, they raced frenetically after it, managing to spill in all directions at once, regardless of rules, tactics or time; regardless of the shape of the ball, which varied, now oval, now round; often expanding in mid-flight, threatening to crush the lightweight figures below, who scampered away – and then themselves grew large and menacing as they stalked a solitary figure in front of a red-brick building rising out of the fog. Setting their teeth into his ankles he promptly slumped over like a wounded animal, silent and resigned, a signal for the packs of roving scavengers to join in, to share in their wild and savage feast.

Soon, however, they yawned and staggered back to their feet. Clambering on top of one another's shoulders, they were like clockwork toys gone beserk, as they hurled themselves into battle. The playing field was littered with makeshift swords, shields, and broken bodies until suddenly from among the carnage a muddied ball was recovered, causing the dead to rise up and give chase as its possessor punted it into the trees.

Struck by the reckless nature of their play, by its violent impetuosity, he noticed nevertheless that wherever they fled, wherever they performed their rousing dance of anarchy, the boundaries somehow contrived to follow them, hemming them in. Without their knowing it – or perhaps they knew but failed to care – he was able to continue tracking them across the wintery fields by following their blazers. Finally he ran them down behind the school pavilion where, oblivious to his presence or the threat it might have posed, they surrounded the embattled figures of Lewis Chamberlain and 'Chicken' Bell.

The boys' fists were raw. He noticed their flushed cheeks and sunken eyes. Like scorpions with their tails locked in mutual self-destruction, they rocked across the hard ground, egged on by the crowd whose own lust could scarcely be contained. Whilst the air resounded with the cracking of shells, with the seeping and spitting of flesh, the rapid rattle and exploding of knuckle, the onlookers braced themselves for the blows they willed, jeering at those that missed their mark.

He could feel the power of their blows in the jarring earth. He could see their eyes roll in the deep, dark sockets, gouged out of bone as white as clay. Above Chamberlain's, a cut burst open, spraying blood through the air, like corn scattered in the sunlight. Immediately those in front began proudly showing off the stains on their clothing.

Gradually, the ferocity of the blows began to subside. Lips paled. Throbbing veins shrank. The crowd's cheers gave way to snorts of laughter which in turn sank into embarrassed silence. Struggling to stay on their feet, the boys now appeared to evoke no more than a cursory interest. An idle fascination began to settle over their supporters who, as soon as a bell rang in the distance, straightened their ties and hurried away, as if washing their hands of the whole affair.

This did not prevent the two from feebly continuing to bounce blows off each other, though their arms were wooden, their knuckles split.

He was aware of their frightened glances seeking him out. Still he made no move towards them. He couldn't. He could see their anger, but couldn't feel their pain. It was as if the fog sweeping over the field was an anaesthetic, dulling his senses; his body, like theirs, floating in an unreachable cloud.

Without warning, 'Chicken' Bell's fist thudded against Lewis's temple prompting a third figure, slim and sallow with large bovine eyes, to step between them. Only to be dragged back by an invisible arm. His own!

Stragglers' mouths dropped open in amazement. A few began to protest, waving their blazers in the air so that the burgundy stripes exploded in a flower of impassioned hostility. With Bell's gaze momentarily diverted, Lewis jabbed his blond opponent in the face. Again the boy with bulging eyes tried to intervene. Again an invisible arm held him back. This time the stragglers fled in horror, a sea of burgundy retreating over the frozen fields . . . exposing vast sheets of ice beneath the fog. He tried to call them back, but the louder he shouted the thicker the ice became. Until at last he was alone. Listening to the groaning and packing of the ice, seeing, without feeling, the youths' blows raining down on him . . .

3

He was awakened by the sound of someone moving under the house. The building, taut as a spider's web on its tall stilts, sent out discreet vibrations that lured him to the edge of the balcony. Peering over the side, Richard felt the blood rush to his head and he let go of the handrail. Groping for the armrest, he sank back clumsily into his chair, his broad shoulders almost shattering the wooden frame. His muscles were tense, his body bracing itself for the blows raining down . . .

He opened his eyes, focusing on the letter he had written to Janice. Among the pages strewn at his feet lay a photograph of himself and Rachel, posing in front of the house. The iron roof and white pre-fab walls had been over-exposed. This gave the impression that the landing stairs were leading off into space; that the building, with its vacant door and window frames, was still under construction, its plumbing clearly visible beneath the floor. The shadow of a giant tree-fern spilled across his legs and into the background, blotting out the faces of the *pikininis* who had gathered to watch between the stilts.

It was not, he knew, the picture Rachel would have chosen. Or one that Janice would necessarily appreciate. Still he felt the glare and blundering shadow, far from ruining it, gave it character, helped to convey the mood of the valley, to capture its rawness and the rawness of its newest immigrants. Rachel looked lean and tall, resilient yet shy, gathering her plaits up into a bun. Her body was angled away from the camera, allowing the sun's rays to steal through a corner of her blouse, flushing out the golden hairs that were glowing like embers beneath her armpit, and the gentle swelling of her breasts.

She wore plastic sandals and a cotton *lap lap* knotted at the waist. He was pretending to undo the knot although his hands were already full, clutching the pig he'd caught scavenging below the landing. His shirt, entangled in the animal's feet, was slimy and torn.

It was this same rawness – he hadn't shaved and his teeth were stained with betel-juice – that made his agreeing to write the letter at all seem perverse. It reminded him of trying to sneak in through the Fenchurch Street foyer of Montgomery Clay & Partners after a late night, hiding his bloodshot eyes behind the pages of the *Financial Times*. Indeed it seemed to drag him even further back, to another age, another more distant life . . .

'*Jambo! Jambo! Jambo!*' Mwangi and all the other Kikuyu children on the farm would shout whenever he and Janice returned home from boarding school in Nairobi. '*Jambo! Jambo!*' singing and swaying, and pressing their dirt-cracked hands into theirs. '*Jambo! Jambo!*' Until one day Janice could stand their 'treachery' no longer, yellling, 'What a sham! An absolute sham. What a sham!' Her shrill voice drove a swarm of chaffinches out of the old fig tree under whose cool branches they had been sitting, sipping lemonade, while their mother broke the news to them of the raid on the Edwards' farm. The Edwards had been away in Mombasa at the time. In the course of the raid the Mau Mau, having murdered both the cook and nightwatchman, had proceeded to set fire to all the buildings, including even the children's tree-house which he, Janice and Mwangi had helped to build during the previous Christmas holidays.

Janice had flung her lemonade at the bewildered Mwangi, and after yelling, 'What a sham! An absolute sham. What a sham!' had demanded to be allowed to continue her schooling in England. Thus dragging him back with her since she was afraid that in her absence he might blurt out the truth – namely that her desire to flee Kenya had less to do with Kikuyu 'treachery' than with the revelation earlier that morning that her best friend, Margaret Harding, was about to leave Nairobi for a boarding school in Eastbourne.

Their parents had sold up and arrived back in England with still no end in sight to the state of emergency declared by the authorities in Kenya. By this time Janice had discovered an altogether different form of treachery: the treachery of being and yet not being fully English. Having failed to get into the school of her choice, she was disowned by her former friend and became a victim not so much of Uhuru as of classic English snobbery. She begged to be allowed to return to school in Nairobi. But by then it was too late.

To mollify her their parents gave her Prince Harry for her eleventh birthday, an old pony they'd bought cheaply from a riding school in the West Country. It was only later that Harry, hastily re-christened Ngai after the High God of the Kikuyu, had let her down. He slid into senility, rapidly at first, and then more slowly, agonisingly slowly, so that it seemed the wretched animal would hang on forever. When, finally the time came for a decision, Janice would have none of it.

'No, he won't be put down! I shan't allow it! I don't care how much he costs. That's not the point, is it? Go on, Richard, tell them. Tell them there are other things in life that matter. Such as the fact he's flesh and blood and has feelings the same as the rest of us. Go on, don't be such a coward. Father and mother always listen to you. If you say we can keep Ngai then we can.'

'Oh, Janice do stop pestering your brother. You know we simply can't afford to keep Ngai any longer. Not with all these vet's bills. It might have been different if we'd still had the farm, but there's no point looking back . . . is there, Richard? One simply has to get on with it.'

Although both their parents – and Ngai – were now dead, it was clear Janice had not forgiven him for his failure to support her. Even after all these years he could detect a note of lingering irony in her letters, in phrases such as 'piling up outside the Elysian gate'; the faint but discernible echo of 'What a sham! An absolute sham!'

For some reason he had begun to associate her sense of irony with the bitter taste of betel-nut. It was a bitterness the villagers disguised with powdered lime although this had the drawback of leaving one's mouth quite numb.

Gathering up the blue airmail sheets, Richard noticed a face turned towards him beneath the balcony. The splash of teeth reminded him of seeds spilling out of a freshly-cut water-melon.

Massaging the blood back into his cheeks he recalled his first encounter with the school's headboy . . .

'No, Mr Green, I would not advise it. If you report them to the headmaster he will expel them. He expels all those boys who are caught fighting. He has no choice in the matter. It is an order from the government. I myself do not believe there is a need for such action. In fact I am sure that between us we can reach a better solution than the one offered by those gentlemen, sitting in their splendid offices down there in Fairfax.'

A diplomat? Or a secessionist? Having won the support of an overwhelming majority of the pupils at the school's last election, Nathaniel Kiakoa was not afraid to speak his mind. For some, it may simply have been a matter of voting for the strongest boy – the young Bolgi's intransigent jaw and broad club fists revealing that he was unlikely to be intimidated by members of the larger, more powerful Endai tribe. Others, on the other hand, may have been swayed by the brief appearance during the election of his uncle, a sergeant in the police force; or possibly by the fact that Nathaniel came from a village which had once flirted with Christianity – the Bolgi believing that in return for their conversion vast quantities of material goods would one day rain down out of the sky – the infamous cargo cult, soon abandoned. It may even have been that the semi-blindness in his right eye, resulting from an early childhood accident, had helped him to win the vote, helped to set him apart from the others. He had had time, unlike his peers, to develop an inner awareness. A promising rugby-league player – competing seven times in a fledgling Highland league – he nevertheless had the capacity to set aside the irresistible desire to win and instead to step calmly into the fiercest brawl in order to separate players older than himself.

Richard could still see that soothing hand reaching out towards him, the smooth, soapy fingers stroking his wrist in a gesture that was intended to pacify not only the *tisa*, but the crowd of irate pupils gathered near the pigsty.

'*Ol manki*, I am asking that you return to your work in the gardens. Mr Green and I shall look into this matter. I'm sure it is not as serious as it seems, though these foolish boys who have disrupted us in our work shall be punished. What their punishment will be I cannot say. That is a job for our teacher. For you there is nothing to worry about. So now, please, I am requesting that you go back to your duties.'

Richard could still feel those deep vocal chords resonating through his arms and shoulders, spreading over the hairs on the back of his neck. He had tried to withdraw his hand but Nathaniel had held on. His head was slightly tilted so that with his good eye lurking in the shadows, and his bad one twinkling in the bright sunshine, his features appeared curiously at odds with themselves: classic, high cheek-bones and a heavy mouth; a virtuous brow and a thick, sullen nose. The habit of tilting his head gave him a slightly bemused air, offset by the severity of the scars that were rampant on both cheeks.

'You see, Mr Green, how peacefully the students depart? They may be angry with these two for behaving like *kanakas*, but they are used to it. It is of no consequence. That is why I say this matter does not deserve the headmaster's attention.'

Yet even as the pupils returned to their chores, their shirtless backs gleaming in the sun, Richard could see the two boys still squaring up to each other. They were of roughly equal build, both short and stocky, with muscles rippling like rapids through their muddy flesh; the one crouching, grim-faced and brutish, the other peering through festering eyes.

Naked, except for their khaki shorts, they had fought their way across the school grounds, leaving flowerbeds, shrubs and fences trampled in their wake, before ending up at the sty, where they'd smashed through the gate, sending pigs fleeing among the banana palms. Although clearly exhausted, neither showed any sign of remorse, their sweat-slicked faces fixed in unremitting hostility.

Meredith had warned him it wouldn't be easy.

'Take the Keramuti flag – perfect example: blue triangle surrounded by an outline of the island. The triangle is Mount Elimbari, the region's most prominent landmark. Its three points are supposed to represent peace, progress and prosperity. Everyone knows they stand for war, payback and the cargo cult. They're the three main pillars of a stone-age society.'

The staff swore it was Meredith that Nathaniel had taken as his role model. This was a view based largely on Nathaniel's refusal to wear school uniform, arguing that while shorts were suitable for the *manki* it was far more becoming for him as head boy to be seen reading out the notices in front of assembly each morning dressed in a pale-blue safari jacket and cotton trousers; with the jacket neatly buttoned, the trousers sporting turn-ups that rested on the eye-catching hooks of light, canvas boots.

It was true Nathaniel sometimes also carried a golfing umbrella like Meredith's, which he sloped over his shoulder as he sauntered up the classroom steps. But then Richard saw this less as a sign of arrogance and more as an attempt by the Bolgi to boost his self-confidence. For despite the outward show of authority, there existed an inner reticence which was enough to make him watchful and alert. Greeting people for the first time, for instance, he stretched out a hand not as an act of formality but in an effort to gauge their mood, to which he would then attempt to match his own. In this, his hands were like voltmeters, measuring the possible resistance.

'Perhaps, Mr Green, you would prefer to leave the matter with me? Such a busy man as yourself cannot afford to waste his time on these petty—'

'Olaman!'

The boy whose eyes were swollen had fallen to his knees and was busy trying to staunch the flow of blood from a cut that had opened below his brow with dirt scooped up from the floor of the sty.

'Really I do not think it is as bad as it looks,' said Nathaniel, who, after a brief exchange in *ples tok* with the injured boy, handed him a clean handkerchief and instructed him to bathe the wound in a basin of water.

'These cuts and bruises, they are easily healed. In a few days it will all be forgotten.'

'Apart from the scar, that is.'

'It will only be a small one. Besides, you will see such scars on the faces of all the boys. Usually they are caused by grass spears when the *manki* are stalking each other in the forest. It is how I myself came to be almost blinded.'

'Then you'll appreciate the school's concern.'

'Of course, but there is little danger of that happening here.'

'Nevetheless, I think we ought to record it in the incident book, don't you?'

'Really, I do not—'

'By way of insurance.'

Nathaniel's fingers sought to re-establish their grip on his wrist. 'I understand what you are saying, Mr Green, but—'

'No buts. War, payback, and the cargo cult. It's time these derelict pillars were razed to the ground. Time people of the Keramuti looked to the future. It's up to you, to everyone at school, to set an example.'

Sensing Richard's determination, Nathaniel tightened his grip further. 'The problem is Nixon already has been in trouble this year. The headmaster will not give him another chance.'

'It isn't a question of another chance but whether the school can afford to take the risk. We have to break free of the past. Free of payback. We have to look ahead. To peace, progress and prosperity.'

The incident having been recorded, the Board of Governors duly delivered its verdict: 'Nixon Kiakoa expelled for provocation, as set out in Article twelve, paragraphs four, five, six and seven of the amendment pertaining to the keeping of discipline in the nation's schools.'

Within hours of the announcement a rumour that Nixon's *wantoks* were planning to attack the school sent the staff fleeing to the headmaster's office. They demanded to know what action he intended to take to protect them and their families. They insisted he call in the local *kiap* and suspend classes if necessary, an act which the pupils who had gathered in large numbers outside, had vehemently opposed, fearing it would mean the postponement of the end of term exams.

Richard wondered whether the rumour of an attack had stemmed from the staff's inexperience. After all, many of them who had only just left college seemed scarcely much older than Nathaniel. Or perhaps it had more to do with their unhappiness at being posted to the Highlands; with the fact that they came from the coast from tribes such as the Bagamatu, Wandabeleb and the Enge, the Petani and Sosomaprik?

Whatever the source of the rumour, their fear found common expression in the sketch pinned by a young arts teacher to the staff noticeboard, depicting Mount Elimbari as a stone axe splitting the island in two. The sketch was soon to be found duplicated in all the classrooms where its message nevertheless did little to deter the vast majority of pupils from attending lessons as usual, or from applauding whenever the lessons ended. Their mindful appreciation of the efforts of the frightened staff was tempered only by Nathaniel's brooding presence, by the lurid swish and sigh as he decapitated the heads of buttercups with the tip of his umbrella on the way back to the dormitory.

It was here in *Haus Waramai* early one evening that Richard found him ordering the *manki* down to the river, with their slivers of soap and towels slung round their necks. Having cleared the building, Nathaniel had proceeded to strip all the beds, piling the soiled mattresses in a heap beside the door. The dormitory smelt of burnt rice. The prefab walls were cracked and the gaps stuffed with paper torn from old exercise books. Without their mattresses the iron bunks seemed to rear up in the grey light. In the corners, cardboard boxes – the pupil's lockers – spewed socks, underwear and faded *lap laps*. There were no curtains over the windows, no locks on the door. Without a ceiling the iron roof continued to pour down its suffocating heat although the sun had set. Outside the mellifluous mountain air was reviving the chorus of cicadas in the grass.

Richard watched as the angry youth, emerging from behind a cloud of dust, lashed out with his umbrella at a khaki shirt lying abandoned on the floor. Missing it, he struck a tin mug, sending it pinging against the door.

'Three years! Three whole years I have given to looking after this place! I have not once had a holiday. Each time the holiday has come I have remained behind to guard the premises against rascals. Now I am beginning to wonder, what is the use of it all? These *kanakas* want to destroy everything. Just today I have learned they are talking of war. But this war, it belongs to the past. For me it is the future that is the most important thing of all. We must forget the past. It is exhausting us. We must concentrate our energies on tomorrow. That is the real reason, Mr Green, why I did not wish you to report those two boys for fighting. Not because Nixon is my brother, but because I knew that if there was a decision to expel either one of them then the *kanakas* would make trouble for everybody. It is all they know, this business of payback. It is the Old Testament conquering the New. Truly it will conquer us all.'

A Bolgi – calling for an end to payback? The staff remained unconvinced, whereupon Richard recounted the story the head boy had told him, of the year he'd spent as a child on the coast, recuperating from his eye operation. For it was while wandering among the collection of old dug-outs and shiny outboards in the tiny fishing village of Malato where his uncle had been stationed, that Nathaniel had caught his first glimpse of what he now called the 'new force' – a revolution he predicted that would one day unite all the tribes, all the different people on the island. They would become *oslem*. One tribe. One nation. Except for those still fighting – they would be excluded.

Which was what he feared most – that the feuding in the Highlands would cause the Bolgi and Endai as well as their smaller neighbours, such as the Mepi and the Mauina, to be ostracised; to be condemned forever as backwoodsmen.

4

'I hope I am not disturbing you, Mr Green. The *manki* tell me Mrs Green has gone to meet the plane.'

The Bolgi's voice bubbled up through the bold chanting of villagers who flooded the landing strip below in a glorious sea of feathers; their slick, black bows like the beaks of bobbing birds, and the paint, grease and grass of their *bilas* swishing against the white Bailer shells which they wore at their throats.

'I think she is very happy always to be receiving so many letters from England. And so many *books*!' ... bubbling, seeping up through the floorboards where fragments of betel-nut lay scattered in the sun.

'Maybe when she has finished with them she will donate them to the school library.' ... bubbling through the bleakness of a grey afternoon, so that Richard, crushing the letter to Janice in his fist, was flooded with an immediate sense of release. He felt the paper curl and shrink in the fire that threaded through his fingers; short blunt fingers with blackened nails, like match-heads flaring with shame. Once his silence had been a lie. Now it would help him to start again; from Meredith's 'stone age' beginning. Here, four thousand feet above sea-level, where the air was clear, the light incandescent, he had no need to fear the past. There was no past. No shameful, squalid History. No guilt. Only the mountains towering up out of the forest, the limestone cliffs, butterflies, betel-nut and ...

And Nathaniel, climbing the landing stairs in his soft, canvas boots, calling out:

'I have brought you some water from the tank, Mr Green.'

'The emergency tank?'

'The others are empty.'

'What, all of them – including the dormitories'?'

Nathaniel nodded. Then as Richard pushed open the screen door leading on to the landing, Nathaniel added: 'It is just a temporary problem. Nothing serious.'

Richard allowed the screen door to swing shut behind him. 'It's the pupils one feels sorry for, having to make the long journey down to the river to wash. Think of the time . . . the valuable man-hours lost.'

'I have thought about it many times,' replied Nathaniel, drying his hands on a plum-coloured handkerchief, which he carefully folded before tucking into the breast pocket of his safari jacket. 'Maybe it is not such a problem. You see the pupils are used to it. All the time in the village they are walking to the river.'

'What about the younger ones? Many of them are afraid of the Waragoi. One often sees the bodies of dead animals being swept away by the current.'

'It's true the *manki* are afraid.' Nathanial's weaker eye appeared marooned in a pool of viscous fluid. 'But I believe it is not so much of a problem as all that as the pupils have all gone home for the holiday. So really there is no need for you to trouble yourself with this thing.'

'Long-term, Nathaniel. I was thinking long-term. Along the lines of a dam, or reservoir. It wouldn't have to be big, just enough to see us through minor emergencies. In fact I've already spoken to the District Commissioner. The only snag is the government's refusing to invest any more money in the area until the tribes have stopped . . .'

'Actually I have seen the cause of this particular problem for myself,' said Nathaniel.

'Ah, well,' said Richard, leaning back against the screen door, 'it isn't exactly a secret, is it?'

'No, but you see,' Nathaniel replied, pointing to a grassy plateau in the distance, 'that is where the villagers are now grazing their animals. They are no more grazing near the spring.'

'But I thought they agreed to set aside that land for coffee?'

The tip of the Bolgi's fingers hovered against the dark clouds massing in the valley below. Soon the government houses, strung out like a silken thread between the trees, would sink beneath a fusion of cloud and forest, with the rain melting on iron roofs, while gnats, moths and flying-ants expired in the rusty dustbowls of mosquito-wire. Naked lights powered by the station generator would blaze in the dark for an hour or two, until the fuel ran out, and candles sketched their haunting shadows on the prefab walls.

Nearby, a 22kg gas cylinder thrust its bullneck up through a spray of *kunai* grass. Its paintwork was cracked and peeled. The brittle green flakes resembled those undigested seeds sparkling in the middens of dung and builders' rubble which lay in heaps along the terrace, as though they too had just passed through the bowels of the villagers' well-fed cattle. Lower down the mountain a second row of houses, with thatched roofs and *pit pit* walls, emerged like a family of long-feathered cassowaries out of the darkening forest. They were smaller than the government prefabs and perched on bamboo stilts. With shaded verandahs they offered picturesque views of the river, but as they were intended as a short-term measure, they lacked indoor toilets and had no electricity. The coastal staff had declined to move into them, doubling up instead in the imported prefabs, allowing the huts to be taken over by the families of village chiefs, or *bikmen*.

'Of course one can see it isn't really a solution,' said Nathaniel, folding his arms once more; 'but then maybe one of these days the villagers will realise they cannot keep cattle *and* grow coffee. They will have to choose one or the other.'

'Yes, it's a pity,' Richard replied, noticing the policeman's belt with its protruding silver buckle which the youth wore under his jacket. In the wake of his uncle's recent dismissal from the force on the grounds of corruption, the belt was far from being a symbol of authority. It pointed instead to an increasing vulnerability – one moment the future wooed like a lover, the next it became a cruel assassin.

'. . . A pity in a way the government didn't build the school nearer the spring. At least we might have been able to exercise some control. This way we appear to have the worst of both worlds – the spring neither clearly ours, nor the villagers'.'

'And it is difficult to guard.'

'Impossible, I'd say. What on earth were the authorities thinking of, leaving it open like that?'

'It is the men from Works and Energy. They are too busy rushing from one place to the other to do a proper job. There are many areas like ours where the people want to improve their standard of living. It is the *kanakas* themselves who should have finished the work. It is they who should have laid the pipe in the ground, and built a proper fence around it since it is their children who are benefiting from the school.'

'In that case perhaps we ought to get the pupils to complete the job.' Nathaniel's shoulders sagged.

'Oh, come now,' said Richard, 'it shouldn't be all that difficult to persuade them. I'm sure they'd jump at the chance. Be a change from the usual scrubbing floors and cleaning the sty. We could make it part of a project, part of the long-term development of the area. Part of your "new force". We could even persuade some of the parents to join in. I wonder what Meredith would say, hearing that Bolgi and Endai were working together? Or the staff – what would they say?'

Nathaniel unfolded his arms. Richard watched as the brooding figure picked at the rough flesh on his cheek.

'Come on Nathaniel. We've got to be positive. Let's give it a go, shall we?'

Nathaniel flicked his head scornfully.

'Why not?' said Richard.

'It's the pupils. They are indolent. They will refuse to work.'

'But they work like Trojans!'

'Only when they have their noses buried in their books. For this kind of thing they are too lazy.'

'I'm sure they could be persuaded.'

'It will not be possible. We shall have to do the job ourselves.'

'The two of us?'

'And those few who might wish to help.'

'But the spring's . . .'

The tribal scars ran diagonally across his cheeks knitting together the warm, dark flesh. Along the ridges, you could see the lumps, like tiny shells embedded in the skin, the result of incisions made at puberty with a bamboo knife. The cuts had been packed with charcoal and left to heal, although as Nathaniel had developed a habit of picking at them, the skin seemed to be permanently torn.

'But the spring's over half a mile away, Nathaniel. It'll take forever.'

'It will have to be done. Otherwise the *kanakas* will destroy our source of water. You see Mr Green, one of these days you will learn to understand these *kanakas*. You have not yet been long enough in the Keramuti. It's true Mrs Green is beginning to understand. In class she is seeing how limited is the pupils' knowledge. For instance, they do not believe her when she tells them how Mount Elimbari was formed, according to the geological timetable. They say that story is not the same as the one their parents have taught them. You, on the other hand, they believe. So it is more difficult for you to see their limitations. They believe you because always you are dealing with topics such as money, growing coffee, buying and selling goods . . . For this reason your teaching is very popular and the pupils look forward to your lessons. When there is homework it is yours they do first. They are hoping it will help them to get a job when they leave school.'

Richard observed the dark clouds sailing up the side of the mountain towards them. He began to wonder how badly the spring or the pipe leading down from it had been damaged.

'I think we'd better make an inspection, Nathaniel.'

'Of course. But the damage is small.'

'I'd like to take a look all the same.'

'You do not wish to know who the culprit is?'

'Well, if it isn't the villagers' cattle tramping all over . . . ?'

'It is not the cattle, though if the government fails to build the tavern the District Commissioner has promised them before the end of the year then they will bring their animals back. They will not care if they ruin the spring.'

'In that case,' said Richard, moving away from the door and leaving a large hollow in the screen, 'who else is there? I simply can't imagine . . .'

The young Bolgi frowned. 'You have not considered the pupils.'

The screen popped behind him. Suddenly the after-effects of the betel-nut seemed to evaporate and it was as if he was seeing the mountains for the first time — a riot of petrified limbs reaching up with pulsating brutality, watching tirelessly over the inhabitants of the Keramuti.

'I also would not have imagined it, Mr Green. Unfortunately there is anger among a few of . . .'

'Anger!' Richard cried above the roar of the aircraft, as it shot up into the clouds. 'What on earth do you mean?'

For a moment the valley seemed to tremble. The sky grew dark and cavernous, ominous and the bamboo fronds seemed to cluster together along the banks of the Waragoi, the forests shrinking.

'Anyway why are you only telling me this now; when the pupils have all gone home? Who are you trying to protect? Who is it this time?'

Nathaniel remained silent as the tiny plane sank from view. The increased gloom helped to obscure the scar left by the landing strip across Elimbari's naked thigh as a steady ooze of villagers trickled down the slopes.

Watching this slow bleeding of the light, Richard noticed the bucket of water beneath the landing. At once Nathaniel clambered down the stairs; not as Richard anticipated, however, in order to rescue it from the multitude of dung-parched insects skimming about its surface. Instead, as he reached the bucket, the Bolgi turned and invited Richard to follow him along the road through the forest.

5

Rachel collected their mail from the grass hut on the edge of the landing strip. After greeting the Assistant District Commissioner, or *numba tu kiap*, who was busy loading a consignment of plastic rugby balls into the back of his jeep, she made her way down to the river. She chose the slightly longer route through the small bamboo forest where spiderwort, orchids and wild lilies grew, and the sunlight spilled like holy water upon the spongy earth that gave beneath her feet.

As she stole away through the shadows she could hear above the noisy chatter of wood pigeons and cockatoos, the villagers arguing with the pilot, who was shouting into the cockpit radio. Avoiding the tangled undergrowth she caressed the tall bamboo stems that leaned this way and that, as though they were the pillars of an ancient temple about to come crashing down. She could feel the tension in them, feel the presence of an unbroken mythology as they sprang up out of the dark earth, soaring forty feet into the air, their ghostly crowns rustling in the breeze.

The hollow stems were used by the villagers to make sacred flutes, or *tambaran*. Often she lay awake at night listening to their sepulchral notes echoing across the valley as the men stealing naked and unarmed through the forest sought to invoke the spirits' blessing. While Richard tossed and turned beside her on the iron bed, she would wonder whether they were doing the right thing, whether their coming to the Keramuti hadn't broken some mystical spell, condemning the spirit-men to wander forever through the mountains in search of a peace they would never find.

Behind her the crackle of the cockpit radio added yet another voice to the increasingly heated discussion. An elderly village woman and her *wantoks* were pressing the pilot to allow on board a large, black pig, which the woman was taking to her son in Fairfax to be slaughtered in honour of his being appointed to the civil service.

As Rachel emerged at the far end of the forest, following a sandy path through waist-high grass leading down to the Waragoi, she could hear the men rattling their bows and chanting and stamping their feet while they hollered to each other across the mountain terraces. It seemed to her that the entire valley was taking part in the discussion, registering its protest at the pilot's refusal to allow the animal on board.

She wondered whether Kumul Air pilots flying the Highlands circuit still carried guns. Or had the privately-owned company bowed to pressure from the Government, following the publication of a lengthy article in the *Fairfax Herald* under the banner headline, CHURCH MYTH OF THE BELLICOSE KANAKA? The article was written by the paper's leading campaign journalist and was based on extensive interviews with a number of anthropologists, many of whom had worked in the Keramuti. It listed a series of instances where 'the largely ritualistic behaviour of the tribesmen has been misrepresented by missionaries'. Rachel remembered how the article said the severing of a finger-joint whenever a family member died was portrayed as an act of naked cannibalism, before it went on to conclude . . . 'Is it at all surprising that the people of this fragile region should have risen up in arms against the missionaries, who sought not to understand their sense of God, nor even simply to demote him in their own religious hierarchy, but to supplant him altogether with a harsh and unforgiving figure who reflected the unforgiving communities from which these zealots came?'

Listening to their chanting sinking slowly beneath the roar of the Waragoi, she wondered how it was that while the missionaries had been driven out, people like Tony Meredith, whose objective was to change the villagers' way of life in no less dramatic a fashion, were nevertheless regarded with veneration. Even teachers, despised and humiliated back in England, found themselves revered. Which perhaps explained why at that moment, with everyone's attention centred on the landing strip, there were dozens of children following her, watching her every movement as she cautiously stepped over the foam-flecked rocks and made her way down to the water's edge, where she slipped off her sandals and washed the dust from her feet.

No sooner had she settled back on the bank and begun to examine her mail than the children swarmed around her. The younger ones, dimpled and warm, brushed her skin with their soft, soil-stained fingers, stroked her hair, sighed and giggled. She could see the curiosity in their eyes, feel the strength of their rounded bodies as they pressed up against her, the bamboo-like smoothness of their bellies brushing against her own. Above all she could feel the natural affection they had for one another. The affection that would one day lead them, with the inevitable passing away of their next of kin, to acts of self-mutilation in their grief. This response, she felt, was not that of a barbaric people, but of a people with a highly developed sense of *one-ness*.

Her father would have understood this pain of separation. He was himself once a missionary who, after twenty years in Africa, had returned to serve in Bolton in Lancashire where she had grown up and gone to school. He hadn't wanted to return, but had considered it his duty. Just as he had considered it his duty to fly out every spring in order to renew contact with his old and largely illiterate flock; physical contact, as the spiritual by itself he conceded was never enough. In doing his duty he had returned late one May evening, buoyant and brown, only to find Rachel's mother had died the day before following a stroke. By the end of the summer he too, a shrunken, listless figure, had passed away, spending his last few hours reciting the names of his former parishioners. He had begged Rachel not to forget them, to look them up. An only child, then in her first year as a student at the Tavistock and living in a London bedsit her father had insisted she had no need to fear being left alone in the world. They, the people of Kisli, in the province of Nyanza, would welcome her as one of the family. For they were her true family. The ones who understood the pain of . . .

'*Apinun, tisa.*'

Rachel looked up over the warm blanket of arms and legs. '*Apinun,*' she said, smiling.

'*Apinun,*' the boy replied, standing stiffly to attention. 'My name is Nimile. Nimile Orapi. I am in the first year of secondary school. But I do not think you will know me.'

'First year you say?'

'That is correct. I am approximately ten years old.'

'Then you are ahead of the others. You must have started school early.'

'I am the first one in my family.'

'That's strange,' said Rachel, as the children fastened their attention on her mail, passing the unopened envelopes back and forth between them, like sacred texts which they were unable to decipher. 'Oh, now I remember; you're the boy who was hurt at the beginning of the year – first day of school. Work parade, wasn't it? Mr Green drove you to hospital in Biyufa.'

The boy dropped his shoulders, carefully turning his head to one side to reveal an extensive though partially knitted wound at the base of the skull where the skin was raw and twisted.

'I was suffering an accident with a grassknife. One of the other boys . . . It was not his fault. We were standing too close together. Those knives are very sharp.'

'How long did you spend in hospital?'

'Just one night. My parents were coming to fetch me. They said it was better if I stay in the village. There is no food in the hospital. At my home we are having plenty of food. And my mother and sisters they are all looking after me. So now . . .'

The boy slowly straightened his head, his eyes reflecting the glittering water of the Waragoi. 'Now I am almost fully recovered. Before, it was hurting very much. But it's no longer so bad. As I have been working hard to catch up with my schoolwork it has been easy for me to forget that such a wound is there. One of the boys from my village brought my books home.'

'And where is your village?'

'It is at Kerenga.'

Rachel stuck out her hand to save a letter dropped by one of the children from slipping between the rocks.

'That's a long way away; the other side of Gelmbolg, isn't it?' she said, recognising Janice's thread-like handwriting on the front of the heavily franked envelope. 'Where Nathaniel comes from.'

'Yes, he is from Gelmbolg, which is not so far from Kerenga.'

'Though Kerenga's an Endai village.'

'Yes, it is.'

'I suppose you're waiting for a lift?'

'No, *tisa*.'

'No? Aren't you going home for the holiday? Or are you planning to stay behind with Nathaniel? I'm sure he'll be only too happy to help you catch up with the work.'

'I'm not staying, *tisa*. I am going home tomorrow.'

'You've left it rather late, haven't you? Why didn't you leave in the morning with the other boys?'

'Because I'm waiting.'

'What for?'

The boy's large eyes fastened on the children who, sensing something in the boy's stiffness, had withdrawn among the rocks. Just then, the aircraft shot out over the end of the landing strip directly above their heads, drowning out the sound of the river and the sound of his own thin voice. Nimile Orapi straightened out his arms and slowly opened his fist. As soon as the plane had gone over Rachel leaned forward to examine the tangle of glossy shells in the boy's moist hand.

'Why, they're beautiful!' she exclaimed. 'Where did you get them?'

'Is *tambu* shell, *tisa*. Small ones called *tambu*. Large ones they are *giri giri*. But there no large ones, although some maybe not *tambu*, they just—'

'Oh I think the small ones are gorgeous. They must be awfully scarce. I mean I see plenty of conch and kina shells but . . .'

'Our people trade with others from the coast. There are many secret routes through the mountains. Even before the government was building the road our people were exchanging *buai, brus, cus cus* fur, shells . . . all such things.'

'How old would you say these are?'

'Some very old, *tisa*. They here before I am alive. Before my mother. Before the Japanese come to fight in our country. Others they just same age as me. They a present from my grandmother to my mother when I was born.'

'A family heirloom. How marvellous. I see you've threaded them together on a – oh I see, it's a necklace. Gosh it's beautiful! The tiny serrations . . . the way they all seem to fit together.'

'Such a necklace is for wearing on special occasions. When someone is getting married, or there is a pig-kill in the village.'

'Has there been a pig-kill?'

'No. No pig-kill.'

'Is one of your *wantoks* getting married?'

'No one getting married, *tisa*. This necklace is special for you.' He urged her with his eyes to take it. 'My mother say I must give it to you.'

'What for?'

'You come to Keramuti to teach. Without you we learn no English.'

'Well, yes . . . but I'm not even a qualified—'

'And we learn no science.'

'I'm really only just . . .'

'You come to Keramuti.'

'Yes, I know, Nimile, but it isn't what you or your mother—'

'My mother say I must give you this necklace.'

Advancing bravely towards her, the boy slipped the hand-warmed tambu-shell necklace into her lap.

The children once more crowded around her, this time not touching, not daring to stretch out their clammy fingers. Nimile turned slowly and began to jog stiffly away through the trees, the soles of his feet splashing like water over the rocks along the river bank.

'Nimile,' she called out after him. 'Thank you, Nimile.'

He did not stop, but kept on jogging until he came to the path leading up to the landing strip. Here he paused, peering through a curtain of pampas grass.

'Thank you, *tisa*,' she heard him call. 'Thank you.'

6

Richard followed Nathaniel a short distance along the road. He then lost sight of him as he darted off into the forest, disappearing in the direction of a prominent algae-smeared overhang which marked the entrance to a series of limestone grottoes. Here in the distant past, or *pastaim*, the Mepi and the Muina had traditionally laid their dead side-by-side, thus reflecting the closeness of the two smallest tribes in the region whose lives were overshadowed by the fierce rivalry that existed between their larger neighbours, the Bolgi and Endai.

Richard waited at the edge of the road, where a myriad of narrow pathways emerged out of the forest, their surface churned to a sticky mire by the hooves of foraging pigs. He brushed the bronzed-green leaf of a tropical chestnut from his shirt, the branches of teak, *kwila* and casuarina trees rasping overhead in the breeze.

Below, a pale mist was beginning to unfold over the river, drifting across the landing strip from where the road began its long, spiralling climb over the mountain. Skirting the grounds of the abandoned New Tribes mission, it plunged into dense, rolling banana groves and swept over a ridge awash with wild lilies and rhododendrons, before swinging towards the station. Here it bisected the clipped lawns of the district offices, ringed with oleanders, poinsettias and marigolds and wound its way up the wooded slopes in a series of loose hairpins, past the fuel depot, the thatched court house, the local market and retail store, the latter's woven *pit pit* walls festooned with adverts for cigarettes and chewing tobacco. Higher up, the road doubled back past the co-operative, where under large sheets of heavy-duty plastic, hundreds of coffee saplings rooted in balls of black earth, awaited distribution among the co-operative's newest members.

The number of hairpins increased as the road continued to lurch upwards, disappearing into ancient stands of walnut and myrtle, as well as thick banks of *kunai* grass. The tall thatching grass gave way to the school's iron-roofed classrooms, to the government houses, and leafy plots of *kau-*

kau, before the trees returned once more. The surface of the narrow road grew increasingly slippery beneath a mulch of *yar*, or casuarina needles, and it was forced to switch back and forth with ever greater frequency in order to conquer the greasy slopes dotted with village hamlets and their steep, terraced gardens. Eventually, at some eighteen hundred feet above the valley floor, the windowless huts themselves vanished into a misty tangle of ferns and moss-draped lianas, leaving the road to slip through the mountain like the blade of a whetted knife.

Nevertheless, it had required a few carefully placed sticks of dynamite to force the mountain to give up its hold on the western half of the Keramuti. The august head of Elimbari, now pale and disfigured, tilted poignantly to the sky, while in the cold, deserted silence the road sprang free, bursting into the valley beyond. Into the arms of the Bolgi. The shell-shocked Bolgi. And into the arms of their neighbours, the Endai.

At one stage the two tribes had posted armed guards on the road in order to prevent anyone from using it. But following a protracted wrangle with the government over compensation for the loss of land, they had finally relented, embracing the steady stream of visitors who were delivered to their door-step – botanists, linguists, surveyors, geologists, anthropologists, engineers and palaeontologists. Indeed returning the compliment they felt had been paid to them by this robust intrusion into their remote and isolated community, the two tribes also embraced a whole new world of – coffee!

'Mr Green.'

Richard turned to see Nathaniel leading a small, spidery figure out of the forest.

'This is my grandfather. He asks if he may speak with you. He has come all the way from Gelmbolg. As you know my father is deceased, so now my grandfather is taking care of the family.'

The spidery figure seemed to float over the dirt-road towards him. He wore traditional dress: a bark belt from which a net apron dangled down between his knees, while in the small of his back an arrangement of leaves sprouted outwards, covering his buttocks. His *bilas* was simple and consisted of a golden-pearl shell strapped to his forehead, a fur armlet, and a tricorn-shaped wig-hat made out of human hair.

Smeared in pig's fat, his skin boasted a healthy, almost luminous quality, marred only by a cragginess around the mouth and cataract-shrouded eyes. His knees were bent, his chest shrunken, while the hole in his septum had become unevenly distended. Where once a set of boars tusks may have bristled against the greased flesh, marking him out as a proud warrior, its raggedness now served merely to underline his increasing frailty.

'His name is Atipu,' said Nathaniel. 'He speaks only the *ples tok*.'

Richard held out his hand. Instead the old man's fingers fastened on to the inside of his thigh.

'It is the custom,' Nathaniel chortled. 'It is the way men who are meeting for the first time greet one another.'

Richard winced as Nathaniel's grandfather began to twist and pull the muscle just below the line of his shorts.

'He does not mean to cause you any pain. He is just a little old fashioned. It is only the old men who are still following this custom. They say it helps them to judge the strength of those who may become their friend. Or their enemy.'

Richard peered down into the mysterious light brown face bobbing serenely on the sinewy neck and shoulders. He had not expected to find such steel in the spidery limbs, such fire in those slender fingers.

'He is the eldest in our village,' said Nathaniel. 'He can remember the time when Malachy Davis came to the Keramuti and together the Bolgi and Endai chased him away with their bows and arrows.'

The veteran Bolgi glanced up at his grandson, made an approving noise in his throat, and then let go of Richard's leg. Retreating once more to the far side of the road, he reached up into the branches of a wild fig, extracting a wooden shaft which was curved and sharpened at the ends. He returned, tucking the bow under his arm. His gums flashed scarlet as he grinned, with blackened stumps protruding like broken arrowheads.

Massaging his stinging flesh, Richard observed a second figure withdrawing deeper into the forest; he recognised Nathaniel's golfing umbrella dipping and diving like the brightly coloured tail-feathers of a parakeet through the gloomy undergrowth.

'It is my brother, Nixon,' Nathaniel admitted. 'My grandfather wanted him to be present during our meeting with you. But now he is running away because he is too ashamed.'

'Well I'm not surprised; after his rather unseemly behaviour.'

'You expelled him for that.'

'The Board of Governors, Nathaniel. It was their decision. Not . . .' He broke off, the sound of branches snapping in the background. He recalled a recent conversation with Meredith.

'A word-a warning, Richie. The *kanakas* ever come looking for compensation, send 'em to the Board-a Governors. They come to you, tell 'em to bugger off. 'Less of course you wanna pass the hat around half-a England, which is what they'll expect yer to do. It's the way it works out here. *Kanaka* gets himself killed in a drunken brawl – the killer's tribe's godda cough up else the buggers go to war. Only way, Richie, is to keep the Board-a governors between them and you. That, or a couple-a blasts from yer shotgun . . .'

As the crackling of branches died away, Nixon vanished into the forest while Nathaniel and his grandfather fixed their eyes on him.

'So that's why you brought the water from the emergency tank! It's your brother. He's been tampering with the spring. He's the one you've been trying to protect. Dammit, Nathaniel, the pupils didn't expel him! Why should they have to suffer? You know what conditions are like without water in the dormitories.'

The old man looked up through cloudy eyes at his grandson who stood quietly picking at the scars on his cheek. A drizzle began to fall.

'A week. That's all we have to repair the damage before the school reopens. Before the Endai find out your brother's the one who . . . For heaven's sake, you must have known. Why didn't you stop him? Why didn't you come and tell me? I thought we at least understood each other.'

Muted sighs and clucks of sympathy drifted from across the road, where a group of villagers had gathered on their way back from the landing strip. Nathaniel's grandfather raised a tremulous hand in the air. Head bowed, the young Bolgi translated.

'My grandfather understands your anger, Mr Green. He, too, is saddened by Nixon's actions. But he says if the school will take my brother back then he will pay to have the damage repaired. He will even pay to have a new fence put around the spring. A proper fence; with steel posts.'

'But why?'

'He only wishes to make things right again.'

'Has your grandfather seen the damage? Does he know whether he could afford it?'

Nathaniel's finger slid haltingly across his cheek. 'He says he thinks maybe you will be willing to help.'

'How?'

Nathaniel glanced uneasily at the group across the road who were steadily growing in number. Wearing leaf skirts, with bandicoot and *kapul* pelts draped between their breasts, the women shivered and swayed as they adjusted the heavy loads of *kaukau* which they carried on their backs. The long straps of the *bilum* bags strung across their forehead caused the tendons in their neck to stiffen like chains. Their skin was smooth, malt brown; their waists slender. Pointillist tattoos decorated their cheeks and breasts.

The men were muscular and stocky and were wearing the same net aprons as Nathaniel's grandfather. In their thick, charcoal-black hair they displayed a striking variety of birds' feathers – the irridescent blues and greens of the kingfisher, the downy pinks of cockatoos, and the russet quills of the *taragau*, though none was as splendid as those of the island's famous *Kumul* or Bird of Paradise, whose gold and orange and fuchsia tail-feathers the men teased up into the air like mist-illuminated rainbows.

The men carried among them traditional rattan-strung bows, shields or *plang bilong pait*, short-handled axes. Here and there a wooden spear bristled among the feathers, the smooth, myrtle shafts tapering into solid blades, heavy as lead, and responsible for most fatalities on the battlefield.

In spite of the weapons, it was largely the bloody splodges of betel-nut, staining their mouth and gums, and which they spat out on to the road with a great ferocity, that made them appear savage.

'Tell me, Nathaniel,' said Richard, as the drizzle intensified, driving the infants in the crowd to seek shelter beneath the loaded *bilums*, 'just how exactly does your grandfather think I can help? By lending him the money? Surely there are others he can borrow from. Your uncle down on the coast. He must have a bit of money put away. And what about all your *wantoks*?'

Nathaniel raised the collar of his wet safari jacket. 'I do not think it is a matter of . . .'

'Or is he suggesting somehow that your brother getting thrown out of school is my fault? Is that why he's being so coy? It's beginning to seem more like blackmail than compensation. Pay up or . . .'

'It is not the money, Mr Green.'

'Then why me? Why hasn't your grandfather gone to the Board of Governors?'

Nathaniel leaned tentatively on his grandfather's bow; the wood was blackened with smoke, its grain smooth as glass.

'My grandfather does not hold you responsible for the decision to expel Nixon. It is the same as when a man from one tribe kills or injures a man from another. That first man's tribe is to blame. So now what he is saying is, it is the school's fault. Not yours but . . .'

'*Fault!*' Richard exclaimed. 'What on earth do you mean? It isn't the school's fault at all!'

'The people from my village, they are saying Nixon was not the only one to blame.'

'But he was caught fighting!'

'Yes, but as everyone knows there has always been fighting between Tapie's tribe and our own. Now we are asking why was only Nixon expelled and not both boys together.'

'Because . . . Well, because . . . Dammit Nathaniel!' he cried, unable to contain his frustration. The bow Nathaniel was leaning on was a symbol of the past, something the young Bolgi was supposed to have turned his back on. Where was that strength now, that exhilarating new force that was supposed to deliver him out of the hands of his militant *wantoks*?

'Mr Green,' said Nathaniel, his skin beginning to gleam in the rain, 'my grandfather says he has seen you and myself playing rugby league at the station. He says you are built as strong as any of the *kanakas*. Your flesh is firm and your bones are hard. He can tell your nose has been broken but that you are unafraid. A broken nose is like a scar. It shows you are a man. That you have suffered pain.'

'I don't understand.'

'Well, there are *kanakas* on the Board of Governors. And the local *kiap* who is in charge of the rugby team is also its deputy chairman. My grandfather says these men will not listen to him. But they will listen to you. Through rugby league they have got to know you and respect you. You were not present at the meeting when my brother was expelled so now he asks if you will talk to them on his and Nixon's behalf.'

Above the distant burble of the river, already swollen by the rain, Richard thought he could hear men singing, chanting discordantly. All of a sudden a battered truck came into sight, its gears grinding as it clawed its way up the steep incline. Its fender had been ripped away, the bonnet secured with bits of wire. A single wiper lurched fitfully through the sludge on the windscreen while the stench of diesel fumes spread rapidly through the undergrowth. As the truck appeared, Nathaniel looked forlorn and bowed and shook his head.

The truck slewed to a halt alongside them, and several noisy and dishevelled men leapt out, clutching bottles of Pacific lager which they cheerfully handed round. Embracing the old man and his grandson, they converged upon Richard, inviting him to join them in the back of the truck, slipping their mud-spattered arms through his. There was mud on their *bilas*, on their lips and in their hair. A wild fire raged in their eyes.

And how quickly its flames spread. In no time Richard found himself surrounded by gregarious Bolgi. He joined in the clapping while they chanted and sang to celebrate the fact that none of them had been seriously injured or killed in their collision with an uprooted tree at the bottom of the Malachy Davis pass.

Rapidly Richard's frustrations with Nathaniel and his grandfather melted away. He began to feel a sense of relief, a sense of euphoria. For he was right. He had been all along. He and Rachel *could* belong, could be a part of the Keramuti. Part of its struggle. Its celebration of life. Unlike the Masai who were isolated, independent, and whose aloofness had led his father to compare them unfavourably with the forward-looking Kikuyu, the people of the Keramuti wanted – demanded – integration. The rapid growth of the co-operative was proof of their longing to share in the new prosperity already sweeping much of the rest of the island. Already he felt a part of that prosperity; part of Nathaniel's new force.

Drinking from a muddy bottle of whisky which the men were now passing round, Richard's eyes fell on a collection of string pouches lying discarded in the back of the truck. They contained bundles of betel-nut, bought in Biyufa. An inch of reddish-brown water swirled round the betel-nut and over the sharpened tips of the men's spears, while tins of bullybeef, which had burst out of their rain-sodden boxes lay gleaming dully on the sacks of rice, flour and salt.

As he listened to the account of their hazardous journey through the mountains, he realised it was their recklessness that excited him. For they showed no sign of fear or caution. In spite of their narrow escape, it was as if the perils of driving through the mud and mist meant nothing to them. They cared little that their truck had slithered to a halt at an alarming angle and they continued to skip joyfully about in the rear. It seemed at any moment that they might begin to roll back down into the valley, far, far down into the growing darkness, dragging him with them.

'*Kanakas*!' Nathaniel hissed as he pulled Richard away from the drunken crowd. 'They say it was rascals who placed the tree across the road. But in fact they have been drinking all the way from Biyufa. Even the driver is drunk. Who knows what will happen when the government gives permission for the Pacific lager company to build a tavern here in the Keramuti. I fear our people will be in big trouble. You can see for yourself how they spend their money. My grandfather is saying nothing, but I know he is disappointed. He wanted you to return to Gelmbolg in the truck with him so that you could meet our mother and grandmother. They are very concerned about Nixon's future. But now it is not possible for you to ride with them. They will be happy to make space for you, but you can see it is too dangerous.'

Nathaniel's grandfather emerged holding up one of the string pouches, filled with betel-nut. Nathaniel felt the weight of it in the palm of his hand and then tied an extra knot in the string.

'My grandfather says these are for you. He wants you to know that whenever you want more, he will get it for you. He says what you buy from the market here at the station is not good. It is usually old and can cause sickness.'

The rain was growing heavier. The grinding release of the handbrake gave rise to a renewed wave of excitement among the chanting Bolgi. Richard stretched out his hand and took the pouch.

'Tell your grandfather I'll talk to the Board as soon as I can. Of course I can't guarantee they'll change their minds, but I'll see what I can do.'

As the vehicle groaned the mood of excitement turned to one of impatience. Once more Nathaniel translated.

'He would like you to come and stay with him for a while in Gelmbolg. He says he knows you are busy man, but he will be happy to wait until you can find the time.'

Richard felt the wet string cutting into his hand. 'I shall come after I've had a chance to sound out the Board. There's no point in turning up before. It'll only raise everyone's expectations.'

With a final handshake Nathaniel's grandfather returned to the truck and Richard marvelled at the ease with which the spidery figure skated over the pools of water beside the road. Suddenly Nathaniel turned to him and said: 'I think it is time, Mr Green, that I visited my *wantoks*.'

A short way up the mountain the vehicle slowed down. Through the trees Richard saw Nixon dash out into the road and scramble aboard, dragging Nathaniel's half-folded umbrella behind him.

Untying the string bag, he extracted a fresh betel-nut. Nixon . . . Nathaniel . . . he murmured to himself, this was the reality, the unsung life of people in the mountains; the life he had chosen for himself. And yet there was also 'Chicken' Bell, Lewis and Austin Chamberlain . . . So that it seemed dream and reality were becoming blurred, the one spilling over into the other. Hard to tell which was which.

Breaking off a piece of the hard, outer shell, he listened to the sound of the pick-up's engine fading in the distance as the the vehicle disappeared into the low black cloud rolling across the face of Mount Elimbari. His fingers felt clumsy, cold and numbed by the rain.

7

He was standing at the entrance to a narrow gorge, whose red sandstone walls had been polished to a glasspaper smoothness. Graffiti sprayed across their surface appeared to glow from within, like a splinter beneath the skin, or the figures of ancient rock paintings viewed by the light of an oil lamp. Sand and dust funnelling down between the high walls prevented him from seeing more than a few feet ahead. His muffled heartbeat was drowned by the noise of hooves thundering in the distance. There was blood on his hands, and on his shirt and tie, to which the sand was sticking.

Then a stiff wind began to peel the sand away – from his eyes, his skin, from beneath his feet, revealing a dimly-lit corridor descending into the bowels of a vast, red-brick building. The bricks were cracked, the ceiling crumbling; whilst extending far into the distance there was a row of scuffed doors, each clearly numbered: 2X, 4L, 3D, 5C . . .

The thundering of hooves was growing louder, dislodging scabs of black moss from the barred windows. The cracks in the walls released a sour-sweet smell, the smell of sweat and lathered leather. He put his hand up to shield his mouth and nose, but it wasn't the smell that was beginning to make him feel ill. It was the noise – with his heart taking up the beat, becoming the source of the pounding. The loud and terrible thunder reverberated through his skull, spreading through his arms, his legs, through his veins, paralysing his entire body. He began to shout. But the voice he heard wasn't his own.

'Ah, there you are, Mr Green. We've been looking all over for you. We thought you must have been ambushed on the playing fields. No further problems to report? Then if you'll come this way. The headmaster would like to see you in his office.'

Her eyes were cold. Her face was flat and featureless. He followed her at a distance, her heels clicking like typewriter keys. They passed an open doorway. He could see blood seeping out into the corridor, trickling from a large coffee urn around which lay scattered cups and curled up sandwiches, saucers of stubbed out cigarettes, abandoned brochures, stencils and misplaced diaries.

A page of one of the diaries lay open. It was headed: 'New Curriculum Definitions'. Underneath someone had scribbled in red ink: Professional responsibility – a team of clapped-out cowboys lashing themselves to the saddle. Discipline – a branded herd. Standard assessment – same brand, same bleat. Policy objective – dried up bore-hole. Opt-out – private ranch, unlimited grazing. Reward – saddle-sores (now you know why cowboys walk the way they do); public derision.

'Ah, Richard!'

He looked up. The tense figure stood sifting through a batch of papers on a wide, leather-topped desk.

'So glad you could make it. Everything going all right?'

It was less a concerned question than a kind of disembodied foreplay.

'A letter. Arrived this morning. Rather disturbing.'

The fingers brushed lightly over the headed paper . . . 'Austin and Lewis Chamberlain. Boys' mother. Writes . . .'

The voice spilled evenly over the desk; the eyes glazed.

> *'Sir.*
>
> *It has been brought to my attention by my eldest son, Austin, that his younger brother, Lewis, was recently involved in an affray at school, as a result of which Lewis suffered the indignity of an official warning – not for the first I am led to believe, though I hasten to point out that no word of these warnings has ever reached me. Now I am informed that Lewis's conduct is being closely monitored by your staff.*
>
> *May I therefore take this opportunity to enquire why similar action has not been taken to monitor the behaviour of the other boy, namely, "Chicken" Bell who I am told has a history of provocative behaviour.*
>
> *May I also know why nothing was done by the teacher on duty to put a stop to this most recent fracas? Indeed I believe it was left to my eldest son to intervene. Surely this is unacceptable? The teacher was present. Why did he or she not take charge?*
>
> *Of course I realise that on the whole the teaching profession is an arduous one, and that its members sometimes feel they are called upon to perform miracles. But as I too am part of a profession, I am only too keenly aware of those who are*

> *content to enjoy the status and protection it offers whilst continuing to operate in a manner of complete indifference toward their clients.*
>
> *I trust therefore that you or the teacher concerned will feel free to offer some reasonable explanation, thereby allaying my, perhaps unnecessary, fears regarding the safety and future conduct of my son, Lewis.*
> *Yours*
> *Mrs W. Chamberlain BA. LLB (Cantab)'*

With the curtains drawn, the office floated in a soft, velvet light, its walls clothed with mahogany. Behind leaded glass windows lurked shelves heavy with Greek and Latin texts, while busts of bearded philosophers looked down from their marble plinths.

As soon as the voice had ceased, the curtains were pulled back and he found himself once more alone in the corridor, struggling to undo the knot of his blood-stained tie. The blood was hard and crusted, and as the knot refused to yield, he was forced to abandon it. He knew there was only one person who could undo it. She was somewhere deep inside the building, a prisoner of its damp-ridden walls. Yet how was he to find her? How was he to help her break out? And in helping her, help himself to escape?

The familiar sound of heels clicking in the distance caused him to set off in pursuit down the corridor. Mysteriously, the sound vanished and almost immediately he was lost, chasing, or rather being chased by the same terrible thunder, the same remorseless pounding as before. It grew louder, more and more violent, a rampant drum-fire sweeping down upon him, until in an act of desperation he smashed the lock on one of the nearby doors and burst into an empty room.

The room was narrow, with high walls and a sagging, wooden floor. Long rows of desks led to a raised platform in the centre of which stood a table heavily stacked with books. The shaky piles staggered upwards like stalagmites toward the naked bulb hanging from the ceiling.

On a bulletin-board at the back of the platform, crammed with photographs under the stencilled heading 'First Form Trip to Moscow', there were scenes of huddled youths waving tiny Union Jacks in the snow in front of the Kremlin. Their faces were flushed with triumph, as though they had single-handedly repulsed the platoon of great-coated soldiers goose-stepping away from Lenin's tomb.

'Sir?'

A voice, sounding like a bell pealing over the dead.

'My apologies for disturbing you. Just thought I'd stop by to offer a word of thanks. Awfully decent of you not reporting the boys to the head – Lewis being on a final warning and all that. Did you know?'

'No, Austin. I believe I didn't. Does it matter?'

He began pushing away the piles of books on the table, repelled by their uniformity.

'Actually, the word is, Lewis is deliberately trying to get himself thrown out. If that is his aim it's hard to know what'll he do next, perhaps . . .' He broke off wondering what it was they wanted of him. Assistance? Why him? – who had less courage than they. Their own was merely artfully disguised, which was not surprising, for they were determined to survive. He would've liked to have helped. Only . . . having to spend so much time with them, listening, learning, growing closer, growing attached; allowing them what amounted to virtually unrestricted access. Access to oneself, to one's innermost feelings, moods, thoughts . . . And then suddenly to discover that the tone of the pealing bells had changed. Where previously there was the promise of a song, of a triumphant march emerging, thunder took its place; the corridors once more ringing with confusion and the clamour of despair. This was called learning.

'Tell me, Austin, why were you so determined to intervene in the fight between 'Chicken' Bell and Lewis? Was it out of a sense of moral outrage?'

The glance reflected a clandestine confusion. They always did, as though the pupils spent all of their schooling smuggling their doubts from one room to the next.

'Lewis is my brother, sir.'

'Ah, the faithful ass! I should have known. And what about your loyalty to the school? To the other pupils? What about your responsibility to them? Because, you see, unless we are able to transcend our tribal loyalties, we shall find our long-standing affair with evolution reduced to no more than an endless succession of Lewis versus Chicken confrontations. Indeed what's required is that we take an overview – show our loyalty first and foremost to the whole human family and not just that branch of it to which we happen to belong. Only then will we be in a position to celebrate our cultural diversity, without exacerbating the differences between people, between Bolgi and Endai, between your brother, Nixon, and . . .'

'Between . . . sir?'

The door slid open. They streamed in in their burgundy striped blazers. He noticed the way they tugged at their ties; the way they threw their bags onto the graffiti'd desks. He listened to the sounds they made – banging into each other, pretending to clear their throats, rifling through their lunch-boxes – bombastic sounds that nevertheless gave little away. Searching rather than revealing, their eyes darted this way and that, pretending not to look yet surreptitiously watching, studying his face for clues.

He began to feel like a circus ringmaster waiting for the roll of the big drum. They were the lions, prowling round the perimeter of the cage; weary of the ritual, the routine that saw them roaring and flailing the air with their paws in forty-minute acts.

And yet no sooner had they entered, than they seemed to slip away again, so bent beneath the weight of their bags that their legs dragged more like caterpillars than lions. They disappeared through the doorway into the void though he could still see them, the rippled segments and soft, satin underbelly crawling tentatively down the corridor. All it needed was a momentary dropping of their guard – You boy! Yes, you – and their threadbare shells would be crushed underfoot.

Indeed those who now appeared before him seemed to have met precisely that fate. For they stood beside their desks silent and exhausted – wearing no blazers, and no shoes, only torn khaki shorts, and bandanas with which they mopped the sweat from their sunken eyes.

He tried to place them. To put names to them. But they slid away to hide among jars swirling with cotton wool and ether, slipping in among the gloomy specimens of those who had gone before. Yet even as they hung suspended within their liquid graves, he noticed one struggling to regain the surface, finally, through the limpid wall of preserving fluid, catching sight of . . .

PART TWO

8

Dear Janice,

I'm sorry you didn't like the photographs. I must admit I had my doubts when I first saw them, what with Richard swooping out of the forest, eyes blazing, blood dripping from the garland of wild boars' teeth draped around his neck. Still, I hardly imagined . . . 'going native'? Good gracious, if anything it's the other way round! It's Richard exploiting the villagers' desire to identify with the forces of progress — in this case, the Keramuti co-operative which sponsored the hunt and whose influence, under Richard's management, has seen its membership rise to almost four hundred in under a year.

Indeed it was a publicity stunt that brought home to me a simple truth. That Richard can dress up in all the *bilas* he likes — in all the beads, shells, feathers, even smear his body in pig's fat — the villagers will always remind him, remind us, that it is *we* who are in charge, who remain *masta*.

'*Apinun, masta. Masta i laik sampela kaukau? Masta i laik baim buai?*'

'*Masta* . . .' The word bursts like a gunshot through the market place. I hear *masta* and my instinct is to dive behind the nearest tree.

Thankfully the children at school now call me by my name, that is . . . wait for it . . . Mrs Green! I live with Mr Green, therefore I must be Mrs Green. I see little point in kicking up a fuss. After all, the women of the Keramuti have their own priorities, even though at times one does despair of them. This is particularly so when they gather in droves to watch Richard do his washing in the sink below the house. The horrifying sight of this bearded man with his arms deep in soap suds goads them into action, at which point I invariably slip away into the dark anonymity of the forest and return only when the women have gone. It is a cowardly act I know, or so at first it might appear. The fact is, Janice, it's really they who should be on the defensive, who have the most to lose. The biggest threat to them comes not from a man doing his own washing, but from a government which is constantly exhorting them to open up their land to large mining, logging and road building projects, so they can 'catch up with their *wantoks* on the coast'.

Nor is 'felling' confined only to trees. The high schools annually cut back up to a third of their roll – lack of resources whetting the blade. As a result growing numbers of semi-educated youngsters now wander about the Highlands with little or no understanding of their position in the new society. Richard calls them 'the excommunicated'. Some see them as little more than *rabisman*, blaming them for the region's worsening crime rate, particularly in those areas near the highway. Here there were so many hold-ups during the coffee season that the large coffee estates issued their drivers with shotguns. Now the government wants to ban all weapons, even the traditional *banara* (bow and arrow).

Naturally all of this raises questions about our own role here. What if we are merely helping to educate a new elite? To create new divisions, with yet another disaffected under-class emerging, vulnerable and confused? These are questions I feel Richard and I ought to be exploring, only he's never around. He's usually charging off somewhere, either in a hurry – or in a huff.

Earlier in the year he created a bit of a storm by calling for the reinstatement of Nixon Kiakoa, and he has since made matters worse by proceeding on the boys' behalf to canvass each individual member of the Board of Governors, so prolonging the whole affair. Fearing a Bolgi attack on the school if he should fail, or an Endai attack if he should succeed, the staff have become increasingly hostile, some going so far as to say he is jeopardising their careers, indeed endangering their lives.

A couple of weeks ago, Huala Doura, a talented young arts teacher, accused him of behaving 'with the reckless arrogance of an old colonial, showing that for all your talk of the future, you are one who is still very much living in the past.'

No sooner had she uttered these words in the middle of a

heated debate than she seemed to regret them and broke down in tears. Whereupon Richard stormed out of the staffroom, reversed the Land Cruiser over 8C's garden project and sped off towards Biyufa, determined to enlist the aid of the chief education officer.

Three hours later a pig sunning itself in the middle of the road forced him to swerve. He hit a bank and catapulted into a ravine. Fortunately, there were villagers on hand to drag him from the wreckage. Using the door which had been torn off as a make-shift stretcher, they promptly ferried him to hospital. Mercifully it was discovered that his injuries were limited to a few cracked ribs and an ugly-looking gash from a metal splinter embedded in his chest.

'Such a lucky man,' I can still hear the ward sister purring; 'so big and strong. In no time we'll remove the stitches and send him back to you; though it's your job, Mrs Green to make sure he gets plenty of rest.'

My job? Quite frankly, Janice . . . It's been two weeks, and though the time has dragged, I can't help feeling a little apprehensive about the reception he might get when he returns; especially as the spring has just been put out of action yet again and the staff's frustrations are threatening to spill over amongst the pupils. Even now a number of them are bravely trying to repair the damage before they sit their end of year exams.

It's hard to know what to do, really, what to say. Unlike Richard, I didn't come out here with any notion of helping the so-called 'Third World' make it into the 'First'. In fact I have to confess there's much I admire about the Keramuti – just as it is; much I'd like to see remain unchanged. Already, however, the changes are all too visible. Traditional gardens, for example, lie abandoned as more and more people turn to coffee, despite news of an impending glut on the world market and rumours that the price may be about to collapse. In that case the rapid growth of the co-operative will almost certainly come to an end.

Naturally I would like to help; if I only knew how. If only I could point out some middle way. Instead I find myself trying to minimise the damage by hiding, refusing to put myself forward as a role model which I believe the villagers will feel

> obliged to imitate. In short, my 'solution' is to devote myself to
> the study of Carl Gustav . . .

She saw Nathaniel out of the corner of her eye, making his way towards the house. With that uneasiness which he had stirred up in her of late, she waited until he began to climb the landing stairs. Then, hating the way the house vibrated, the way it seemed to become an extension of the youth's vanity, she hurriedly folded her letter to Janice and set it aside. She made a mental note of things to ask when she resumed her letter to Janice: how Kingsleigh's centennial dinner had gone, whether she'd got to meet the Chamberlain boys' mother; whether anyone had yet put a stop to the antics of 'Chicken' Bell, or she had managed to find an alternate route, avoiding the sight of him taunting passing motorists; wondering at the same time what Richard would make of it . . . regard the youth as yet another victim of 'ex-communication'?

Nathaniel's knock was soft, barely audible. She stood up, and for a bizarre moment it seemed as if this was the signal the pupils had all been waiting for, as she saw them rush out of their dormitories and run screaming across the school grounds. They swept down the road – a wave of molten lava pouring down the side of the mountain.

'Nathaniel?' she called out, leaving the balcony where she had been sitting. 'What on earth's going on? Why are they making such an awful noise?'

He came to attention behind the screen door. 'Actually I'm not certain, but I know that Mr Green has just returned from Biyufa.'

'What? Are you sure?'

'I am sure,' he replied.

She noticed he'd had his hair cut. His face appeared leaner and sharper. Even the focus of his weaker eye seemed less vague. His polished boots creaked as he grinned – he no longer wore canvas but black leather, with steel toe-caps.

'But I thought the sister . . . well, you were there. She said it would be the end of the week before they took the stitches out.'

The starched epaulettes of his olive-green combat shirt (yet another alteration to his dress) arched slightly as he shrugged his shoulders. 'Perhaps he will allow the medical orderly at the station to do it.'

She looked dubiously at him, then saw that he hadn't meant her to take it seriously. 'The fact is just a few moments ago I saw the co-operative truck arrive with some new machinery. I spoke to the driver. He says he left the *masta* at the station. He says Mr Green went to talk with the ADC about the rugby league fixtures for next week. So now I am thinking of going to meet him as he will not be able to walk up the mountain alone.'

'I imagine the ADC will give him a lift.'

'His jeep has broken down.'

'I thought your brother'd helped to repair it?'

'It is the roads . . . they are shaking everything loose.'

Rachel sighed. 'In that case I suppose . . . No, wait a minute. How do I know this isn't just an excuse for you to hang around the co-operative?'

Nathaniel pressed his hands to his chest. 'If you like we can go together.'

Returning indoors to fetch her sandals, Rachel paused in front of the tiny mirror propped up on the chest of drawers in the bedroom. She tucked her blouse into her *lap lap* and tied up her hair. It was a ritual she performed with modesty as well as severe misgivings, knowing that she was erecting a barrier between herself and the villagers. It was a barrier she loathed and which the men and women she passed on the road would instinctively seek to break down, sifting through the loose strands of her long hair, just as she'd seen them sift through their coffee beans drying in the sun. Somehow her pale green eyes lacked the fire to ward them off.

Cocking her chin and setting her long, thin face with its pointed nose and frugal mouth, she managed to stare into the mirror with a contrived belligerence. Now and then Richard would catch her doing this and throw his arms around her. But she would pull away. For it reminded her of the smoke-blackened fingers of the men growing increasingly emboldened as they pawed at her hair; of the women smiling as they looked on, stoking the fire of indignation smouldering within her.

'Right then,' she said, re-emerging on the landing. 'Shall we go?'

Nathaniel swept down the stairs ahead of her. At the bottom he waited until she'd passed. Then, as was the custom in the Keramuti, he followed behind. As they slipped beneath the house, the copper pipe looping down through the floorboards to the gas-boiler reminded Rachel of the drip at Richard's bedside. He'd tried to make light of it until the sister, carefully unwrapping his bandages, had exposed the ripped flesh ruggedly sewn together.

Turning down the steep incline, once more she began to feel the blood draining from her face, began to feel an overwhelming sense of weariness and despair. For a moment she was tempted to stop and put her head between her knees until the moment of weakness had passed. It wasn't so much the futility of Richard's crusade as the knowledge that the Bolgi, said to be once the best hunters in the region, had detected a sign of guilt, and set a trap into which Richard had duly blundered.

True, a disproportionate number of the school's 'excommunicated' came from Bolgi villages, while those living in the remote areas around Gelmbolg regarded Nixon's expulsion as a further example of Endai domination. Yet was it right to enlist the *masta*'s help in order to restore the balance between themselves and their more powerful neighbours, to attempt to use the *masta*'s influence when he was just as unable as they to control the force of events?

'Tell me, Nathaniel,' she said finding it difficult to hide her frustration as they slithered over the road's uneven surface, 'how much longer does your brother think he can get away with this sort of behaviour? It really isn't fair you know on the rest of the pupils, having to put up with blocked lavatories, food encrusted plates, rats, scabies. We're jolly lucky we haven't suffered an outbreak of—'

She saw, or rather heard – too late – the rush of stones, felt the force of Nathaniel's steel-capped boot as he skidded and caught the back of her sandal, snapping the strap in two.

'Sorry, Mrs Green!' he exclaimed. 'I am very sorry.'

She squinted up through the sun at him. The air was dry, the sky an acid blue. His eyes rested uncomfortably on her feet poking out from beneath her *lap lap*.

'I am truly sorry.'

She threw up her hands as he began scratching at his cheek. 'Oh, look, it doesn't matter. It was only a cheap pair.'

'But if you allow me, I shall buy you another as soon as I am able to go again to Biyufa with Mr Green.'

She stamped her foot into the sandal. Warily they continued their descent; the road dwarfed overhead by the massed ranks of shimmering peaks. A line of flagpoles running along the top of the westernmost range marked the number of years in the island's life as an independent nation. Accompanying members of the local government council, Richard had helped to erect the most recent of these, unaware, it seemed to her, that what they were celebrating was really an illusion. For men – mankind – ultimately were *all wantoks*, relying, depending on each other, even if it was a dependency few cared to admit. They preferred instead to hide what they saw as a sign of weakness, maintaining the illusion of power for which they would fight, obliging others to fight back. When she and Richard had first arrived in the area, they'd marvelled at the lush terraces, abundant with melons, paw paw, bananas, *kaukau*, beans, peppers, pumpkins, tomatoes . . . Now increasingly there gathered burgeoning battalions of coffee trees, threatening to alter not only the shape but the entire history of the valley; promising to make it... still richer? More powerful? Already the school, the co-operative and surrounding villages were dissatisfied with the old land-sharing arrangements. Each wanted to own more. Each had been forced to post guards. To fly its own flag as it were.

As the road finally unwound along the valley floor which was speckled with the faded stains where villagers had spat out their betel-juice Nathaniel interrupted her thoughts. 'Actually, to tell the truth,' he said, 'this time it was not Nixon who was responsible for damaging the pipe. I believe it may have been someone who did not want to write the exams; who was afraid of failing. You see, Nixon is no longer interested in returning to school as he has found a job at my uncle's new garage. Those who are blaming him do not realise this. Even the people of Gelmbolg do not yet know. In fact he has turned his back on the Keramuti and gone to live in Biyufa.'

Rachel continued to drag her foot through the dust thrown up by her broken sandal. Marching a careful four paces behind Nathaniel added, 'He has already visited Mr Green in hospital and told him the news. So now your husband need not disturb the Board of Governors any more or Mr Meredith. He need not worry about my brother's future.'

'Why, that's a relief!' Rachel exclaimed, as she caught sight of the Waragoi, bright green and flecked with silver. It was a moment before she realised her ears were no longer filled with the incessant screaming of cicadas but by the roar of the river's turbulent waters, bubbling, bucking and foaming.

Among the shadows below the huge sentinelled rocks, the water took on a dark, threatening hue and became both calmer and more sinister as it gathered in murky pools to lap at the foot of Mount Elimbari.

It was here she saw the children scrambling down, the same noisy throng she had seen earlier spilling down the road. As then, they filled the air with a distracted screeching that seemed to rise up out of the earth.

She noticed that many of them had torn off their clothes, concealing their nakedness by daubing their bodies with mud. Their emblazoned cheeks, fragile chests and half-moon bellies were smeared with the sludge which they'd scooped up from the river bank. Aware that she was in fact witnessing a traditional display of grief she immediately sensed that their traditions were failing to give them solace as of old; as though by dragging the dead child up toward the road they endeavoured not so much to drag it back to life with them, as to hurry fretfully after it; mourning less its passing away, than its thoughtless desertion of them.

It was through this inability to turn back that she realised their immunity had been cruelly shattered – the immunity which the long years of isolation in the mountains had given them. For it was obvious the child's was no ordinary death, following illness or disease. Nor was it the result of a warrior's spear flung in the blinding heat of battle. Instead, as the small, shrivelled body drew near, hoisted up on to the shoulders of children scarcely much older than itself, the watery mucus that dribbled from Nimile Orapi's nose symbolised a foreboding she felt explode deep within her.

As they paused in front of her – was it to hold up the future they foresaw with all its bitterness? – she found she was unable to respond, to reach out. It was as though she had no right to offer them any words of comfort that might soothe or blind their open wound. Blinded by her tears all she could do was stand by helplessly as they began the long climb back up to the school, the girls with muddied breasts and matted hair pausing briefly to take her hand in theirs before returning to the bleak and clotted stream of fellow mourners.

9

It was not until the children had passed beyond the landing strip, winding their way towards the heart of the mountain, that Rachel at last found the courage to look up. The village women, who every afternoon spread their washing over the rocks to dry, had melted into the forest, along with the pigs and the *pikaninis* who looked after them, and the wood gatherers and the casual workers employed by the ADC to cut back the undergrowth from the banks, their grass-knives flicking back and forth over the shallows like tadpoles.

She stood alone at the edge of the Waragoi, at the edge of the foam-flecked torrent as it raced away through the trees; alone with the dead child's mudstained exercise book lying at her feet.

Just then she caught sight of Nathaniel crossing the wooden bridge over the river, the heavy tread of his boots echoing over the loosely-laid planks. He strode towards the solitary figure on the far bank, who sat watching the tail-end of the procession evaporating beneath the sun's unconsoling eye. Quickly she waved. Relieved. Enthusiastic.

With some difficulty Richard got to his feet. Brushing away her tears, Rachel hurried along the bank, scrambling over the rocks and through the soft mud in between. The shadows were already beginning to lengthen, creating a mood of sombreness. Panting, she suddenly found herself unable to run any further and watched instead as Richard shuffled towards her.

There was something about the way he leaned on Nathaniel's arm. It was a warning, or rather confirmation that the Bolgi were not yet finished. That despite Nathaniel's assurances, the fight to have his brother re-instated would continue, until either Richard saw the hopelessness of it, or the Endai's patience gave out and they drove him from the Keramuti, as they had once driven out Malachy Davis.

Had she crossed the bridge to take his arm she had no doubt he would have looked on it as an act of moral support; would have interpreted her simple joy at seeing him return as a sign of her continuing commitment.

Commitment she was no longer prepared to give, at least not indefinitely. Hobbling up to her with his bootlaces trailing in the dirt, he let go of Nathaniel's arm, and promptly stumbled.

'Richard!' she cried out.

A read smear on the front of his shirt shone like an autumn leaf as he managed to steady himself.

'We weren't expecting you back so soon. My God, you look awful! You look—'

'In damned better shape than the poor blighter they've just fished out of the Waragoi,' he remarked, holding out his hand with mock formality.

Rachel ignored it. 'You mean they let you . . . but I thought the sister . . . ? Your stitches? Surely . . . ?'

His hand settled on the young Bolgi's belt. 'It's all right, Nathaniel. Mrs Green'll help me the rest of the way.'

Nathaniel's fingers locked around Richard's wrist.

'Honestly,' said Richard, 'we can manage. It isn't far.'

'Then I shall walk behind. Just as a precaution. You are not yet strong enough.'

'Nonsense,' Richard exclaimed, shaking the youth's belt so that the noise the heavy buckle made reminded Rachel of an animal rattling the bars of its cage. 'Of course I'm strong enough. Why shouldn't I be?'

'You have lost a lot of blood.'

'Ever heard of transfusion? It's like . . . topping up the oil in your engine.'

'Your body is still in a state of—'

'Look, I feel fine.'

'Though one can see it is not easy for you to walk.'

'A little stiffness, that's all. It'll wear off. Now I suggest you take yourself off back to school. The pupils'll be wondering where you are. *They're* the ones in a state of shock; the ones who need comforting.'

Nathaniel's epaulettes cast a shadow on the road behind him as they rose like giant moths stirred by the evening breeze. 'I shall wait half way. Mrs Green is herself upset over Nimile Orapi's death. I fear she may not have the strength to . . .'

'Really, there's no need. We can manage.'

Tucking the mud-stained exercise book under her blouse, Rachel waited at the side of the road while the two went on arguing. They were both commanding figures, well over six foot, with broad, sloping shoulders and large hands, their bones embedded in taut, hard flesh. Neither seemed in any way daunted by the walls of Keramuti limestone towering over them, reducing their altercation to a minor farce, to the level of a noisy side-show.

The one was showered in dust, so that his beard seemed wild and extravagant; the other appeared sharp, disciplined, with the policeman's belt and pressed epaulettes, ironed bootlaces and flat, shaven crown.

Unlike Richard's eyes – grey and lifeless, reminding her of the shells of the river crabs she sometimes found washed up among the rocks – Nathaniel's gave off a sharp yet troubled light. They seemed to betray the humiliation he felt as he finally stepped down, turned and began making his way up the wooded slopes. Rachel saw him trip over the shiny roots of an old beech, reminding her of her broken sandal and bruised heel. 'Sorry, Mrs Green. I am truly sorry.'

Watching him vanish among the trees, she noticed the long shadows of the mountain sweeping down through the undergrowth, like the blades of the workers' grass-knives.

'Don't think I could face a crowd of hysterical children right now, Rachel, do you?'

She saw him dip his hand into his shirt pocket, toss aside bits of stalk and leaf until the healthy shell of a betel-nut nestled like a bird's egg in his palm. He sank down on to a patch of grass beside the bridge, pulling her down with him, though his strength was negligible and she felt the heat rapidly draining from his body.

At the bottom of the valley where the mountains briefly parted, allowing the Waragoi to burst through a buckled gorge, the evening light continued to fall in angled shafts among the rocks and trees, slanting off the velvet leaves, off the tangled buttress roots, and conical roofs of huts overlooking the river. It was as if she'd opened the centre of a child's book and paper houses surrounded by mountains in faded water colours had sprung up in her lap, compelling her to run her finger along the edges, the edges he failed to see, refused to see. Her thoughts were interrupted by Richard's mumbling.

'. . . was the only way I could get to see him . . . wasn't all that far . . . done it in a wheelchair if there'd been any. Ward sister wouldn't hear of it. Said the boy's family could take care of it themselves . . . said she'd warn all the nurses. Four Square church – thought I ought to go down on my knees and say a word of thanks. Knew her stuff though . . . had to sneak out while she wasn't looking . . .'

All the while he flung pieces of shell into the stagnant pools of water nearby, where silver-winged dragonflies zigzagged over the copper ripples, before dipping down and then with a flash of scarlet peeling away into the night.

'. . . just didn't want to appear arrogant that's all . . . taking up more of his time than one was entitled to . . . especially after Meredith . . . God, what a show *that* was!'

Without his noticing she began slowly unbuttoning his shirt. It was damp and smelled faintly of surgical spirit. Gradually with the tips of her fingers she traced the gathered flesh, feeling the anger and frustration steadily mounting in her as she counted the stitches. Until, no longer able to withstand their silent reproach, she cried out:

'Dammit Richard! Knew her stuff? Yet as soon as her back is turned you're out of the door like a shot! What is it you owe the boy? All you did was log the incident in the book. Anyone would think you were the one who drew up the regulations. It's as if you were responsible; had a duty to his family to somehow . . . I don't know . . . resurrect him from the dead.'

A group of village men advancing over the bridge forced her to withdraw her hand.

'*Apinun masta*.' They each saluted Richard in turn, pausing at the side of the road, their faces bearded and rough.

'*Masta* play rugby long Sarere?' asked one.

Suddenly it occurred to Rachel that none of the children's shrieking she had heard earlier had come from the boys, despite the fact they were the ones who had pulled Nimile Orapi's body out of the water; the ones who had carried him up the mountain on their shoulders. The shrieking, she realised had come from the girls. Or rather the women. For although they were still at school their hands were already calloused from digging, their cheeks tattooed and breasts swollen; their bodies, like their mothers', slow and heavy with responsibility . . . for the cooking and ironing, not only of their own uniforms but also the boys'; for the scrubbing of classroom floors and monitoring of homework; attending to the needs of the *manki*, advising on illnesses, as well as unplanned pregnancies – the quiet, no nonsense conspirators of abortion.

For their part the boys, bow-legged and caked in mud, had remained largely silent. And although they'd marched at the head of the procession it seemed to her they'd been unable to bring themselves to cry out; unable to burst the chains of their masculinity. She wanted to shout out, to tell them – that the past, History – that ancient log of hunting and war – was a cruel deception, a gargantuan illusion for they had come to regard their silence as a form of strength, as a virtue; asserting that it was somehow manly or brave. Even virile.

'. . . would you believe . . . refused to help,' she heard him grumble, as the men, having solicitously examined his clawed flesh, continued on their way, grave and subdued beneath the shadow of their long spears.

'... even to ring up the Ombudsman's secretary ... claimed the Ombudsman had nothing to do with it. Left me no choice really ... was the only way I could get to see him.'

'You might've waited until they'd taken the stitches out,' she replied, fastening his shirt.

'There wasn't time. He's flying out this evening.'

'Out of the country?'

'Biyufa. He has this circuit ... all the major towns; keeps an office in the capital.'

'Then you could have written.'

'And waited six months for a reply? The exams are only a few weeks away.'

'You don't seriously think Nixon could pass? After all the work he's missed? For heaven's sake, Richard, you almost got yourself killed in a stupid accident! And now this, which has nothing at all to do with not wanting to appear arrogant, of course. Discharging yourself from hospital – I suppose that wasn't arrogant, either?'

'I'm sure they'll understand,' he shrugged, at the same time spitting, a blob of crimson juice on to the ground beside him. 'I mean you should've heard us ... Meredith ... arguing. Brought everyone running ... doctors, nurses. In the end even the registrar agreed ... thought Nixon should appeal. Soon as Meredith left I got one of the nurses going off duty to take a letter round to the garage. Seemed at first Nixon didn't want to know. Wrote back saying he was happy where he was. Said it was only pressure from his *wantoks* in the village made him dig up the pipe ... made it look like he wanted to go back to school. Claimed he really wanted to be a mechanic. I had to send another letter. Told him the only way he would ever get an educated girl to marry him – he'd written some remark about the young nurse – was if he completed his own education. It seemed to do the trick. Turned up this morning at the hospital. Said his uncle was waiting in the queue outside the Ombudsman's office. Just as well. By the time we arrived it stretched all the way round the compound. All sorts of claims, mostly against the mining companies ... summary sackings, injuries at work, failure to comply with health and safety procedures ... cases have been piling up ever since the government outlawed payback. Don't think anyone could've realised the effect it would have.'

'Payback was a brake, Richard. It helped to slow down the speed of change. It put a value on people's lives; it was sometimes outrageous I know, but at least they *had* a value – the old, the young, even the excommunicated. Without payback they become vulnerable, open to exploitation. Take Nimile Orapi's death. Without payback the child becomes . . . well just another . . .'

'Statistic? I think we should let the people of the Keramuti decide.'

'Decide?'

'On the price they're prepared to pay.'

'You mean the price of your crusade to have Nixon reinstated?'

'I mean of change and development.'

'Oh I see, like how many lives to extend the highway; or to build a new bridge so the co-operative can buy a bigger truck.'

Juice dribbled down his chin as he replied: 'You may sneer, but the co-operative's given these people something they've never had before: economic muscle. It's given them the chance to deal with suppliers as equals. Not only do they no longer have to put up with the bullying and intimidation that takes place whenever they try to sell their crops, they don't have to pay exorbitant prices for things such as seeds, fertiliser and insecticide. What's more, by running the smaller, local markets, issuing licenses, that sort of thing, the co-operative's able to raise extra revenue – money that can be spent on improving local facilities. It's also helped to break the Endai monopoly on pitches. The villagers now enjoy fair competition, which is what they want, Rachel; what they'll pay for. That's why we're here. To offer our help and expertise.'

'Help? I thought you said Nixon wasn't interested in returning to school. You said he wanted to be a mechanic.'

'I expect it was a bit of bravado. After all everyone knows what happens to them when they're kicked out of school. End up begging on the streets. I imagine he was putting on a brave face. Well, he doesn't have to any more. He can fight back. With the Ombudsman's help he'll be able to challenge the Board of Governors. Who knows the Ombudsman may even recommend changing the Board's composition, getting rid of the Endai majority.'

'Richard!' she cried, feeling herself overwhelmed by his stubbornness, both the fountain of so much of his energy and the source of its dissipation. 'The Endai are the largest tribe in the Highlands. Why shouldn't they have a majority? It isn't as if the smaller tribes have no voice. After all, the most powerful figure in the school is a Bolgi. Nathaniel is the one they all look up to. Endai. Bolgi. Mepi. Muaina. It's all part of the balance, the glue that holds them together. Who are we to interfere? Has the West done any better at looking after its own minorities?'

'What are you saying? Like Meredith – that we shouldn't get involved?'

'I'm saying it may be prudent to examine one's motives, that's all.'

'I told you, I'm only trying to help.'

'So are the staff. So's Meredith.'

'Sure. Clean hands no heart. Frees them of responsibility. How convenient.' Tearing up a fistful of grass from the bank, Rachel allowed the purple stalks to tumble gently into her lap. They gave off the same dry scent as the feathery pampas which leant like drunken men over the edge of the terraces; she must unearth her bitterness before it too sank its roots into the fecund soil.

'So, rescuing Nixon from a growing band of excommunicated is your idea of exercising responsibility, is it? Then what about Nimile Orapi? Are you going to accept responsibility too for the child drowning in the Waragoi? After all . . .'

Her anger seemed to grow, to rebound against the obdurate cliff that was his forehead.

'. . . if it wasn't for the damage done to the pipe there'd have been no need for the children to use the river. Nathaniel assures me Nixon had nothing to do with it, though the boy's record hardly inspires confidence. If the pupils haven't said or done anything about it up to now I suspect it's only because—'

'They're just as afraid of ending up on the scrap heap.'

'Yes, but they don't feel as guilty about it as you do.'

'Why should they?'

'Why should you?'

He spat again on to the ground beside him. Rachel brushed the purple blades of grass from her lap. The last rays of the sun were now streaming through the undergrowth throwing into sharp relief not only the immense smooth-shaven jaw of Elimbari but the tiny, splintered figures of the women returning home along the mountain pathways.

'I mean, here you are accepting responsibility for the trials and tribulations of a young Bolgi whom you hardly know, while at home your sister struggles on alone. You never write. You scarcely even bother to read any of her letters.'

'Cattle drives . . . ? Bore-holes? Or is it black holes?' Richard appeared not to be listening.

'It isn't only Janice,' Rachel went on. 'There are teachers all over the country who feel the way she does. All those strikes . . . Why else would so many of them be talking about leaving? It's precisely because Janice cares – even for the likes of "Chicken" Bell – that she's finding it difficult to carry on. Eighteen years! My God, no wonder she's exhausted. We've barely managed *one*. I'd have thought under the circumstances she deserved a little more support. At least as much as you're prepared to offer Nixon.'

Juice continued to dribble down his chin as he replied: 'Did you even know there was an Ombudsman? One of the nurses only happened to mention it when I asked, jokingly of course, who I'd complain to if I went down with food poisoning. Now do you imagine the Bolgi would have come to me if they'd known he existed? Things are happening so fast, Rachel. It's hard for them to keep up. Hard for us all.'

'Some of them must have known. You said there was a queue.' Irritation welled up in her voice.

'In Biyufa.'

'Yes and pretty soon the news would have spread to the Keramuti. Why force the pace, making it even harder for them to keep up?'

A woman and a child passed by behind them, briefly raising their heads beneath the heavy loads of *kaukau* and firewood. Rachel waved. Bent from the waist, with cracked feet and knotted calves, they trundled on, smiling.

'In any case, I still don't see how you can be so sure Nixon doesn't really want to be a mechanic. What if *you're* the one who's trying to put on a brave face? Trying to save his pride? It seems to me you've become obsessed with this whole . . . ?'

She realised he was no longer listening. His expression had become like the glassy face of Elimbari while his hand lay lifeless in her lap.

'Richard?' she sighed, as she lifted up the bruised fingers and felt in them the weight that was slowly crushing her. 'Richard?'

'*Apinun, tisa,*' said a voice softly to her left. By the time Rachel managed to swivel round the laden figure had already begun her steady, bent-kneed climb. Trapped by Richard's fourteen-stone bulk she wanted to call out after the young girl, to scream at the already bowed shoulders, the arched back and rough, malt-brown skin . . .

But then her anger suddenly evaporated, just as the strength of the Waragoi appeared to ebb with the passing of the sun. As the valley slipped softly into the dusk she felt the constraints of her body leave her, felt a new and unexpected buoyancy take its place, the tips of her fingers tingling where they met the earth. The backs of her knees, her bottom, and shoulder where he continued to lean on her, seemed to dissolve, to melt away.

At the far end of the Waragoi – effulgent now as the sun rebounded through the gorge – she saw the green water rise and come calmly sliding towards her, passing through her. Neither submerged nor afloat, neither carried along by it nor left stranded, she felt its power flow with a great solemnity and evenness. Then with the sudden roar of the current in her ears, she felt herself soaring above the uppermost peaks, above the dazzling green ribbon. With her arms floating clear of her body, she saw beneath the distant spray, an arc rising in a phosphorescent rainbow, joining the outstretched fingers of one hand to the other, passing beneath her feet, over her head, to complete a flawless circle.

'Richard?' she whispered. 'Richard?' But her voice sounded muffled and fell away, silenced by the torrent of water plummeting over the precipice below, by the humming of the light as it travelled round her, anointing her with iridescence. Now she saw a sparkling, imperial red, now an apple green. Then gold and yellow, all fragrant in their feathery dance; light and yet firm in their flowering – in the flowering that was both herself and everything around her, gradually opening; till she felt the innermost coolness of their mauves, their silvers, saffron and rose, the colours that were herself unfolding . . .

10

His reflection in the window revealed the same blood-flecked tie as before. But as he reached for the knot it came away in his hands like a piece of old skin and floated to the floor. Lying among the scraps of rubbish it seemed to mock him; to warn him that no matter how many layers or disguises he shed, there'd be no escaping his confinement without Janice. He had first to help free his sister – victim turned predator – whose heels he could hear ringing in the distance, driving him deeper into the building, past locked doors and grey windows.

A key. If only he could find a key that would unlock one of the doors. No sooner had he begun examining his pockets than he discovered they'd been sewn up. And so instead he beat his fists on each of the doors in turn as though they were the keys on a soundless xylophone. Soon his fists were stinging and he was using his feet, leaving black marks from his boots on the paint.

Suddenly a door did open, though barely a crack and just long enough for a green leather satchel to be tossed at his feet, before it was shut again and he was left to disentangle himself from the straps. He looked up at the shut door, the silence broken only by the relentless clicking in the background.

He tried to open the satchel but its straps were twisted. In desperation he picked it up and swung it forcefully against the door, showering the corridor with books. The books floated past him like butterflies in a sunfilled meadow. Lunging at them he caught only a brief glimpse of their titles – The Unknown Self, Memories, Dreams, Reflections, The Act of Will *– as they glided by, passing effortlessly through the grey windows. All the while the clicking grew louder, like the chamber of a revolver being loaded.*

He shook out the satchel and a letter fell to the floor. It carried the embossed heading of a firm of solicitors. Unfolding it he read: 'Subject: Last Will and Testament of Richard Albert Green; born 31 May 1910, died June . . .' Click . . . Click . . . Click . . . He could hear his sister's footsteps growing nearer. 'Regarding deceased's account with Barclays Bank.

Account held main branch, Nairobi. Substantial funds . . . assigned family of one, Mwangi Njombo . . .' Her footsteps no longer sounded sinister, but sad, slow and elegiac, like a child who'd been slapped in public by its mother, sobbing as it followed her home.

Folding the letter, he heard her call out. 'Richard, couldn't we at least talk?'

She was short, slight in build. Her hair was tangled and grey. She wore a faded smock and a pair of dungarees which flapped over her bare feet. The clicking he had heard had been the sound of pencils – the pockets of her dungarees festooned with registers, mark books, diaries, pens, and boxes of pencils. These seemed not so much to weigh her down as to suck out the blood through her skin, like leeches, leaving her pale and emaciated. Once more he began to search for a way out. There had to be a door, a window, even a fanlight he could crawl through.

'I shouldn't bother,' she sighed, her eyes shrunken and drained. 'There's nowhere left. If you're thinking that old standby, the "Third World", will do, remember . . .' She jabbed him in the chest with the point of one of her pencils, 'it's in here, Richard. Not out there. The Third World's in here!'

A line of boys began to file between them, pausing in order to allow her to place a hand on their forehead, as though 'anointed' in this way they were acknowledging their debt to her; acknowledging more that she possessed some mysterious hold over them than their faith in education, since it was clearly a matter of routine judging by their bored expressions. She continued to exert the same hold over him, even as he fled along the corridor now flowing with bodies, like chains of molecules warmed by the sun.

'Good Lord, it wasn't as if I was asking the earth!' he heard her call out as she hurried after him. 'All I wanted was you to support me against father's economic tyranny. I mean what would it have cost to keep Ngai alive? The family's subscription to Country Life? Ngai was alive, Richard. A life! Flesh and blood. Not just some wretched figure in a pocketbook.'

'What about father's life then?' he yelled over the heads of the pupils who continued to bow before Janice's outstretched hand while ignoring him altogether, brushing past him as though he were invisible. 'Did you ever stop to consider how much his life might have been worth every time you galloped across the road in front of his car? Of course you knew he'd swerve, knew it wouldn't be your life that was in danger. Dammit, Janice, if you wanted to go back to Kenya so much . . .'

'I didn't want to go back,' she said.

'The Edwards would've been only too happy to have you stay. Getting burnt out didn't see them joining the exodus.'

'I said I didn't want to go back.'

'You were unhappy. You hated England. Said the English were—'

'I am English. Besides, you were just as unhappy, remember? Only you managed to keep it a secret – the way father did.'

'I don't think you could say father's unhappiness was exactly a secret.'

'No, but what a pretence! Having everyone believe he'd sold the farm so that he and mother could be near us while we were at school; when really it was that damned court case. The shooting of Mwangi. Made it so embarrassing meeting old neighbours who knew the truth and then pretended not to know. Heavens, everyone knew! Everyone that is, apart from mother. And you and I. Knowing and yet not knowing. Wondering where all the money was going . . .' She broke off as a group of boys burst out of a nearby classroom, saw them standing outside in the corridor and scrambled back to their desks.

'Sorry, Janice,' he said quickly, spotting the chance to get away; 'as you can see, I've a class waiting.'

'What for?' she replied, grimly surveying the boys as they hurriedly spread open their books in front of them like prayer mats. 'Deliverance?'

'History, actually.'

'Ah, of course – the Crusades! Enter Richard the Lionheart! Enter the gallant knight.'

'I'm only trying to do my job.'

'Come to offer his charges fresh hope. Come to calm their fears. Not of rotting in some damp cell, mind, some dank ideological dungeon; of being condemned to a life of darkness. No, theirs is the fear of unemployment, of old age and infirmity, of socialism, higher taxes . . . In which case . . .'

'I think perhaps you'd better leave, Janice. This is hardly the time . . .'

'In which case they'd be entitled to feel aggrieved. Cheated even. After all a man of your education and background. Well paid job in the city. Throwing it all up to cower in paradise. No wonder mother despaired. Couldn't make sense of it. No one could. Good Lord, at least Gaugain could paint!'

'Mother was ill. She had difficulty making sense of anything. She was confused. Father's death meant – '

'She felt betrayed. Felt he'd taken the easy way out.'

'Father wasn't the type. Everyone knew that. His war record spoke for itself. A man of integrity. Remember the story of how he and mother met? Who knows what pain he suffered, what despair? Perhaps if you knew all the facts, the truth – as you say, knowing and yet not knowing where all the money went – perhaps you'd understand.'

'The truth!' Janice cried, the echo reverberating down the corridor. Immediately it was taken up by the boys who leapt to their feet, banging the desks with their fists and chanting:

'The truth! The truth! The truth!'

Suddenly Janice's attention was drawn by the leather satchel which had mysteriously re-appeared in the doorway. She darted forward, scooped it up and sent it hurtling through the window.

'Right then,' she yelled above the crash of flying glass, 'let's see if you have the balls to tell the truth!'

The boys sank silently behind their desks, their faces burning. It seemed to him their eyes were filled with terror, as though the enormity of their demands had only just begun to dawn on them.

A drained and trembling figure, mocked by the jagged halo behind her, Janice snatched up a splinter from the windowsill and slid it carelessly through her smock. Her lips twisted into a curiously triumphant smile, so that it was a moment before he felt the fire. To his horror he saw the blood seeping through his own shirt, a voracious flower opening its crumpled face to the laughter of the pupils. He ran blindly out into the corridor where in the dull, grey silence he could hear the sinister flutter of petals, the harrowing click click click.

11

Malachy Davis had been taking part in the island's annual Second World War fly-past when the Tiger Moth he'd spent years restoring in a corner of the Biyufan airfield crashed into the Kagamuga river. He was sixty-nine. By that time, having been with varying degrees of success explorer, prospector, planter, trader, and hotelier, he'd managed to leave a modest legacy to his two sons. The eldest soon fell out with his brother over the running of a mining concession and applied to settle in Australia. A few months later the entire island community was stunned when he hanged himself after learning that his application had been turned down on the grounds that no official record existed of the marriage between his father and mother – the daughter of a local Kagamugan headman.

The wooden bungalow Malachy Davis had lived in with his family after the war stood on sagging supports at the far end of the Provincial government compound, its paintwork faded, the iron guttering choked with leaves, so that the rain left russet stains on the plywood ceiling.

There were other stains, more widespread, that seeped like time into the bleached and broken floorboards; stains that were the fingerprints of a people's patience. The signatures – recorded for all to see – of Kagamugan villagers who, anxious for their children's future, had gathered daily upon the crowded verandahs of the old building, their weathered faces and broken teeth adding to its atmosphere of decay. And yet now that the spacious though mournful rooms had been taken over by the Education Department, it seemed they also brought with them fresh hope. Hope so rampant that one hesitated before knocking on the door, uncertain whether anyone or anything – let alone the whole paraphernalia of a government office – existed on the other side or had merely been conjured up by the people's eternal optimism, by the immense power of their dreams.

'Thought I'd give it a bit-a time, Richie; thought perhaps the novelty would wear off. Christ, I didn't think you'd become addicted to the stuff! Just goes to show – the bush, I mean, what it can do to a man when he has all that time on his hands. Course with some people it isn't the time. It's the silence. Begin to hear voices. Lucky yer got Rachel to keep yer company. Even so, yer bound to get a little bored now and then. Which is why I don't want to kick up too much of a fuss. All I'm asking is yer don't chew the stuff in front of the kids. Remember, being a chalkie's like taking part in a mannequin parade. You're out there, strutting your stuff on the stage. The audience – in this case the *kanakas* – they watch. They imitate. Last thing the Department wants is you imitating them!'

Meredith pitched forward in his chair and banged the heavy glass which he gripped in his right hand down on the desk in front of him, as though it were a rubber stamp whose ink was fading. Richard gave a start. He had refused a drink and yet the heat in the office had the effect of a dozen whiskies: his blood was throbbing, his legs were like string. Richard watched as the tall, bony figure proceeded to reach down into the drawer, pull out the bottle he kept hidden in a disused file, and pour himself another drink before sinking back in his chair. He raised the glass to his blunt lips so that the light filtering through the whisky spilled down the front of his chest, landing like powdered gold on the surface of his silk cravat.

Richard thought Meredith was probably in his early fifties. He had never said. Probably never would though he had plenty to say about most things. Meredith's outspokenness betrayed, Richard thought, an element of desperation. It was simple really. In a country where people conducted virtually almost every single aspect of their lives out in the open – courting, dancing, feasting, mourning, giving birth – Meredith found himself incarcerated in a run-down government office. He watched life like a laden coffee truck storm past him; life that was swift, urgent, driven by the villagers' desire for something better than mere mannequin parades.

Meredith lived alone with an old male servant, Jonah Rea, who had been with him back in the days when Meredith, then still a young admin officer on secondment from the Australian government, had tried unsuccessfully to initiate a ban on civil servants chewing betel-nut. It was an act that had led his Fairfax colleagues to demand he be sent back home. Instead he was transferred to the Education Department and a year later made an inspector of schools.

It was said the two men quarrelled frequently and that late at night neighbours could hear the sound of bottles being smashed inside the house. However whenever Richard had had reason to call – sometimes on shopping trips he and Rachel would be invited to lunch – he'd detected little sign of enmity between them, Jonah, a devout Christian who neither smoked, drank nor chewed betel-nut, going about his domestic chores with an air of quiet unflappability. Indeed with most of Jonah's family having perished at the hands of the Japanese, and Meredith leaving home at the age of seventeen following a violent quarrel with his step-father, it seemed to Richard that the two solitary figures had found in each other's company a solace and understanding, a moral sensibility that allowed them to shelter under the same roof – Meredith's untamed belligerence notwithstanding . . .

'. . . Godda set an example for Christ's sake, Richie. Can't have yer walking about with yer mouth looking like a lump-a butcher's meat. It's not only disgusting, it's bloody unhygienic too. Look around yer. *Kanakas* spit the stuff all over the damned place!'

'And have been doing for years,' said Richard, glancing wearily out of the window, where a group of villagers stood with their painted faces pressed against the glass, like wild flowers. Their still, dark-ringed eyes reminded him of the elders of the small Muina village with whom he had sat until the early hours of the morning debating whether the co-operative needed to purchase a pulping machine of its own. A vital investment in his view, given the inflated charges of the Biyufa middle-men. Although the *bikmen* had agreed, it had been the women squatting like tree stumps in the shadows of the fire who had held things up by urging caution. Their soft, mesmerising eyes were frightening in their stoicism, in their slowness to anger, for despite the men's impatience – he could hear the hot steam of betel-juice being spat on to the scorched stones – it seemed that nothing would ever be decided. Finally, with dawn stealing across a bruised sky, a consensus had been reached, allowing him to set off for Biyufa with the completed purchasing order in his briefcase. Fourteen sets of signatures – the minimum required – from fourteen different villages, gathered in a little over twenty-one days, while Meredith's three month-old telegram summoning him to an urgent meeting lay where it had fallen, among the betel-nut skins in the cold fire.

'The point I'm trying to make, Richie, is . . .'

'Look,' said Richard, fingering the dealer's receipt nestling in his shirt pocket, 'you knew perfectly well when you asked Rachel and me to help out that we'd never done this sort of thing before. All this mannequin stuff.'

'Then if I can put it in rugby terms – I hear you and the ADC are getting quite a little team together up there – you're the bloke with all the experience. You've been on the pitch, what is it . . . twenty-seven, twenty-eight years?'

'Actually it's thirty—'

'Whatever it is, it's a lifelong familiarity with the game.'

'That league or union?'

Meredith paused only to drain his glass. His long jaw resembled a windswept beach over which the sea-green of his eyes appeared to ebb and flow, while what little remained of his sandy-coloured hair reminded Richard of a fragile barrier reef lining his freckled skull.

'Thing to remember is, over here you're on the pitch not as a player but as a referee! The minute you join in as a player, they'll trample you into the ground. 'Course I realise you're a bloke with tons of energy, likes to get involved – chaps next door in the Department of Industry and Agriculture have been filling me in on your work at the co-operative. Reckon they don't know how you do it, the way you been expanding, pulling *kanakas* out-a the bush, bringing in more'n more money. Great! I think it's great. Makes me feel kind-a embarrassed when I think of the row we had back at the hospital.'

'All I asked was that you ring the Ombudsman's secretary.'

'Helluva time to pick an argument, Richie.'

'Sound him out on—'

'What with you just been stitched together. You know, I wish you'd taken that holiday I offered you. Could-a gone down to the coast, sunned yourself on the beach. I'm sure Rachel could-a done with the break.'

The sound of scuffling breaking out on the verandah caused Meredith to pause once more.

'Anyway,' he said, flapping his arm, seeming to forget that he still held the glass. It promptly slipped from his hand, striking the edge of the desk before rolling on to the floor; 'that's all history now. I mention the business about the co-operative because I want yer to know I – we all – realise you're doing a fantastic job and that the chalk-bashing is really beyond the call of duty. It's a burden you're free to walk away from any time; no recriminations. 'Course that'd be the last thing I'd want yer to do. However . . .'

Angry shouts rose above the languid whirr of the office fan as it fitfully stirred the stale air. Meredith sighed and pushed himself up out of his chair. With the knuckles of his left hand pale as driftwood, he leant over the side of the desk and reached out to retrieve the empty glass:

'There's still the issue of the boy. Now either you never got my telegram or . . . ? Well, anyway, the Ombudsman's office has been in touch.'

'They contacted *you*?'

'Rang me up from Fairfax.'

'Why you? I thought . . .'

'Sure, we all know what you thought. Whole bloody hospital knows.'

'You said you didn't want anything to do with it.'

'I said it had nothing to do with me. There's a difference. However, seeing how much it meant to you – you know, couple-a inches and Sister Boniwe reckons that metal fragment might-a done yer some real serious damage.'

'It was an accident. Could have happened to anyone.'

'Yeah, well, first thing the sister did after discovering you'd gone walk about was ring me up and ask if I knew what was going on. Said she couldn't understand the fuss you were making. I said I didn't understand myself. Thought perhaps yer felt under some kind of obligation to the boy.'

'What did the Ombudsman's office say?'

They could hear the swift padding of feet over the bare boards; the shouting grew louder, gusting through the compound.

'They said they'd got my letter, asking to be kept abreast of developments. Told me you'd been to the circuit office; that you and the boy had filled in all the forms.'

'And?'

'Also that yer handed over a personal statement detailing your role in—'

'Did they reach a decision?' Richard interrupted.

'Yer won't like it, Richie, but the Ombudsman reckons it's out-a his jurisdiction. Says it's a departmental matter. Which is what I've been trying to tell yer all along. Could-a saved yer a ton-a trouble.'

'He say anything else? Suggest other avenues we might explore?'

Meredith swayed over the large, leather-topped desk. 'He suggested yer might go back to the Board-a Governors, though frankly . . . Have you any idea how frustrating it's been watching you keep the fuse burning? Waiting for it all to blow up in your face?'

'Look, you agreed the boy deserved a second chance.'

'On principle, yes. But the Board of Governors ought to be the judge.'

'What about the boy's parents? Don't they deserve a chance?'

'Like I said, it's up to the Board.'

'But you're the Chief Officer. Surely you could—'

'Twist their arm? Sorry, we've been over all that before. Another time, another era. *Kanakas* got a right to make their own mistakes.'

The shouting and the patter of feet on the verandah being pursued by the menacing tramp of boots now spread rapidly through the compound. Richard rose, pushed aside the cane chair Meredith had once referred to grimly as, 'Wayne's last stand', and made for the door.

'Christ, yer godda give 'em time, Richie to get used to all the changes; to become inured, less thin-skinned. Time to develop the necessary immunity.'

'Immunity?' replied Richard heatedly, swinging round abruptly as he reached the door. 'Suddenly life's a disease. For God's sake man they don't want immunity! They want exposure. All immunity's done has left them isolated and poor. Ask the boys waiting for me at the Land Rover. First time any of them have been outside the Keramuti. You should've seen their faces as we drove into town. Their eyes . . . you could tell they were high as kites.'

The door burst open and he felt a blow against his shins. A wave of dusty flesh knocked him back into the room. Through a haze of milling bodies he saw that a scrawny youth stood trembling before him in the doorway, almost naked.

'I'm sorry, Mr Green, we did not mean to disturb you,' Nathaniel apologised hurriedly, grabbing hold of the emaciated figure and pulling him outside.

'Wait a minute,' said Richard, following him out. 'What's going on?'

Nathaniel twisted the smaller boy's arm behind his back. 'This is someone you have met before. A rascal. Tonight he shall have a bed in the Biyufa jail.'

Nathaniel's rascal was a brackish-coloured figure, rough-skinned, with sharp bones and thin, scarred legs. His jaw and left eye were swollen, his arms grey with ash. The squashed butt of a cigarette protruded from behind his left ear. Encouraged by the crowd's growing hostility toward the Bolgi, he spat defiantly at the feet of those who had helped to corner him – Nathaniel's fellow pupils, all first years, whom Richard had entrusted to Nathaniel's care, and who now huddled together near the door, their faces creased with terror.

'He is the one who ambushed us a fortnight ago near the Kagamuga,' Nathaniel announced, his eyes glowering in their dust-reddened sockets. 'I'm sure he did not expect to see us again so soon.'

As the sun streamed through the broken eaves, its heat seeming to strip the bark off the nearby eucalyptus trees, Richard recalled the incident Nathaniel was referring to when, driving along the highway, the Bolgi had made a sudden grab for the wheel.

'No, do not pull over, Mr Green! It is a trick. A dangerous trick. You must not stop!'

He recalled a tenuous figure emerging out of the mist.

'There will be others hiding in the bushes. They are the same people who have been robbing the trucks from the coffee estates. One of them pretends to be in trouble and then when the driver stops the others jump out and steal his money.'

Gradually the figure became more distinct . . . drab, grey flesh, wrapped in rags hanging like moss from a pandanus tree.

'Please, Mr Green! It is too dangerous.'

With cupped hands the gaunt figure waited in the middle of the road; his eyes hollow bowls, reflecting the emptiness of those who have nothing left to lose but their lives.

'As you know there is no panel beater in Biyufa,' Nathaniel now reminded him.

For although he hadn't stopped, he'd been forced to swerve. The Land Rover – that had replaced the wrecked Land Cruiser – skidded over the greasy surface, bouncing off the side of a deserted stockade before returning once more to the road.

'It means we are obliged to drive all the way to the coast if we wish to have the vehicle repaired.'

Avoiding the Bolgi's bewildered gaze, Richard set about trying to free the young rascal.

'But Mr Green . . .'

'I think it's best. After all, it happened so fast how can you be sure he's the one we saw?'

'I *am* sure.' Nathaniel insisted.

'But it was raining.'

'It is easier for them to stop the trucks in the rain.'

'Using children?' said Richard, sceptically.

'The robbers will use anyone to help them achieve their aims.'

'You saw them? Hiding in the bushes?'

Nathaniel's tenacious grip tightened on what was left of the rascal's torn collar. 'In any case he is the one who caused us to drive into the stockade. Now the Land Rover is —'

'Us? Caused *us* to drive . . . ? I was the one behind the wheel.'

'The Land Rover does not belong to you, Mr Green. It belongs to the co-operative. To all its members who have contributed to the cost of purchasing it. We should not be the ones to pay for the repairs.'

Richard pointed to the half-naked figure whose scarred legs threatened to slip between the broken floorboards. 'You aren't seriously suggesting that he pay?'

'He is not alone in the world. He has *wantoks*. It is their responsibility. If they refuse then we can have him charged.'

They heard a drawer slamming inside the room. 'For Christ's sake, Richie, tell 'em to bugger off!'

The crowd, many of whom had begun to surge noisily on to the verandah, grew silent. Richard saw their confusion. It seemed to be embodied in the collection of run-down bungalows which had been converted into various government offices. There was the Department for National Development; for Works and Energy; Mines; Tourism; Culture and Recreation . . . The doorways of each hung open, like the mouths of animals that had fallen asleep in the sun, while those in charge, the permanent secretaries and under-secretaries, lunched at the Flight Deck Hotel, or boarded Kumul Air flights bound for the capital. They were fleeing the besieging villagers who remained uncertain of what was happening to them, uncertain of this strange new force that was propelling them in a direction few seemed able to predict. Nevertheless they continued to plant new coffee trees, to open new trade stores and roadside cafés, because these things were new and excited them, as they excited Richard by their eagerness to break out of the past – even if it meant on every journey along the highway one had to confront the spectacle of emaciated pikininis begging from the countless trucks bounding into town with their new-found wealth.

'Richie!'

Having stumbled across to the door, Meredith pointed to the far side of the compound, where a posse of policemen were clambering out of a blue Suzuki jeep.

'I suggest yer let the kid go and then hop it round the back. Unless yer wanna spend the rest-a the day explaining yourself to these fellas.'

The peaks of their scarlet caps gleamed beneath the silver leaves of the ragged eucalyptus trees as the police rapidly threaded their way between the wooden buildings. The clump of their boots on the concrete pathway, the jangle of steel cuffs, caused the crowd to shrink back into the shadows. Hurriedly Richard prized the beggar out of Nathaniel's grasp and shoved him into the arms of the retreating villagers. Grabbing Nathaniel by the arm, he dragged the Bolgi forcefully across the verandah, instructing the rest of the pupils who'd remained cowering by the door to follow them. At once their bare feet thundered over the floorboards.

Clambering over the railing, they leapt to the ground and fled round the back of the bungalow, barging past isolated groups of villagers who sat in the shade rolling cigarettes and chewing betel-nut. A grey-haired woman urinating in the long grass looked up and saw them take a short cut across the overgrown graves of Malachy Davis and his son, Wayne, before ducking beneath the compound fence. Minutes later they reached the Land Rover and scrambled aboard in silence.

12

They sped out of town along the Keramuti Highway, showering the inhabitants of a nearby slum with dirt and gravel. The light burst like a string of Chinese crackers along the razor wire that separated the road and its growing fringe of cardboard shanties from the airfield, where heavy twin-propped aircraft squatted like caged animals on the tarmac. As the town receded in a bruised and angry light it must have seemed to the boys to be a savage creature best left undisturbed. It was a mongrel mix of plate-glass windows and murky lean-to's, whose smells and stains – from market stalls selling exotic potions, to chemists, curios and do-it-yourself butchers dripping their sodden meat in the sultry air – saturated the wide, unpaved streets, lined on both sides with heaps of sand, cement and aggregate.

And yet, although they were racing away across the Biyufan plain, they still couldn't escape the savage creature – a fiery leash unfurling in the sky so that the greater their speed, the longer, more blistering the leash, stretching all the way back to the very throat, of the untamed beast.

Observing Nathaniel staring rigidly ahead Richard wondered whether Meredith had been right after all; whether perhaps he ought to have taken things a little more slowly, given them time to adapt, time to develop the necessary immunity. Clearly had it been within their power they would have rid themselves of anything that reminded them of the town's unexplained savagery. Even now it appeared they had shut their eyes in order to deny its existence. At least until they had returned home, to the security of the mountains, where they would proudly recount the story of all they'd seen.

It was this ability to leap back and forth he realised he envied; the ability to explore areas that were unfamiliar, without losing one's way; being able to return to the inner sanctum, where you would be welcomed no matter the scars, or the hurt caused by your leaving.

As the afternoon wore on and the mountains ringing the great Biyufa plain emerged pale and exhausted against a silver sky, the boys fell asleep in the back of the Land Rover, their bodies cocooned in the silken dust that spiralled up around them, seeming to suck out all the moisture from the air before settling on to the branches of the surrounding trees. The dust appeared to age the trees, leaving them shrunken and withered. Only these were coffee trees and the company estates that owned them stretched as far as the eye could see, so as they sped through the vast emerald landscape they passed only a few deserted villages scattered by the roadside with empty stockades and derelict stalls.

'Once,' said Nathaniel, the first to rouse himself, 'the Kagamuga was a special place. The *kanakas* were afraid of it. They would not come here unless there were many of them together. Then they had to pay a lot of pigs and shells to the mudmen living beside the Kagamuga river, because they were the ones who looked after the spirits of all the people who had drowned – in the Waragoi, or the Waramai, which runs near my village at Gelmbolg, or any of the other rivers running down from the mountains. Until Malachy Davis came to stop the Japanese from reaching the Highlands, no one had ever crossed the river without first paying the mudmen. Malachy Davis did pay, but only some months afterwards when he wanted the mudmen to join as soldiers. Everybody knew it was too late. That's why even many years afterwards they were not surprised when they learned that his plane had crashed into the river. In fact it was not Malachy Davis who paid but his son, when he hanged himself. It was the son, the elders say, who really paid for his father.

Richard eased his foot on the accelerator, wound up his window so that the roar of the wind was restricted to a thin whistle through the vents, while Nathaniel's voice rose with a rueful resonance above the monotonous whine of the engine.

'Today of course you can see the Kagamuga no longer belongs to the mudmen. Neither the land, which is in the hands of the big companies nor the river, which is being dammed now that the government has received a loan from the World Bank to build the hydro-electric station. The people are unable even to use the mud from the river's banks in order to make their traditional masks. Those masks were very important to them. They represented the faces of the drowned spirits. By dancing in them they give those spirits back part of their bodies so they could join in the special sing-sings with their *wantoks*. Nowadays the mudmen just use handkerchiefs. But it is for a different purpose altogether. The traditional sing-sings are being replaced by drunken celebrations when they have stolen money from passing motorists. The mudmen have become rascals and bandits. Of course they will not admit it. They say they are making drivers pay for the road which goes over their land. It does not matter that the government has already compensated them, that it has given them other land. They see the profits which the big companies are making and so they want more for themselves.'

As they reached the foot of the Malachy Davis pass, the bonnet of the Land Rover shot up in front of them like a wall of scum-laden water, knocking the boys in the back out of their sleep. Cursing the hot steel burning their hands and feet, they quickly fought to regain their seats, their hissing and sighing fading like steam as the vehicle slowed.

'What are you saying?' said Richard, glancing up at the summit, crowned in the dazzling sunshine with pandanus trees; 'the mudmen are being greedy? Or that they should return to the river? Go back to looking after the spirits of those who've drowned?'

The Land Rover lurched up the narrow pass, brushing the side of the mountain. Nathaniel stretched out an arm, making a spring between his body and the dashboard. Above the impassioned revving of the engine his voice sounded phlegmatic, almost whimsical:

'Mr Green, is it true you once lived in Africa?'

Richard shouted as he felt the wheels slipping, spitting stones against the underside of the chassis: '*Born*, Nathaniel! I was *born* in Africa.'

'And your parents?'

'In Nottingham. At least Father was. Mother was from Wiltshire. They went out to Africa after the war.'

'They were not afraid?'

'Father'd already been. Left home when he was twenty-one. Refused to follow his father – my grandfather – down the mines. Instead he joined the Kenyan police. Eight years later when war broke out he joined the army. Fought in North Africa.'

'Against the Africans?'

'Against Rommel. My father was wounded saving the lives of four East African volunteers. So they packed him off to hospital in England. He hated it – England, Europe, the war. Threw his medals into the river near Bath. That's how he and Mother met. She'd seen him out of the hospital window. Livid apparently – rushed out, lifting up her skirts and waded into the water to search for them. Found one – the George Cross. Turned out it was the day her father'd been buried. She'd just come back from the funeral. He was quite wealthy. Left her some money.'

'Ah, the bride price!'

'You could say that. They bought a farm with it in the Highlands.'

'Africa?'

'Kiambu. It's where I was born.'

'Then it is in your blood.'

'Farming?'

'Africa.'

'They sold it while I was still in junior school. It's ironic really, they used to grow . . .'

His voice trailed away as the large coffee estates began to shrink in the distance. Nathaniel leaned forward to get a better view of the road ahead. Both above and below, the slopes were littered with the debris of mudslides; the dark red earth bristling with boulders and the roots of up-ended trees. 'Do you think,' he said, his eye following the tortuous thread as it looped back and forth, ducking behind concrete reinforced banks and splashing through streams, making its way steadily toward the summit; 'do you think one day you would like to go back? To see the place where you were born?'

'I did try once,' said Richard, glancing in the rearview mirror. 'That's how Mrs Green and I met. At Nairobi airport. In fact we'd sat next to each other on the flight, but didn't talk. It was only after we landed, on our way through immigration that we . . . she was behind me in the queue, you see, and was getting rather impatient – not with the immigration officials; with me as it turned out. She thought I was being rude. In fact I was at my wits end as the authorities were refusing to allow me back into the country.'

'You see,' said Nathaniel, 'one can never go back. It is the same for all of us. You. Me. Also the mudmen of the Kagamuga. They cannot go back. Once their land was sacred. Now it has become something else. Many say the land has died. I do not agree. It is still alive. It has just become something else. Something different from what it was before . . .'

The young Bolgi fell silent, as though the thought were cushioning his body from the jolting of the Land Rover as it scrambled in and out of the tight bends with its tailboard chains clanking. Then, as he spread his palms over the hot metal of the dashboard, he sighed.

'You know, Mr Green,' he said, 'I remember the last time I returned to the village with my brother and grandfather. My *wantoks* were very angry with me. They said I had forgotten them. They said that in all the years I have been guarding the school they have hardly seen me. When I said I guard the school because it means the school pays my fees and therefore I do not have to be a burden to them, they replied that I was becoming independent, like the white man.'

'I would've thought that's what they wanted. What the country wants. That way it'll achieve its own – economic – independence. No more genuflecting to the West. That's why I'd like to see organisations like the co-operative do more, why I'd like to see the people keep control of their own resources. Because then any profit they make they can reinvest in order to build up the country as a whole. Unlike the English whose tradition is merely to feather their own nests.'

'The English are rich.'

'In memories. They are the *kanakas* of Europe. Always looking back.'

'They are still ahead of us,' said Nathaniel.

'They've had a few hundred years' head start.'

'It will not be easy to catch up.'

'No, but then *you've* managed it – to catch up with the rest of the boys in your class, I mean. I imagine all those years ago when you came close to losing your eye, you must have thought you'd never go to school, especially after your parents decided to send your brother ahead of you.'

'It was a difficult decision for them to make.'

'It's you who's done all the difficult work. Paying your own fees . . . By the way, what will you do when you go to college? You are going on, aren't you? You must. Your future, it's . . . well, it's the country's future. That, to me, is what *wantok* really means. Not just sharing a common language but a common destiny.'

'I shall hope to go,' said Nathaniel, buttoning the sleeves of his heavy combat shirt as the temperature began to drop. The Land Rover continued to climb, to scrape its sides against the bare rock which threatened at any moment to collapse on top of them. 'At the same time I cannot say that I wish never to go back to my village. Sometimes at the beginning of the holidays when I see the other pupils returning home I want to go also. The only problem is I don't want to be ruled by *kanakas* for the rest of my life. It is not just the Kagamuga or the Keramuti which is changing, Mr Green. It is our whole nation. It is being reborn. Unfortunately the *kanakas* cannot see it and may destroy everything. That is why I want to finish school, because it's better I find a new life for myself, maybe overseas, as you have done. Though of course if you remain here for a long time in the Keramuti then you, too, will find yourself becoming a prisoner. The *kanakas* may address you as *masta* but they will treat you as one of their own. Everything you do will depend on their command and wishes. You will become a part of village life, which means they will become responsible for you, but also that you will be responsible for them. That is what we understand by the word *wantok*.'

A light mist drifted across the road. Slowly the dust on the windscreen began to dissolve, leaving watery threads dangling from exposed chips in the glass. Through the mist they could just make out the Biyufa plain stretching far away below them, a golden, brandy colour with the sun still shining on it, as though into an open cask that had just been steamed and scrubbed. The highway was its trademark, burnt into the wood, into the smooth staves held together by the glittering hoops of the horizon. Overhead a white-tailed buzzard slope-soared on a pocket of warm air, producing a flurry of activity from the boys in the back. As Richard steered the Land Rover towards the top of the pass, Nathaniel, who did not allow his eye to wander from the road, said stoically:

'Many times on the weekends I am travelling this way with Nixon. Now that he is working in my uncle's garage he is free to come and go as he pleases. The people in Gelmbolg are not happy about it as you know. But sometimes I think he is happy. Then other times when we are talking he is sorry for all the trouble he has caused and says if the Ombudsman will give him permission he will come back to school.'

Glancing in the rearview mirror, Richard saw the mist drawing like a cataract over the eye of the plain. 'I'm afraid it doesn't look too good, Nathaniel; the Ombudsman's just turned us down. As for Meredith . . .'

'You will go back to the Board of Governors?'

'There's no point. All they've done is stall. I'm going to try the Minister.'

'You are not afraid?'

'The Minister's one of the most popular men in the government.'

'I mean of becoming a prisoner of these *kanakas*?'

'Perhaps if I had *wantoks* who might be hurt as a result. Fortunately in this case there aren't any.'

'But Mrs Green. Is she not . . . ?'

'Apart from Mrs Green that is. And even she . . . well, the fact is Nathaniel, we aren't married. Mrs Green's real name is Tormey. Rachel Tormey.'

As they rounded the final bend before the summit Nathaniel slipped an army-surplus jersey over his head and said: 'Actually last week when I was talking with Mrs Green . . . eh, Mrs—'

'Ms Tormey.'

'She told me you have a sister. One who is regularly writing to you from England. She said she is concerned that you do not write back and asked me to remind you of your *wantok*. You see, Mr Green, even you cannot escape. Because really we are all like the Kagamuga. It is only on the outside that we change, become different. Independent, as you say. But always we belong to the same heart. Outside we are someone else. Inside we remain the same.'

And so. At last. The summit! Richard pulled over to the side of the road and turned off the engine. A wooden plank nailed across the window of an abandoned roadworker's shack had the words, 'twelve thousand feet above sea-level' scrawled across it in brown paint. He wondered whether it meant anything to the pupils as they scrambled over the rocks, picking nuts from the pandanus trees silhouetted in the mist. As they paused to empty their bladders, they reminded him of bronzed gargoyles, their glittering arcs shooting skywards before tumbling into the marble folds of the mountains where the cloud lay foaming at their feet.

'You see, Mr Green, even you cannot escape. Because really we are all like the Kagamuga. It is only on the outside that we change, become different . . . always we belong to the same heart . . . Outside someone else . . . Inside the same.'

13

He was arguing with a hotel doorman whose only words of English appeared to be 'No ticket'. The more he tried to explain that he didn't need a ticket, the more fiercely the red-faced doorman shook his head, shouting, 'No ticket! No ticket!' Until finally someone he took to be the hotel manager, wearing a lounge suit with a pink carnation in his lapel, marched through the heavy doors and in a bid to disperse the crowd of curious bystanders, began distributing free tickets from a flowerpot at the top of the marble steps. The bystanders glanced briefly at the tickets before tearing them up and hurrying off into the night.

On his hands and knees he began scouring the steps for the broken stubs, trying to find two halves that would match. The doorman was laughing, hitching up the trousers of his gold-braided uniform and shoving his face against his.

'See? Is a mirror. Is two halves. You, me, is two halves!'

Staring into the doorman's marble-blue eyes he suddenly found himself transported into the foyer, from where through a revolving door he caught sight of her. She was standing alone in a crowded dining hall, on a raised platform which appeared to be roped off from the dining area surrounding it. Around her guests in dinner jackets were filling their glasses with champagne.

She was dressed in a white, satin robe. She had her hair tied back off her face and wore long, liquid-silver earrings. Twirling a glass in her hand, she appeared engrossed in the stream of distorted images which the light set off, magnified with each suck and sigh of the revolving door on to a large video screen in the foyer. Images of patrician figures with gargoyle cheeks, of fresh-faced waiters in school blazers pouring drinks that left cancerous stains on gowns and dress shirts . . . of dinner tables rising like debris in a storm drain, nicotine-stained teeth embedded in a blancmange of pork fat; gold fillings, rings, ribbons and sequins . . . all appearing in the same order, the same harsh light and impulsive disfiguration. Until she began to twirl the glass faster and faster in time with the revolving door and the one merged into the other, becoming a stream of . . .

'Miss Green?'

He watched as Janice caught hold of the glass.

'It is miss, isn't it?'

Leaning out over the scarlet ropes, his sister poured herself a drink from one of the bottles on a nearby table.

'Miss Green I've been meaning to have a word with you.'

The ropes seemed to propel her back into the centre of the platform where the light was at its brightest, picking out the elegant, golden-haired figure who had clambered up to greet her, dressed in a dark blue suit with padded shoulders and a wide, silk bow.

'Chamberlain's the name. Mrs Winifred Chamberlain.'

Immediately the rest of the room was plunged into darkness. Hurrying over to the revolving door, he found it locked, and began banging on the glass, trying to attract his sister's attention.

'Oh, let me say right away, my dear, I do not mean to attack you. My letter to the headmaster was merely the enquiry of a concerned parent.'

There were muffled boos from the guests as Janice shrugged and swallowed her drink.

'After all, there isn't much else one can do these days is there, except to enquire politely? It seems our role remains largely a financial one. That is, we pay the fees. And Kingsleigh does not come cheap, believe me.'

The booing stopped. Janice was peering over the rim of her glass. 'Is that how you see your role?' she asked. 'Merely paying the fees.'

The slim, suited figure, whose smile, like her bow, seemed frozen, reached out and stroked Janice's shoulder. 'Surely my dear you do not believe there is anything more that we can do, other than attend open days, prize giving, centennial dinners? Besides, I would have thought that as a professional you'd be more concerned with guarding your territory, rather than throwing it open to the public.'

Horrified by the dark bruises appearing wherever the diamond-encrusted fingers caressed his sister's pale skin, he banged louder on the door; the noise of the cheering from the crowded tables drowning his frantic tattoo on the heavy glass.

'On the contrary,' said Janice, 'we have far too many professionals running organisations on behalf of the public as though they were their own personal fiefdoms. In my view it poses a serious threat to democracy; with people entrusting their right to know to assorted guardians; losing touch, *with the passing of time, so that in the end it becomes a vicious circle. People throw up their hands in the air and cry it's all much too complicated. Far easier to leave everything to the politicians; to the so-called experts. Do you think I know any more about bringing up your sons than you do? Or that the Minister for Education is any better qualified than you are to decide which subjects they ought to be allowed to study?'*

The diamond-laden fingers continued to stroke Janice's shoulder. *'You'll forgive me, it's all very well suggesting that parents take on a greater share of the burden of educating their children. In primitive societies, where aunts, uncles and the like are able to help look after the young that may be possible. But heavens! In an age of working mothers? Do you imagine I'd have reached my position in the legal profession if I'd had to take care of Austin and Lewis all day? Every day?'*

His sister seemed oblivious to the bruises spreading over the exposed parts of her body; only her knuckles glistening, white as she clutched the scarlet rope.

'Actually, I find your interpretation of our task rather illuminating. If I am guilty, it's merely of expressing a similar view.'

'No doubt for very different reasons.'

'Reasons?' He became conscious of an uneasy silence on the other side of the glass. 'If you don't mind my asking, Miss Green, what are your reasons?'

Janice let go of the rope. *'One, because modern education is responsible for the artificial extension of adolescence. Two, because it is purely in the economic interests of society to extend it. And three, because schools have become responsible for the creation of yet another class of misfits, delinquents, drop-outs, excommunicated, call them what you will, whose parents are either unable to cope alone, or are too busy furthering their careers.'*

'Janice!' he shouted as the silence was broken by a wave of booing from the audience. 'Janice! That's not fair.'

His sister stared intently at the boys' mother. *'But then I suppose that's the price we pay for our prosperity. A price that puts a question mark next to each pupil's name. With each examination they pass, the question goes unanswered. Like comets flooding the heavens with a rush of light, our children's spirits sparkle, splutter, then die. Their momentum may carry them on, but like moles, their eyes grow dim in the dark.'*

He continued to bang on the door, but as the booing from the audience grew even louder he allowed his fists to slide down the misted glass.

'I can see, Miss Green, you have given the matter a great deal of thought. Naturally you are a specialist in your field, which makes your disillusion-

ment all the more regrettable. Perhaps you are in need of a break? If I were you I should get away for a while, join your brother in the South Seas.'

'You may be a specialist in your field,' said Janice, her silver earrings spiralling like beads of sweat down her cheeks. 'In mine I doubt very much whether one exists. We seem to have become little more than agents of the market place. Education? By all means, as Gandhi might have said. Only let's not fool ourselves in imagining it's what our children are getting. Which is why your son, Lewis, has my sympathy. Believe me, of the two, Austin the school prefect may be the easier to work with, but it's Lewis who's noticed the emperor doesn't have any clothes. By getting himself expelled he's made it clear he doesn't want any part of our illusory world. It's rare these days to find such perception among the young.'

As the audience began to hurl their glasses on to the platform, followed by coins, napkins and still-burning cigars, he noticed the boys' mother was trembling, her lips, torn flaps of skin hanging from a discoloured jaw. Blood trickled slowly from her nose.

'I have to admit, my dear, I've never really understood Lewis. He isn't terribly communicative. Do you think all children are as guarded in their . . .'

'We only guard what others threaten to destroy.'

'But a garage mechanic! Oh, I realise how much he's hated school. But Lewis is no more cut out to muck about in the grease of Fielding's Garage than I am to sit around the house all day. He's intelligent. He sees things . . .'

'I said he was perceptive.'

Her body sagged amidst the debris raining down out of the shadows, as the audience continued to voice their angry disapproval. Many of them were leaving, shouldering their way through the revolving door, scornful of his eagerness to get in.

'Are you saying society's drop-outs have a keener sense of vision than the rest of us?'

'Their blindness will come. Through rage, rancour and frustration.'

'And the rest? The Austin Chamberlains of this world?'

'Gentle as lambs to the slaughter.'

Over the heads of the departing guests he saw the boys' mother reel back against the ropes, lose her footing and tumble to the floor. The booing continued, one moment growing fainter, the next louder, as the door spun round and round, spilling guests like broken teeth from its glass jaw. Even as Janice, bruised and weak, stumbled over to help the debilitated figure back on to her feet, glowing cigars were still being tossed on to the platform.

'I'm sorry,' he heard his sister say, 'I didn't mean to upset you. I hope you'll accept my apologies.'

'Janice!' he yelled through the glass. 'No, Janice, wait!'

The women looked up. Just then the lights in the hall flicked on and he found himself staring at walls lined with mahogany cabinets. Behind the leaded glass windows lay shelves stacked with voluminous books, marble busts, and silver trophies.

'A little toast then,' said the taut, funicular figure behind the leather-topped desk, raising a glass of sherry to his lips.

'A toast to the boys' futures.'

'To Austin and Lewis,' said Mrs Chamberlain.

'To Fielding's Garage,' said Janice. 'If you like I'll have a word with Archie Fielding. Perhaps he could persuade Lewis to attend night school. It might offer him some incentive. I know Archie. He's an old friend of the family. Regularly services the car; been taking it round there for years.'

It seemed to him the boys' mother wanted to laugh. Instead, as she turned and caught sight of him waiting outside the headmaster's study, her face became hard and immobile. He glanced anxiously across at Janice, at the headmaster. But they too had become marble busts, staring down from the shelf with wide, unseeing eyes. Horrified, he fled through the deserted building, through the long, dark corridor and down the steps. Where once again he bumped into the hotel doorman.

'No ticket!' he shouted furiously. 'No ticket! No ticket!'

14

Rachel sat looking out at the rain slanting across the balcony, wiping the dust from the night's weary face as it pressed against the louvre windows. They were only partially closed, tilted upward like a lover's lips, poised and glistening. Rachel gave an involuntary shudder. Her reflection in the watery glass – gaunt cheeks, modest brow, bony shoulders – stirred up old feelings of inadequacy.

Nevertheless she loved the rain. Loved everything about it, its ardour that bordered sometimes on severity, though mostly teasing, soft and subtle. She loved its reliability, the loyalty with which it returned, sweeping through the valley, bringing with it a taste of freedom, of life beyond the mountains; bringing with it the warm caresses of the coral sea. She loved also its smell, that fresh-stale smell which was the smell of the old and the new mingling. She loved the fragrance it unlocked from the soil; the fresh life it brought to the leaves of plants and trees. Above all she loved the rain's company, especially late at night, when she sat alone in the house and it tapped on the window like a friendly and thoughtful neighbour.

'*Dear Mrs Green . . .*'

She could see the classroom lights in the distance, burning with a profligate air; the mountain darkness swallowing the trees in the background whose branches sighed and groaned in the wind. Below in the valley she could hear the steady chug of the station generator.

'*Dear Mrs Green, I am begging to offer my humble apologies . . .*'

The rain grew stronger, throwing up great drops that burst through the wire mesh to land in a fine spray upon her cheek. The wind rushed in through the cracks and under the door so that the pages of the children's books on the table behind her fluttered like the wings of dying insects while the light bulb lurched back and forth in its moth-cluttered orbit.

'*. . . I am begging to offer my humble apologies for not doing my homework. As you know the pipe from the spring is damaged and because* *of this we are having no water in the dormitories. So now there is no choice for us but to sacrifice our valuable learning time in order to go down to the river.'*

As the rain drummed with increasing ferocity on the iron roof, Rachel gently smoothed the pages of the mud-stained book in her lap before closing it and slipping it beneath a pile of old papers on the shelf beside her. A startled cockroach scuttled across the living room wall, its path obstructed by the numerous bits of sticky tape securing Richard's photo montage – a litany of majestic mountain tops that did little to lift her spirits but merely reminded her of her own isolation now that Richard spent much of his time shuttling between Biyufa and the Keramuti on behalf of the co-operative.

Even at this late hour, he was probably still somewhere on the Highway, stopping off either to unload supplies at one of the co-operative's new depots, or to unpack the chains from the back of the Land Rover so that he could help pull the poorly equipped village trucks out of the mud as they struggled back from the town with their loads of rice, beer, sugar, salt and bullybeef.

She recalled a recent trip when she'd gone with Richard to do the monthly shopping and also to be present at his medical. After a night of heavy rain they'd found the Highway strewn with vehicles, all buried up to their axles in mud. Richard had insisted on helping to tow them free, wading through the deep orange slush in order to secure the chains. The Land Cruiser was hauling, spitting, slithering as he willed it forward, inch by inch, vehicle by vehicle; the entire morning spent locked in furious battle. As she watched him throw off his shirt at the doctor's to reveal a dirt-stained neck and scarred chest, it seemed as if he'd been fighting to pull the whole of the Keramuti out of the mire.

Yet he had done nothing to alleviate the misery of Nimile Orapi's family. He had still not called on their village, on any of the dead boy's *wantoks*. He had left it to her to accept their invitation to do so, though she knew it was Richard they wished to see; knew it was Richard who ought to have undertaken the journey – deep into the heart of Endai territory. A journey of atonement.

Instead discovering that it was no longer possible simply to retreat into the forest, it was she who found herself squatting in the village square, trying to describe the moment when she'd first realised it wasn't the screeching of cicadas she'd been hearing, or the tearing of metal blades in the nearby quarry, but the children screaming as they dragged Nimile's body out of the river. It was she who spoke of the mucus and the mud, of their terror as they fled back up the mountain, leaving her to reflect on her inability to reach out to them, to protect them from the dissolution of their past.

Fighting back her tears, she spoke of the progress their child had made at school, of his quick thinking and talent for firing the rest of the class with enthusiasm. She spoke of his level-headedness and the stoicism with which he had accepted the injury to his neck, showing no sign of bitterness towards the boy responsible. She recalled their first meeting when he presented her with the tambu shell necklace. And their last, the day before he had drowned, when he called to ask if he might start a garden for her at the back of the house, thereby saving her the trouble of walking all the way to the market.

She talked through the long, hot afternoon . . . of the school's sense of loss, of its fears – especially of Endai retaliation. She talked of her own fear of spending more and more time on her own; of the Keramuti stealing Richard from her; of his drive and energy, and her despair at never being able to make him slow down. She talked of the accident, of how lucky he'd been to escape with his life. But she did not talk of the guilt. Richard's guilt. Her broken pidgin wasn't up to that.

Nimile's family did their best to comfort her and put her at ease. She soon realised that they were not interested in revenge. Nor did they raise the question of compensation, as some, at any rate Nathaniel, had led her to believe they might. All they'd wanted was an assurance that Nimile's death hadn't been deliberate; that it had been an accident. One which the authorities, from whom they had heard nothing, would in due course investigate.

Eyeing her with their robust, peasant's compassion, they assured her they were determined the school should remain open. They even expressed the wish that it be expanded so more of their children could attend. The lack of places, they believed, was holding up development in the area. Refraining from smoking or chewing betel-nut, they further impressed upon her that as she and the *masta* were *olsem*, it was through her that they understood his grief. These feelings of hers which she had described, of pain and sorrow, were enough to make them understand his own suffering.

Enough? His suffering?

Watching the women with their mournful eyes and bracing thighs sheltering behind the men, it struck her that their tolerance concealed a streak of cruelty. A cruelty they practised upon themselves. For it was as if there was no limit to what could be asked of them, to what they would allow to be asked; no limit to what they and she and women throughout the world might be expected to endure. The men – those taut figures silently hoisting

Nimile's naked body on to their shoulders – were to be excused because they were unable to release their anguish. It was their fate to be pardoned, as it was the women's role to pardon.

Rachel felt that it wasn't until this division was healed that the cruelty of it all would end. Only then would it be 'enough'. All else – Richard's eagerness to help, Nathaniel's ambition to see the 'new force' triumph over the old, the villagers' own efforts to embrace the world of coffee . . . she couldn't help feeling all this would come to grief. Even Richard, she suspected, sometimes sensed as much. If only he'd take heed of the . . . dreams? nightmares? hallucinations? – what did it matter what one called them, for they were the voices, not of the dead, but of the living that came whenever he'd overdone the betel-nut. If only he would listen to them.

The wind tore at her raincoat as Rachel stepped out on to the landing. Wrapping an old *lap lap* over her skirt to keep off the mud, she kicked off her sandals and slipped into Richard's wellingtons before climbing down the stairs. She bent her head into the driving rain.

With the station generator now regularly running until midnight the school had been forced to introduce a 'lights-out' policy – nine-thirty during the week, eleven-thirty at weekends – in order to dissuade pupils from studying late into the night – a habit encouraged by the ever present threat of 'excommunication'.

Passing along the rain-swept pathways, however, Rachel was surprised to discover the classrooms already deserted. Exercise books lay neatly stacked on top of the desks. The floors had been brushed, the blackboards cleaned, bins emptied. Even the doors had been locked, the windows secured. Clearly the pupils had gone to bed early.

Glancing at her watch she realised it had stopped. She had no idea how late it was, how long she had sat with Nimile's book in her lap, listening to the rain. Just then she heard the generator's dying cough and saw the lights splutter and fade, plunging her into darkness as she stood alone in the empty grounds. Clicking on her torch, she watched its tiny beam leap feebly into the night, like a voiceless scream. She paused to scrape some of the accumulated mud from her boots and set off briskly back to the house.

Above the howl of the wind she could hear water spilling over the edge of the playing field, channelling the soft earth into the open drains which surrounded the classrooms. It was into one of these drains she thought she'd stumbled when she suddenly lost her balance and saw the torch spinning from her grasp. Struggling to her feet, she felt a hand reaching into the hood of her raincoat, dragging her backwards. Instantly she felt that, like the earth, her body too was disintegrating, sliding away in thick handfuls, soft, sinister and irretrievable; a landslide of her own flesh that was crushing her, sweeping her in the direction of the trees below the school.

Fighting to breathe, she felt a burning sensation in her throat, felt her mouth and lips being crushed by rough, intractable rods of flesh which she instinctively bit as she tried to break free. The hand disappeared but not the burning sensation which clung to her lips; the taste of her own saliva impregnated with raw tobacco, causing her to choke. At the same time that her arms were being pinned behind her back, her *lap lap* became entangled in her boots, enticing the iron hand to tear the sodden bit of cloth from her, all the while preventing her from calling out, though to whom? she thought in a moment of lucidity. Who would hear her above the drumbeat of the rain, above the boom and boil of the Waragoi?

Tumbling to the ground, she jarred her knee. Had she lost one of Richard's boots in the struggle? Dragging her arm out from beneath her, she tore at the invisible face, at the cloying rag of flesh; tore at the beard which seemed to come away in her fingers, forcing her attacker's hasty retreat. But not for long, as once more she felt the heat from his breath at her neck, smelled the sour stench of tobacco, laced with beer. A hand pulled at the confusion of *lap lap* and skirt which cut into her waist, lifting her forcibly up off the ground.

She tried to dig in her feet but failed and slipped. Wrenching her arms free she dug instead into the flesh; into the hard, wet bone that was crushing her, fighting as she had never before been made to fight. Yet somehow it had gone on forever – this endless struggle to breathe freely, to strip away the clumsy armour of sex, status, role, to strip away the numerous layers one clung to for protection; to reconcile the outer and the quiet, forgotten inner self; to unlock that inner chamber and inhabit it not to escape but as a means of self expression. A self-consuming struggle of which this now was the final round, the decisive one, and she had to win.

She started to run not knowing that it was only having one boot on that was hindering her as she fled across the melting earth. She realised and kicked it off and immediately felt the jagged limestone cut into the sole of her foot. The branches of the densely packed trees flashed in front of her, like whips in the hands of the wind as she ran, stumbling into the conduit along the side of the road. It was in running she told herself that her victory lay, in escaping through the night; if only she could get her legs to carry her. But suddenly they were caught, held fast again by those same course fingers whose pungency she could still feel crushing her lips – now lashed by the soiled strips of her hair, blinding her as she screamed, heard nothing, and tried again to run.

But the hand clung mercilessly, like a distraught beggar dragging her down into the depths of his poverty until it withdrew suddenly, mysteriously. She felt the vibrations in the road, saw the drunken figure with his broken beard and taut, hungry body lit up, and she fled blindly down the path towards the house. The truck rumbled past on its way back from the tavern, the roar of its engine drowned by a deep, dirge-like chanting booming across the valley, cutting the spell, the nightmare; allowing her to scramble up the stairs and lock the door behind her.

Hours later she woke. A pool of water had formed around her on the living room floor. She lay there staring not at anything in particular, but taking in the room as a whole – its drab walls, Spartan furnishings, fly-paper dangling from the ceiling – while the night wrapped itself like a fetid bandage around her limbs. It was not the tawdry emptiness that drove her even deeper into herself. It was that something kept telling her it hadn't happened. Or rather tried to tell her and failed, though in a sense it hardly mattered. What was important was that she would have to convince Richard nothing had happened. Therein lay the great emptiness. All the house could do was remind her of it.

Even the balcony – where, in the afternoons, she would sit reading, her attention soon wandering from the closely printed pages to the large, child-like scrawl of cliffs in the colouring book sky; her curiosity roused by a kite circling above the kunai grass, a pig foraging beneath the house, by children stealing through the trees – all the balcony could do now was remind her of the pernicious mould spreading within the Keramuti's own clumsy armour.

Feeling as if part of her had already bade farewell to the island, she rose and slowly gathered together the clothes she had torn off and flung across the room. She groped for them in the dark rather than light a candle or use the torch. In any event, she remembered, the torch was gone. She'd have to get one of the pupils to look for it in the morning; try also to recover Richard's wellingtons. With her swollen hands stiffened by the dried mud, she stuffed her skirt, *lap lap* and torn mac into a carrier bag and pushed it underneath the rest of the rubbish in the bin. Naked, she stepped into the ice cold shower.

Sobbing as the water ran in glutinous streams from her hair, between her breasts and down her legs, she held out her hands to support herself. Opening her mouth to the icy current, she felt it slither like a snake into the fire of her body, writhe, and then vanish, consumed by the intense burning that refused to go away. She knew it wouldn't go until she'd been allowed to tell him, been allowed to share it with him, so that he too could suffer some of the pain.

Yet she knew that she couldn't tell him. Not until they had left the Keramuti. For he would find excuses: 'It's all the changes; the excitement . . . probably becoming a bit over-excited. Then again who wouldn't? What with so much to play for. So much at stake.' She knew she would never be able to stand the deception.

Of course there was always the chance that if she told him, he might agree to leave. On the other hand it might be a decision he took on the grounds of: 'Well, if you really feel we must', in which case she'd rather they stayed; was spared his sympathy – a crude attempt at understanding while lacking the ability to share or to suffer the real pain with her. It would only lie there between them, flaring up every so often in the middle of an argument which had nothing to do with it. No, not until they'd returned home, until he had decided of his own free will to return, would she be able to tell him.

And if he chose to stay, to make his life in the Highlands? That way she would know. She would suffer the hurt for years to come, while he, like so many others whose role it was to be pardoned, would continue to run away from it and deny the pain even existed. Not until he'd stopped hiding among the people of the Keramuti would she be in a position to tell him, to share the burning, so that at least some of it might go away.

Naturally she did not think it all out so clearly. It was in the water as it flowed down over her belly, between her thighs. It was in the hours she'd lain staring at the grey emptiness of the house, the incessant fire sweeping through her, forcing her to hold open her body where previously she had fought to keep it shut.

She swallowed the cold, writhing water, urinating where she stood, seeing it run down the inside of her legs, across her feet, across the stark, white plastic. She felt the intense heat of it across her skin and forced her fist into her mouth to prevent herself from crying out.

PART THREE

15

The taxi drew up in front of a shabby, wooden building on the outskirts of Fairfax. The driver, a plump figure with sideburns and downy shoulders, shrugged as he contemplated the broken shutters and worn, sagging stairs leading up to the deserted verandah. But then, adjusting his sky blue *lap lap*, causing the profusion of bracelets about his wrist to jangle against the gear leaver, he leaned out of the window and said brightly, '*Suposim yu laik sumpela pus pus tunait, yu nogat fa long wok.*'

Richard followed the direction of the driver's outstretched arm, but all he could see by peering down a nearby lane were colonies of flying foxes hanging from the trees like paper lanterns. The driver chortled, tucked his fare into the *brasbel* wedged between his ample thighs and pulled away into the night.

The building was the Alice, a two-storey hotel situated near the edge of the mangrove swamps in the old part of the town. Completed before the First World War, it had survived not only the Japanese and American bombings of the Second, but, once peace had been declared and the island placed under Australian trusteeship, subsequent invasions by planters, traders, brokers and merchant bankers – from China, Britain, France, Malaysia, Singapore. This was followed in the late 1950s by adventurers in the so-called 'Swetim' goldrush, which as a result of outbreaks of cholera and dysentery had claimed more victims among the islanders than either the War, or the devastation wrought by Hurricane Betsy in 1948. It had also survived the 1960s' riots by indentured Indian labourers, and a fire which had gutted most of the old town. A collection of wooden shacks and iron-roof stores whose blackened shells still littered the undergrowth, the Alice seemed to crouch over the town's decimation, like a bereaved mother, scarred and pale; an ageing *wantok* slowly toppling over into the mangroves, tormented even as she sank by a tantalising glimpse in the distance of the vibrant, tungsten-lit arc that was modern Fairfax Bay.

Unlike the old town, which was flat and suffocating, and stank of rotting fish, or the central business district where buildings tore like the rugged teeth of a ripsaw through the forest canopy, the bay area thrived in a climate of prominent exclusivity. Here, among the foothills of the Ruatok mountains, their bungalows overlooking the white beaches and palm-fringed coral sea, resided government ministers, judges and the high ranking civil servants tended by trained cooks and Filipino maids; also university professors, lawyers, bankers and foreign dignitaries. Scented not with foul mangroves, but with honeysuckle, jacaranda and frangipani, their floodlit patios blazed a spellbinding path through the night, saturating drives and seductively sloping lawns choked with mangoes, avocados, figs, lichees, guavas. A sea of swollen fruit burst up against the French windows, casting into the air a deliciously sweet spray that brought with it the inevitable fear of plunder; the teeming branches savagely trimmed so as not to afford armed gangs passage over the steel fences slung like nets around the crime-ridden capital's lush oases.

In his room in the old town – broken fan, enamelled chamber pot, leaky shower – Richard drew the curtains, peeled off his sweat-soaked clothes and lay down naked on the bed. The two-and-a-half hour flight from Biyufa, via Tuarua and Sina had left him feeling disorientated, heavy. The air as he'd stepped from the plane clamped like a hot rag over his face. It wasn't only the air, but the stench of mangroves, of rotting fish, the perpetual stickiness. Outside he could hear the strumming of a string band, the swish of tyres on the steaming asphalt, the sigh and clap of bus doors disgorging people on to the concrete pavement; the click click click of stiletto heels. They were sounds which reminded him that, in spite of the national flag he'd seen fluttering over people's houses on the way from the airport, he had flown into what was in effect a foreign country; a country whose streets were stained with the same crude patches of betel-juice but which, like the 750cc motorcycle he could hear hurtling down the dual carriageway, appeared so much more self-confident, so much bolder, faster and noisier. The noise and the adrenalin it released kept him awake so that his pulse seemed to be in time to the beat of the neon light on the wall opposite his bed; a rapid interchange of green and red . . . of thoughts on the minister he was hoping to meet, and Rachel who'd refused to accompany him:

'I'm sorry, Richard, but I've all these books to mark, lessons to prepare.'

'I am pleased to meet you, Mr Green. You have journeyed far.'

'Besides, what makes you think you can simply walk into the Minister's office . . . ?'

'Indeed I have read your letter with great interest. You have put a very forceful case.'

'*After all, his secretary's already made it perfectly clear. There's nothing they can do to help.*'

'*Naturally I shall do everything in my power – such a miscarriage of justice must not be allowed to pass unnoticed. It is not only the boy who suffers, but as you point out, the parents also.*'

'*What's done is done, Richard, and can't be . . .*'

The neon light flickered, faded, then flickered again, remaining stuck on red . . . One long, excruciating blush seeping into the wall, into the sweat as it trickled down his cheeks, burning, refusing to fade, refusing to switch back to green:

'*What's done is done, Richard, and can't be . . .*'

He rolled over and lay on his side. Behind the shower he spotted a small, tailless gecko, its body almost translucent as it zigzagged across the frosted glass. It was like watching the shadow of his thoughts, watching fragments of the day being gobbled up like flies. He thought back to the tattooed faces hollowed with pain behind the glass doors of the Biyufa departure lounge; the delectable smiles of the plane's cabin crew; the rivers and muddy estuaries bleeding into the sea, into the brief tropical sunset obliterated by a violent downpour; the taxi driver: '*Yu lakim sumpela pus pus tunait yu nogat fa long wok.*' Fragments flushed out into the open where they froze in the gecko's path, struck by the fear, by the firmness of Rachel's decision not to fly down to the capital with him.

'*What's done is done, Richard, and can't be . . .*'

Rolling over on to his stomach, he buried his face in the warm dampness of the pillow. The neon light still blushed upon the wall. Still the fragments froze. Outside, Fairfax – capital and nerve centre of this vast web of island tribes – remained cut off, estranged. Like the fragments, familiar and yet . . .

He shifted to the edge of the bed; lay there poised, remembering how Rachel had been there to steer him through the same unexpected strangeness which he'd encountered on his return to Nairobi. He remembered how, seeing his sudden loss of nerve outside the hotel where the taxi from the airport had stopped to let him off, she'd offered him the use of a friend's house in the suburbs. The following morning she'd invited him to accompany her on a trip to visit a few of her father's old parishioners, insisting on doing all the driving herself while he sat staring at the wattle-fringed landscape. It was the landscape into which he'd been born, into which Mwangi Njombo's mother had delivered a son of her own, while picking coffee early one afternoon . . . only to pick him up, eight years later, out of the grass where he had fallen wearing Richard's old school tie over his blood-stained vest. It was a landscape of simmering ridges and blood-red earth that had seemed at once both alien and familiar, both welcoming and hostile, the slopes dotted with crumbling farms and dusty shambas. Rachel had recounted the area's history with skill and ease – from Mumbi, wife of Gikuyu who was the father of the Kikuyu, to Johnstone Kamau, better known as Jomo Kenyatta, son of Muigai Kamau, grandson of Kongo and great-grandson of Mangana Kamau. Her long, sometimes passionate commentary smoothed the road ahead, dampening down the dust, finally coming to an end as they pulled up outside the farm gate. Here, seeing him immobilised with fear behind the wheel – only on their return from Kisii, on the shores of Lake Victoria, did she permit him to drive – she'd climbed out and gone round the front of the car, pausing he'd thought in a moment of panic, to fling open the iron gate where Mwangi had always waited for him to return from school. Instead she'd merely squeezed a pebble from her sandal, before sliding in behind the wheel and driving quietly back to Nairobi.

Later that night when he had drunk too much and lay, as now, on an unfamiliar bed, in an unfamiliar town, it was Rachel who once more stole through the blur and fog of his estrangement. With her earthen-red hair sweeping down over her shoulders, obscuring the swell of her breasts, she had stepped out of her travel-stained clothes and lain down on the bed beside him. Her pale thighs curved like slender waterfalls round the golden promontory she shielded modestly with her hand; the same uncertain hand, warm and trembling, searching, finding, guiding him somewhat clumsily yet with great gentleness, till she burst upon him with a bitter-sweet cry; a cry he only later understood, when after they had lain for some time together in the dark, her head cradled upon his chest, she spoke in a low, crushed voice.

'That man you were talking to in the curio shop . . . Nguli Mangana. You could say we . . . I mean he's good looking wouldn't you agree? Those carvings . . . he's quite well known. Not that that had anything to do with it. We just felt drawn. First time I'd slept with anyone. Later I discovered he was the grandson of father's first convert. That's how I knew . . . father's dream . . . his seed if you like . . . had found a way of surviving; of rooting itself in the continent. In a land it had no place, no right. I mean who are we to . . . ? People couldn't understand why after I was born, when Mother was so terribly ill and had to leave me in the care of the servants, Father refused to ask the church authorities to allow him to return home. It was Mother in the end who wrote, begging, though by then . . . I don't think she ever really recovered. Soon as I found out Nguli's connection with father I fled. Caught the first available flight to London. It's the first time I've been back. Took a while to pluck up the courage . . . gained I suppose from realising the seed had failed. Stony reception you might say. Barren ground. Nothing left to be afraid of. Africa's taken its revenge on the church . . . at least on the Reverend James Tormey.'

The following morning over the phone the Minister's secretary expressed surprise that Richard had travelled all the way from the Keramuti.

'But surely, Mr Green,' his voice rising in horror, 'you received the Minister's letter? I can assure you it was despatched quite some months ago. Perhaps on your return to Biyufa you might check with the postal authority there. It is possible they are waiting for someone to come and collect . . .'

'Just fifteen minutes,' said Richard, gripping the receiver with both hands. 'And I promise not to take up any more of your time.'

There was a silence on the other end of the line, broken only by the sound of the air conditioning humming in the background.

'Unfortunately that is not possible, Mr Green. You see the Minister is attending a departmental meeting this morning. This afternoon he will be in Cabinet and then later this evening he is due to fly out to Canberra where he is taking part in an inter-governmental conference. Perhaps if you had telephoned first from Biyufa.'

'The lines were down!' Richard shouted above the noise of the traffic outside the hotel.

'So you boarded a plane and came all this way?'

'I needed to see the Minister.'

'I am surprised you managed to get a seat on the plane at such short notice. Normally one has to wait for some weeks.'

'Look, it *is* important. The Minister is my last hope.'

'You will appreciate the Minister is a very busy man.'

'Yes, but then all I'm asking is—'

'I would like to help, Mr Green, but I'm afraid—'

'Fifteen minutes, that's all.'

'I'm afraid your journey may have been a wasted one. You see—'

'Five minutes! Just give me five minutes!'

'—you could not have picked a worse day.'

In the end, however, the Minister's secretary had relented. But not before Richard had taken a taxi from the hotel to the Minister's office, situated on the eleventh floor of a fifteen-storey glass tower overlooking the Bay marina, and placed an envelope containing two hundred kina on the secretary's desk.

At once the secretary, a small circumspect figure with thinning hair and heavy eyes, rose from his chair, swiftly picked up the envelope and without even bothering to examine its contents, slipped it back into Richard's pocket, informing him with a lugubrious sigh that he would once more brief the Minister on the case of Nixon Kiakoa and that if he, Richard, wished to join the many people who would undoubtedly be present at the airport to see the Minister off, then he, the secretary, would endeavour to steer the Minister his way.

'But be warned Mr Green. This has nothing to do with diaries or written appointments. It is the world of the *kanaka* and will be a push and shove affair.'

16

The pushing began unexpectedly early when, on his way to the airport, the taxi stalled in a thunderstorm and Richard had to help the driver manoeuvre the vehicle on to the gravel shoulder so they could dry out the plugs and get the engine started again. By the time they arrived, his sodden clothes stank of swamp water and engine oil, and he had to force his way through the tightly-packed crowd in order to attract the secretary's attention. Instead he attracted the attention of the cane-wielding policemen, who, alarmed by the rapid and unruly progress of the tall, bearded figure across the busy terminal, set out to intercept him.

Fortunately it was the Minister himself, the Rt Hon. Kairu Wii, who intervened. Observing the disturbance from the entrance to the VIP lounge, where supporters and well-wishers had gathered to see him off, he waved the police away with a gesture of amusement and sympathy, at the same clearing a path through his official entourage.

'Mr Green. You have arrived at last. What a pleasure!'

'Minister. Secretary,' said Richard, fighting to get his breath back. 'I'm sorry, but I had hoped to be here much . . .'

The secretary's heavy eyes rose, hovering despairingly beneath arched brows. Richard hurriedly straightened his jacket, tugged at his tie – the knot wet and oil-stained. He threw up his hands.

'There is no need to apologise,' said the Minister. 'We should have been far more disappointed if you hadn't got here at all.'

'Oh?' said Richard, hopefully.

'Yes. My secretary has been telling us all what a determined fellow you are. A man who will go to great lengths to get what he wants.'

Richard glanced uneasily at the secretary, who adjusted the front of his waistcoat. He wore a striped charcoal suit, gold cufflinks, and like the rest of the Minister's entourage checked his watch repeatedly.

Greying, rangy, unshaven, the Minister cut an altogether less circumspect figure, dressed in a pair of creased trousers, navy blazer and bright floral tie. His slip-on shoes were wet, while his tie hung skewed to one side of his button-down shirt. His movements – he was continually darting forward to shake hands with well-wishers – were sudden and uncalculated, and suggested someone of immense vigour, both assiduous and able to enjoy himself, despite the crush and the large numbers of cane-wielding policemen, and the suffocating humidity. Even as the human broth washed back and forth beneath the sluggish fans, the Minister's spoon-bulging eyes, magnified by large-framed spectacles, retained a lively and hungry air, warmed, Richard thought, by a touch of self-deprecation. For the Minister had the boyish habit of prodding his glasses with a splayed thumb.

'So, Mr Green, now that you have succeeded in fighting your way through the crowd, perhaps you would like to make your pitch. Bearing in mind our time is short.'

'Pitch?' replied Richard, glancing once more at the Minister's secretary. 'But I thought . . .'

The secretary quietly tapped his watch face.

'Forgive me,' said the Minister hurriedly, 'but when time is short one must learn to apportion it with care. The pitch is a technique you will no doubt already be familiar with. I first came across it last year, whilst attending a management course at Berkeley, California. There I met a Hollywood writer who could reduce an entire script to a three-minute pitch. He thought it was a wonderful way of concentrating the mind. I thought it would be a way of getting to see more people than I would otherwise be able to – ordinary people, people who cannot read or write or might be intimidated by the bureaucracy of government. Often such people though uneducated are born orators and know how to present a case.'

'With all due respect,' Richard frowned, conscious of the Minister's secretary's dark gaze, of the ceiling fans spinning round, like the hands of a clock beginning to race ahead, 'but I do think I explained the situation quite fully in my letter. All I'm asking is . . .'

'Yes, yes, Mr Green. I have just once again this evening on my way to the airport read your letter. The events in themselves are clear enough. However, if I may be permitted for a moment to focus on the background, if I may be permitted to ask you . . .'

The Minister broke off as all heads turned to the ceiling, a voice announcing over the tannoy that passengers on Kumul Air flight 043 to Canberra, Australia, were to proceed to the departure gate. With a sigh the secretary gestured towards the VIP lounge and the Minister nodded: 'Yes certainly, go ahead. I shall catch up with you in a few minutes.'

While the same announcement was relayed in pidgin and *ples tok*, and the Minister's entourage squeezed past two tall policemen at the door, the Minister himself leapt forward to exchange greetings with those who had managed to force their way to the front of the crowd. Richard observed the people around him for the first time, for he had not noticed them before as he had been too busy shouldering his own way through the massed ranks. The crowd was dominated by villagers dressed in their finest *bilas*, with thick, furry *pur purs* and long, white feathers streaking upwards like flashes of lightning hung over from the storm. Banks of black faces glistened with tears, for the most part silent, though noisy rumblings of sorrow and desolation broke out immediately the officious voice over the tannoy faded. People rushed to the front of the terminal building to stare out at the sleek bodied Tristar floodlit on the tarmac.

'Thank heaven for the rain,' gasped the Minister, returning with a handsome set of boars' tusks entangled in his tie, 'or we shall all be cooking in this glass *mumu*. You know, Mr Green, where I and many of these people who are here to see me off come from, the climate is altogether different. There is none of this humidity. It is the humidity that keeps my wife at home, although she could live much more comfortably in a smart Bay bungalow. All the time I am here, while she is there – not a happy situation, I'm sure you will agree. You are married, my friend? With children? Surely the fact that you have expended so much energy on the boy . . .'

'I have a partner,' said Richard. 'We live together.'

'Happily?'

'As happy as . . . I mean . . . Well, it's an arrangement that suits us.'

'And your family? They approve?'

'You mean the *wantoks*? That's not quite the way it works. Anyhow I rather think we ought to be discussing the case of Nixon Kiakoa.'

The Minister smiled; his lean and bristled jaw lending a shrewdness to his cheerful gaze. 'The background, Mr Green. It is sometimes useful. With your letter there was much I had to try and fill in for myself. Now that I have had this opportunity of meeting you, there is only one further thing I need to know. If I may be permitted to ask: why did you come all this way? No, no, I do not mean from the Keramuti. But from England. What drove you into our arms?'

'*Drove* me?'

'I do not think we could have enticed you. Paradise this and paradise that. You are not a man who believes in paradise, are you Mr Green?'

'I'm not sure I understand what you're getting at.'

The Minister put his arm around Richard's shoulder. There was something of Nathaniel in the gesture, Richard thought; something of the Bolgi's watchfulness.

'I see you find the background difficult. Never mind. If I may make a suggestion. We switch roles. Let me be the one to make the pitch, while you decide on the outcome.'

'But that's . . . It's out of the question. I mean what on earth would you be pitching for?'

'Your understanding, my friend.'

'But how can I . . . ?'

'Just first hear me out.'

'Surely it means you've already made up your mind?'

'Just a few minutes,' said the Minister, running his fingers like a tailor down the front of Richard's jacket, frowning, though whether at the absence of a button or the damp crackle of the sealed envelope in his pocket, Richard couldn't tell. For the Minister's eyes were obscured by the light reflecting off his spectacles.

'To begin with, Mr Green, just now I asked why you had come to our country. By the same token one may ask what made me want to become a politician. The answer is that I had a desire to serve my fellow man. *Not*, however, because I saw poverty in the village where I grew up and swore that I would fight it. Nor because I wanted to repay the debt to my *wantoks* who helped me through school. No. I simply wanted to serve. A noble thing in itself which has no need of all this, shall we say, psychological baggage? Dreams of liberty . . . equality . . . a desire to atone for past mistakes . . . Throughout history these have proved to be powerful forces. But the engine of service has no need of their fuel. Indeed it is possible these ideals may be so mixed with impurities that they clog up the engine. Which is why I say: service for its own sake. If you ask a mother why she does the things she does around the home, she will reply "Really you might as well ask why I love my children!" It reminds me of the way parents answer some of their children's more tiresome questions with the simple word "because". In that word is everything – love, affection, tiredness, power, humour. Above all, trust. Of course sometimes it is not enough, when the child wants – *needs* – more. But the parent has work to get on with and no time to explain. Usually it ends in tears. If you are lucky the tears end. All is forgotten. On the other hand . . .'

The voice over the tannoy announced the second call for passengers on Kumul Air flight 043 to Canberra, prompting a fresh outbreak of sobbing among the Minister's well-wishers, now cordoned off by the police with their peaked caps and long canes poised like lightning conductors.

'My wife and I,' the Minister continued, with a grimace that altered the angle of the light reflected by his spectacles. Richard saw for the first time a despondency snagged upon the lines beneath his eyes, a greyness silting up the warm flesh; 'we have brought up five children. Four of them have good careers. For this we are grateful. People look up to us. They say we have been blessed. Sadly, two years ago our fifth born, who did not make it to his final year in school, joined a band of rascals and ended up spending some time in jail. Why, I asked him, did he do what he had done. He told me he didn't know. I insisted there had to be a reason. He just smiled and said: "because". You see to him the word had become a hoax; a fraud perpetrated upon him by parents who always have been too busy to explain. My wife has since given up her career as a nurse in order to be at home whenever he should need her, but I fear it's too late. The damage has already been done.'

'But surely,' remarked Richard, as the Minister paused to prod his glasses with his thumb, the nail cracked and stained with nicotine; 'all these so-called rascals want is a job. With your connections it shouldn't be all that difficult to fix him up with something. Not only would it keep him out of trouble, it would help you to win back his trust again; show him you cared.'

The Minister's expression hardened. 'Naturally you are not the first to suggest such a course of action. Even my wife has begged me to find him a job. But then as a servant of the people I would have to ask myself, whose interest am I looking after. Theirs? Or my own? Whose failure would I be covering up? The boy's? Society's? Everyone has a different answer. Tonight, Mr Green I would like to hear yours. You are to be the judge. I have made my pitch. Now it is up to you to decide.'

'But that's impossible. It wouldn't be fair, either to you or your wife. I couldn't possibly.'

'It is as we agreed. I pitch. You decide.'

'It isn't that simple. Really this is a private matter.'

'I am a public servant. People have put their trust in me.'

'Then let them decide. I couldn't possibly make such a judgement.'

'You have thirty seconds, Mr Green. I see my secretary is gesturing frantically to me on the other side of the lounge. It seems everyone has already boarded.'

'Look, Minister,' said Richard, having to raise his voice above the villagers' intensive sobbing, the fans flashing overhead like whips; 'if you do not re-instate Nixon Kiakoa, then I'm afraid his *wantoks* may decide to take it out on the school. By the time you return there may be no school. If you are not concerned for the boy's future you might consider the damage to your government's image – both here and abroad – should fighting flare up in the Highlands.'

'*Abroad?*' repeated the Minister, in a voice not unlike that announcing the third and final call over the tannoy; a voice that was both bold and blunt, though clearly flagging wearily. 'The West hardly knows we exist, Mr Green. Here there are coral islands which people in Great Britain or the United States of America have never even heard of and yet in thirty or forty years' time they may be completely submerged as a result of the Greenhouse effect. In my view it is not *our* image but that of the West's which is at stake. As one of the youngest members of the international community – the fifth born if you like – all we can do is hope. Hope that we will get the same chances as others have had. Hope that our trust will not be betrayed.'

'The Alice Hotel,' growled Richard, flinging his jacket across the back seat of the taxi. As the vehicle pulled away sharply from the terminal building his jacket slid to the floor spilling the sealed envelope he had intended for the Minister.

'I'm sorry you were not able to reach a verdict, Mr Green,' he could still hear the Minister calling out as he was shepherded away to the plane, 'perhaps I shall have to . . . serious effort . . . re-write my pitch . . .'

Richard scooped up his jacket and folded it across his knee. The main road from the airport hummed with traffic that dodged and weaved in the bright, tungsten light splashing like surf over the sand-dune barriers. In garish day-glo strip, the spindly-legged hoardings promoted restaurants, discos, bars and night-clubs – a shoreline booming with promises, hissing and bubbling in a florid fanfare of excitement, but which found him reluctant even to get his toes wet, shutting his eyes and listening instead to the tyres peeling back the water from the tar.

Once more he longed for Rachel's passionate commentary, for her plain speaking and earthiness; her courage in the face of disillusionment . . .

'The land here is like nothing one sees anywhere else, but the story it tells, the story of the Kikuyu, is universal. It's the story of a people rooted in the earth, feeding from the breast of Mother Earth, from the spirit mother, whose presence even among these dusty shambas is as tangible as the ground the Kikuyu walk on – is the ground they walk on. The ground that feeds them – physically, spiritually.

So what do we do? We "buy" the land as we once "bought" its people – no longer slaves but orphans. We plant tea, coffee. Build game parks. Turn the land into a vast orphanage. The dust isn't that of a hungry land, Richard.

Africa's rich and will feed – once it's been reunited with those who understand it. It'll flower – once the sterile cloud cover of the Bible has passed and the politicians and businessmen who thrive on its ambiguity are exposed to one simple truth: that for people such as the Kikuyu, the Kisii – the Yamani, Innuit, Dani, Sioux – the land can never be bought. Can never be individually owned. To fence it off is to imprison the universal mother. To shackle the spirit.'

Once more he longed for the scent of her earth-red hair, sprinkled like spice over the swell of her maize-soft breats. He longed for the softness of her ivory-smooth belly, and the shy dance of her fingers over the nest so brazenly perched in the flow of her waterfall thighs. Once more he longed . . . Only to be met with:

'Yu lukim summoa pus pus tunait?'

It was the same driver as the night before, wearing the same cheerful, sky blue *lap lap* and tapping him on the knee with the envelope he had retrieved from the floor. Richard looked up. They had arrived at the hotel. Quickly he tore open the envelope, handed the astonished driver a fistful of notes and got out.

As the taxi sped away, its horn blaring, Richard stuffed the rest of the money into his pocket. He paused as a gang of rascals emerged from a nearby bar and began picking their way towards him through the debris washed up on to the pavement by the earlier storm. There was a light sea breeze carrying the unmistakeable stench of mangroves – into which he plunged, anxious to escape the bright neon-lights, the jangle of traffic, juke-boxes, and the violent retching of a drunk on the hotel steps.

The mangroves lay behind the hotel, cutting off downtown Fairfax from the sea. Stumbling along the dirt lane that petered out at its fringes he could just make out in the lingering murkiness of the storm, the knotted mass of roots delving into the black mud bared between tides. The sinuous fingers reached into the fetid half-life of swamp lizards and nightworms, of eels, crabs, water rats and frogspawn; reaching down into the black soul of his longing.

Clapboard houses strung out along the side of the lane sank lower upon their stilts the nearer he got to the edge of the mangroves. Obscured by wild palms and trumpet creepers the houses at first glance appeared to lie derelict and empty. Yet he could hear *sotto voce* laughter on the verandahs, spilling like balm over the bark of bullfrogs, softening the relentless whine of mosquitoes. Through the shadows he could vaguely see isolated figures hanging about in the doorways, shielding their eyes whenever a car swung into the lane, its headlights plucking a rusted roof out of the darkness, a broken shutter, the bare legs of a woman in high heels.

Reaching the end of the lane, Richard stared out across the empty, yet seething expanse of mud, at the satin-shrouded corpse of the rotting land slashed with blades of water and emitting a suffocating stench from its wounds. He stared at the starless sky pressing the roots down into the blood-sucking swamp where squadrons of insects feasted on their steaming flesh. He covered the lower part of his face with his hand, but the gasses bubbling to the surface seemed to have penetrated his skin; his fingers had become the festering roots reaching into the rank and soggy mass of his lungs. He began to choke.

'Hey mister!'

He turned round and the lights inland leapt brutally upon him, hurling his shadow like a stream of bile into the mud.

'What you do this place? Is not safe.'

She emerged from behind a tangled mass of vegetation, gold and silver jewellery glittering.

'Too many thieves and rascals come here. They kill you. Take all your money.'

Although long-legged and slim, with gentle curves and a girlish fringe, he could tell at once she wasn't young. There was a polished rather than instinctive languor to her gait, a tension in the corners of her mouth which an oily mauve lipstick failed to alleviate; and while her cheeks jutted out like coral shelves any beauty they once may have possessed lay buried beneath a thick sediment of rouge. Her eyes, though, were soft and lucid, and he thought he detected in them a submerged longing, mirroring his own, though it might only have been the shadows, or the reflection of a flickering street lamp in the rainwater at her feet. Wearing a cut-away blouse with billowing sleeves buttoned at the wrist, a gold laminated belt and green leather skirt, she made her way slowly towards him, hugging the shadows of a wild oleander bush.

'What you looking for here? There nothing in this place. Jus mud. Stinking mud. No good for fishing. For swimming. No good for anything.'

She was not from the island. Her features were too fine. Her voice lovelorn yet capricious. Malaysian, he thought. Possibly Thai. Or Filipino.

'You not afraid the *puk puk* crawl out of the swamp? The rascals feed you to the crabs? Many man die here. No one find their body. They jus disappear.'

A thick plait funnelling down over her right shoulder, the end tied by a ribbon, reminded him that for all his longing, the pleasure of dipping his hands into the heavy richness of Rachel's hair would in future be denied him. For she had had it cut – an act that smacked of self-mutilation though she claimed it had become a nuisance and was difficult to keep clean. No more would he thread the tumbling tide between her breasts, glide the glowing stands towards the estuarial sea of her thighs. No more would he smell in it the salt or scent of her desire.

'Mister, you come looking for girl? Only black fella come this side. Better you go centre of town. Find good girl in club. They no walk the street.'

Her accent was a curious mixture of pidgin and Oriental. It had a hard edge to it. An edge that was vulnerable, yet also merciless.

'Maybe you nogat enough money? Maybe you want cheap girl? Here all girls cheap. Only twenty kina. Best one forty kina.'

She stepped out of the shadows of the wild oleander, her heels swaying precariously over the rain-softened ground. Just then a car entered the lane and came cruising slowly towards them, its headlamps peppering the sky with flying foxes whose wings made a noise like rippled applause. The car's tyres sounded like a curtain being drawn back from a stage where she stood alone, squinting in the spotlight; caught between a strange beauty and inescapable ugliness; frowning yet unafraid, for even as the car drew near, finally turning into the drive from which she herself had emerged, she continued to weave her licentious way towards him.

'You gat forty kina, mister? It not much money.'

He admired her courage, knowing from the leaflet he'd found in his hotel room that often the police patrolled the district in unmarked cars. It was the sort of spirit he wished Rachel would show more of, instead of slinking about the house, complaining of continually being in the spotlight. But then it seemed of late that something in her had given way . . . given up. She seemed to have reverted to that quiet, moody figure whom he had first sat next to on the plane, huddled behind a book that was brandished like a shield. He'd been put off by her thinness, but later had become intrigued by the complete, almost painful self-absorption. He discovered during their subsequent journey together up country that she had not been altogether unaware of his interest in her, but that she'd been deterred by the fact he'd been drinking, though by the time they'd landed she had softened towards him, having seen the fear and tension drain from his face as he slept with his hands tucked between his knees, his feet resting against hers.

'Thirty kina,' said the woman, fingering the hem of her skirt. 'It not much. In town you pay hundred and fifty kina. More. All depends.'

He wondered what she saw. The same fear and tension? The same slow fuse still burning . . . He wondered how one saw anything at all in this sultry half-light, in this harsh, primeval cul-de-sac.

'Come,' whispered the woman, softly. 'For twenty kina I show you good time. Nice room. You stay long as you like.'

And in the foul stench of the mangroves she held out her hand.

17

He was driving along a dual carriageway; a bromine haze blurring the blue-grey columns clustered together like porcupine quills on the horizon. His eyes were fixed on the road, on a blond haired schoolboy standing in the outside lane with his back to the traffic. The traffic was heavy, swift and seamless.

He could see the boy surveying it over his shoulder, his body lean and supple, swaying with a nonchalance that mocked the silent frenzy of those waiting nearby at the bus stop, waving their scarves, bags and newspapers in despair. Even as a smoke-belching juggernaut surged forward with its horn booming, he continued to lounge in the middle of the road, waiting until the vehicle was almost upon him before skipping lightly on to the central reservation, where with a lofty sneer he raised his fingers in the air, jeering at the horrified driver.

Stranded on the reservation he appeared to become impatient. Soon he was plunging back with reckless ease into the path of oncoming cars. His movements were slick and fluent, though the teasing shuffle of his feet, the theatrical turning of wrists and swivelling hips weren't quite the gestures of a skilled matador, but rather of a ballroom dancer whose partner was proving embarrassingly clumsy – the traffic one moment veering to the side, the next accelerating as if in an act of hypnotic madness, only to stall at the last minute, before being spun on its way, breathless and angry, disbelieving as he taunted them for their lack of nerve; disbelieving as . . .

Suddenly it was he who was speeding towards the boy. He who was at the head of the long line of cars, his fist punching the hooter so that the vehicle, drawing on his terror as fuel, accelerated, hurling him back in his seat. He caught a glimpse of his face in the rearview mirror, his cheeks turning to jelly in the wind. He tried to lift his foot from the accelerator but his leg remained locked, his body rigid as the car sped low and fast towards the boy.

Just then he heard a scream. He saw Janice grabbing the wheel from him, shoving her foot on the brake. The vehicle's nose dipped and reared as they skidded to a halt.

He watched the youngster pick himself up out of the gutter, coolly brush the dirt from his blazer, then stoop to retrieve his satchel from under the front wheels. Holding the green leather satchel aloft, he cleared a path through the crowd of onlookers and halted beside the driver's window.

'Damned fool!' he heard himself shouting above the roar of the traffic. 'It isn't just your own life you're gambling with you know. What if we'd overturned? Smashed into the central reservation? Or into another car?'

The blond head with its imperious cheekbones hung as still as a portrait behind the glass.

He found himself struggling to wind the window down.

'Listen, you arrogant little . . .'

Eager young faces began to crowd round the car, soft and innocent in their curiosity.

'Next time you want to find out just how much your life is worth . . .'

The window refused to budge. He tried the door.

'For pity's sake, Janice, will you open the . . .'

Slowly the car slipped into gear, and the faces began to drift away, like bubbles in a stream.

'Next time I won't bother braking!' he hollered as the blond head faded in the rearview mirror.

'Damn it, Janice, what does the blighter think he's playing at? What if something had gone wrong . . . the brakes had failed? What if old Archie Fielding . . . ? I mean I know he runs a tight ship but . . . I should've thought the old boy'd retired by now. Way cars have changed. More than just machines. Weapons if you ask me.'

'In that case,' said Janice, appearing to control the vehicle without any effort at all as they glided smoothly through the heavy traffic, 'maybe we ought to consider bringing back the flag. You know . . . hiring someone to march out in front . . . one of your excommunicated perhaps?'

'I'd have thought the Highway Code was sufficient.'

'Might as well issue everyone with a gun licence. What we need is something to show we care.'

'Of course we care. That's why there are speed limits; laws to ensure that people wear their seat-belts.'

'Then why aren't you wearing yours?' she asked, her hands cool and composed on the wheel; in marked contrast to his own as he struggled to unravel his belt. 'And why are more people than ever before being killed on our roads?'

'Well, I expect it's because . . .'

The belt seemed to expand, to grow longer and longer, spilling out of his lap and on to the floor, where it threatened to become entangled in the pedals.

'I expect that with the scale of things . . . the increase in roads, traffic, the . . . Look here, Janice, there's something wrong with this damned belt. It won't . . .'

'You make it sound as though it were inevitable,' she replied, seemingly unaware of the difficulty he was having preventing the belt from pouring out of the socket above his head, from wrapping its silvery coils around his arms and legs, until he could no longer move, but sit trussed up like an insect in the larder of a spider's web.

'As though it were somehow built into the system – or should I say, billed – being part of the price of our living in a car-owning democracy. Mind you with so many being killed . . . maimed . . . you'd think people would begin to query the bill. Or don't they realise they can? Have a right, a duty to? Perhaps they're just too exhausted. I mean people talk of compassion fatigue. What they mean is they're tired of acting in a humane way; of having to remember who they are; how far they've climbed up the evolutionary ladder. These days it seems easier to fall back on the older instincts, the crudest instinct of all: survival. Isn't that what our lives have become – or should I say, gone back to – the struggle to survive?'

'Janice!' he cried out in alarm, as he felt the belt beginning to contract, its taut fabric cutting into his skin, forcing the air out of his lungs. 'Janice, what's going on? Where are we going? Where are you taking me?'

'And yet,' said Janice, showing no sign of hearing his panic-stricken calls; 'the fact remains, it only takes one person to die, to be sacrificed upon the altar of expediency, for the rest of us to feel the pain. Trouble is we hide it. From ourselves as well as others. We've grown used to hiding it . . . become immune, even to our own suffering. We've become the victims of our own indifference.'

'Janice!' he managed to shout, though by now the belt was winding itself around his neck and lower jaw, cutting into the corners of his mouth, into his gums. He could feel its slime slowly hardening, like glue. 'For heaven's sake, will you help get me out of this damned . . .'

But the words soon froze, and he began to choke on the blood drawn by the belt's ever-tightening coils.

All at once sunlight was bursting through the windscreen. As Janice disappeared from view he felt the car kick and surge. His body remained rigid in the front seat, his cheeks pummelled by the wind as he found himself *bearing down once more on the blond schoolboy, standing mockingly in the middle of the road, his head thrown back, his satchel slung over his right shoulder. He could hear the jeers and taunts of the boy's companions, the stricken screams of onlookers at the bus stop; could feel the engine bursting with—*

'Good Lord!' cried Janice, 'I know I'm always late for school but this is ridiculous. Slow down, Richard, before you get us killed. Look, there it is – Kingsleigh; with its ancient ramparts pawing at England's caged sky.'

Staring at the red brick walls and reinforced buttresses, he realised that neither he nor his sister was in control of the car any longer. Janice herself had become imprisoned in the belt's interminable coils. And yet the vehicle was still moving, being dragged towards the school by a steady stream of traffic. At the head swept a convoy of school buses with their transparent bellies of pupils, confined to uniforms and uniform transhipment, dragging them between the banks of steel and glass, between traffic signs, billboards, overhead cables, manhole covers, bridges, tower blocks and tenements; dipping them like cattle in a bath of noxious fumes. Introducing yet another generation to the study of the market state. To the science of immunity.

To Chicken.

18

They marched in single file along the road to Gelmbolg. At the head, Richard flexed his rough, oil-stained fingers and to the boys the black, bitten nails seemed to clash like axe-heads in the early dawn.

'*Tisa planti kros,*' they whispered. '*Bambai yumi mekim wanem samting?*'

'*Hayi, yumi yet nogat taim long tok. Yumi wokim strong.*'

Their faces swollen and lined with sleep, they pushed up through the mist rising from the slopes of Elimbari. They knew he had flown back from a meeting with the Education Minister in Fairfax only the day before, and that he'd been up all night trying to repair the Land Rover. It had been commandeered in his absence by some of their *wantoks* who, hearing that war was imminent in the Keramuti, had walked out of a meeting of the local independence celebrations committee, forcing Nathaniel to drive them back to the village.

They also knew it was not the blown cylinder-head gasket – 'The *kanakas* did not give me a chance, Mr Green, to check the oil and water' – which had caused him to set off at such a furious pace, ignoring their pleas to wait for those who had still not fully woken or were still tying their bedrolls. Although they could not possibly have known, the contents of the note dropped anonymously in the night while he had lain sprawled beneath the engine, shortly before setting out they had seen him hand the bit of paper to Nathaniel. As they chased up the mountain his long silence left them breathless with anticipation.

Already they had climbed beyond the last village, beyond the last remnants of frozen forest, stealing through the sinister tangle of moss and spidery lianas, before striking out across a bleak, boulder-strewn plateau where solitary tree-ferns lurked in the mist. A thick, white mist was wrapped like a surgical collar around the neck of Elimbari, so that the mountain appeared sullen and withdrawn.

'Well, Nathaniel,' said Richard, without pausing, though he could feel the fire sweeping through his lungs as he drank in the thin air, 'you've read the charge against you. How d'you plead? Guilty or not guilty?'

At that moment the first bayonet-like rays of the sun struck the ground ahead, reflecting a hoary sheen back off the road, which crackled beneath their boots; beneath the feverish whisperings of the boys to whom, as he glanced back over his shoulder, Nathaniel shouted:

'*Ol manki yu no tok! Yu wokim strong! Yumi wokim olgeta fopela ten miles long Glembolg.*'

Dressed in camouflage fatigues – some, like Nathaniel, carrying umbrellas over their shoulders – the *manki* responded by swinging their boots at loose chunks of gravel, scattering the road with debris.

Richard brushed the dampness from his beard, hooked his thumbs under the straps of his oil-stained pack and lengthened his stride. It occurred to him that Nathaniel, while not quite *longlong*, had yet to prove himself a brilliant scholar. Indeed the staff had repeatedly questioned his performance in exams, pointing out that others not only outshone him but through their answers revealed a greater understanding of the material. They relied less on learning by rote and more on insight, on the ability to discriminate, to discard facts that were either misleading or irrelevant. Yet he was the one who had gained *their* respect. They, the more intellectually gifted, had elected *him* as their leader.

But then was this really, he wondered, the source of his frustration with Nathaniel? This lack of brilliance? Or was it simply that, in spite of all his efforts, the young Bolgi remained unable to cut the umbilical cord?

'The truth, Nathaniel,' he panted as they surged up the mountain. 'I want to hear the truth. Was it you who gave the pupils the order to tear up the pipe? Or is the note an attempt by your Endai friends to discredit you? Surely you're the last person who'd want the school to close?'

As shadowy slabs of limestone loomed above their heads, Richard heard a voice behind him croaking in the damp air.

'It is true, Mr Green,' said one of the boys, 'Nathaniel is the one who gave us the order. But we would have done it in any case, even if he'd tried to stop us. In fact, the Endai boys did try but it was important for us that the school should close so we could go home and be with our families during the time of fighting. As the Endai have received no compensation from the government, they are blaming us for Nimile Orapi drowning in the Waragoi. They say it is the Bolgi who must pay compensation because when the pipe was first broken it was a Bolgi who was responsible. Now the men of our village are making preparations for—'

'*Ol manki!*'

The sound of Nathaniel's fury reverberating among the cliffs caused the boys to huddle together, their fatigues wrinkled and damp. Far from imparting an air of military-like crispness, they resembled a pile of old leaves about to be tossed on to the fire.

'*Ol manki*, you know nothing. All you are doing is spreading rumours, saying things to gain attention. You think all this is just a game which you can stop when you are tired. You do not understand. You will not be allowed to stop, or escape the consequences of your actions. They will remain with you for the rest of your lives.'

The boys seemed to teeter on the edge of the mountain. To their left the rockface tore up out of the earth, dripping with a thick, black ooze; while to their right, in the far distance where the light was vivid and unhindered by mist or cloud, lay an endless succession of valleys like beads of mercury spilled from the rocky palm of Elimbari and caught in the nooks and crannies of gnarled rock that reached up toward the sky.

'These small boys,' said Nathaniel, turning to Richard, 'they are too excited. It is this opportunity of going home, of meeting their friends and *wantoks*. Unfortunately they do not realise that as soon as the fighting is over they will have to go back to school again. Life is not a holiday.'

The *manki* stared out across the deserted slopes, determined it seemed to Richard not be drawn further into the argument. Not only had they no need to argue, no need to fight back in order to preserve their dignity, but they no longer had to prove their courage either. For as the broken pipe showed, they already possessed all the fighting spirit that was required of them.

'Really their happiness is just foolishness,' said Nathaniel. He plunged the point of his umbrella into a nearby crevass and prised apart the sheets of brittle rock. 'It is the happiness of those who are still playing with grass spears; for whom war with the same boys they are sitting next to in class is just a game. Tomorrow they will be friends again, helping each other with their homework; forgetting that today their brother was killed by the *wantok* of the one whose pen they are borrowing.'

'On the other hand,' said Richard, observing the *manki* impatiently swinging their bedrolls against the skyline, 'it may be they're happy for the simple reason they do not have as much to carry as us. Forty miles. It's a long way.'

'Well it's true their bedrolls are smaller than ours but then so are their muscles. By this afternoon they will be complaining that we are walking too fast. We shall most probably have to carry one or two of them on our backs.'

The strain of wanting to laugh yet being reluctant to became too much for them. With hoots of derision, the *manki* scuttled down the side of the mountain.

The silence shattered, the sun burst over the top of the nearby ridge whose slopes seemed to yawn; their sheared teeth bristling against the sky. As the last traces of mist evaporated the air became dry and ashen. Richard rolled up the sleeves of his denim shirt and followed the boys down into the valley.

'You see, Mr Green?' said Nathaniel, stopping briefly to retrieve an exercise book that had fallen from one of the boy's packs, 'it's just like a *sing sing* to them.' Richard watched as the youth examined the book's plastic cover, shook the dirt from it and then carefully tucked it under the epaulette of his right shoulder. 'All they know is what they read in school.'

Richard shrugged his shoulders and walked on. He wondered just how far the *manki* would be prepared to go in challenging the authorities. What, for instance, if they stepped up their call for abolition of work parade? – 'We are scholars, why should we be forced to work like *kanakas*?' Or demanded an end to all further 'excommunications'? The pipe which, by providing water directly to the dormitories, had done so much to improve their living conditions, now threatened to make things worse, to make a mockery of the progress they'd achieved. Something Nathaniel clearly hadn't thought of when he had given them the order to dig it up.

'Actually it is not their fault,' said Nathaniel, puffing at his shoulder. 'It is our parents who told us we must return home. Unfortunately the authorities did not want to give us permission. So it was decided that we—'

'You mean *you* decided.'

'There was no other way. The authorities did not understand our argument.'

'Neither do I,' said Richard. 'You, of all people! How could you even think of it? After all the trouble we went to.'

'It's true it took us a long time to dig the trenches, and to pour the cement. But you see the authorities think that if they can keep us at school then the fighting between the tribes will stop. In fact they are just using us as hostages.'

'And you think by smashing the pipe . . . good God, man, what if they decide to shut the school down altogether? "For me," you used to say, "the future is the most important thing of all." Well there can be no future unless the fighting stops; unless the school remains open. Without it the Keramuti will be left behind.'

'All the pupils would like to see the fighting end, Mr Green. But it cannot be. Not for a long time. There has been too much suffering on all sides.'

'That's what the *kanakas* say. What about you, Nathaniel? What's dragged you back into all of this, after you fought so hard to escape, taking all these boys with you? God knows, some of them may end up paying for this folly with their lives.'

Swiftly they descended into the low-lying savanna where, although it was only mid-morning, the heat lay trapped like water in a reservoir, the earth giving off an effervescence that prickled the skin. As the familiar chorus of cicadas in the tall grass greeted them, Nathaniel snapped open his umbrella.

'I do not think they are in any danger. There is never any fighting in the village, only in the forest or in the mountains. The village is where the women and children carry on with the business of cleaning, cooking, washing and so forth . . .'

'The watering-hole of *kanaka* boredom, you used to call it.'

'It is the only place that is safe.'

'But surely the school . . . ?'

'Usually, yes. But then sometimes there are arguments which cause our parents to worry, like the one last year between Nixon and Tapie. They become angry with the government and say it is not doing the job properly of looking after us.'

'It's not being made any easier by your *wantoks*' behaviour. Is that why you lied about the pipe? To protect them? Thinking perhaps I would blame myself. Absolve you and them of all responsibility?'

'You should not blame yourself,' replied Nathaniel, sheltering in the umbrella's eagle-like shadow.

'Then who is to blame? The chief education officer? The Board of Governors? the Ombudsman? Nimile Orapi – for drowning?'

Nathaniel shifted the umbrella from one hand to the other. As the road stretched out beneath the glare of the sun they seemed like insects glued to the tongue of some prodigious lizard, basking in the primordial sun. Indeed the whole landscape, with its steamy grasslands, scattered sprays of fern, snagged kapok seeds, and savage peaks appeared to be locked at some primordial junction; the light an iridescent haze, the air coarse, pungent and heavy, with the ground snapping crystal-like beneath their boots.

Seeing the boys a short distance ahead of them throwing off their bedrolls, Richard wondered whether Nathaniel had been right, whether the pace he had set was indeed proving too much for them. But then he noticed that they were pointing back up the road. The circles of dust around their eyes magnified their excitement as he and Nathaniel finally caught up with them and they pulled him feverishly by the arm, like an infant being plucked out of harm's way by its mother. For speeding towards them came a pick-up, its hooter blaring as it plunged down the hazy slopes.

Knowing they would have to walk no further, the pupils applauded, drowning out the noise of the tyres drumming through the dirt. As the vehicle drew level it slithered to a halt, punching the air around them, transforming the light into a transparent bronze, through which he thought he recognised Nathaniel's grandfather. But as the dust settled he was surprised to find himself staring into the reddened eyes of the boy Tapie and his father, whose steel *tamiok* glistened in the sun on the dashboard. Immediately he felt himself being dragged aboard by the *manki* who had already prepared a seat for him in the back.

'It is better you sit outside, Mr Green. You can see that Tapie and his father are afraid. This way they will feel safe as they drive through our land.'

Within minutes he was clinging to his seat in the back of the pick-up as it bounced along the road, bubbling in a boiling cloud of dust.

'It is a long way by foot – even if you – are used to it.' Nathaniel's voice hiccupped in the torrent of air buffeting their faces. 'It is – the same for the Bolgi as for the Endai. So – whenever it is possible – we give each other a lift – and the fighting – is forgotten.'

Richard nodded and shut his eyes. His nose, mouth and ears were clogged with dust. As his arm slipped over the side he could feel the rest of his body becoming increasingly numb.

'Actually, Mr Green' Nathaniel continued, 'my grandfather was afraid because some time ago Miss Tormey visited the village of the drowned boy. So he thought maybe you would be persuaded to join the side of the Endai. He says it is possible for a man to fall under the influence of a woman in this way. But now you are coming to our village perhaps he will see that this has not happened. Perhaps he will realise it was not necessary for us to mislead you. I am sure he will be pleased to apologise. I, too, am sorry. You are right. Much effort has been wasted. Perhaps together we can rediscover the road to the future.'

Richard opened his eyes. The primordial junction: had it come unblocked?

19

The village of Gelmbolg straddled a narrow limestone ridge, one of many running parallel across the western Keramuti. The succession of white, sunflecked crests lent the impression that the earth was moving in waves through the dappled shadows and deep swell of the undergrowth.

It was a small village, even by Bolgi standards. Nestling just below the clouds, it had an old, dilapidated *manhaus* surrounded by casuarina trees and a pig stall fenced with wooden palings backing on to a disused hut under whose fringe of broken thatch stood a row of water-filled gourds. The centre of the village was criss-crossed with paths whose destinations among the dark stands of trees and scattered rocks seemed uncertain. Pigs wandered freely among them, uprooting bulbs and tubers, causing the soil to remain spongy underfoot, glistening where slugs and snails had spun their give-away trails and the fat fingers of hungry infants had left the broken shells in their slime.

Just below the village, on the eastern side of the ridge, were lush, green terraces simmering in a watery haze. While on the west, vast slopes of coffee, bounded by forest, testified to the area's burgeoning prosperity. Not that the Bolgi considered themselves prosperous. For it was maintained that a village's wealth depended less on its earnings from coffee than on the number of pigs it owned, since it was this which ultimately determined the success of the Moka.

The Moka, which had existed from *bipo taim*, that is, from as far back in village folklore as could be remembered, was one of the most prestigious events in the Highland calendar, a celebration often lasting many weeks, occasionally even extending for several months. It was a period when all work ceased and hundreds gathered in their finery to feast; to sing and to dance like spirits amidst the smoke of earthen ovens steaming in the undergrowth; above all, to bear witness to the lavish dispensing of gifts, it being the duty of those hosting the celebrations to apportion carefully between their neighbours all the wealth they had managed to accumulate.

Kina, conch and bailer shells, shell belts and necklaces, stone adzes, lengths of beaten tapa cloth, dyed beads, opossum furs, *buai*, *bilums* and *brus*, live cassaweries, parakeets, as well as the rarest plumes, including those of the Bird of Paradise whose glamorous silken sprays for once failed to compete with the most highly prized gift of all: the village pig. Or rather pigs, since as many as several hundred might be herded together in the village square to form the central focus of the festivities.

There were strict rules governing the Moka, determining who was to receive, who was to contribute, and how much. The family contributed to the village, the village to the clan, the clan to the tribe, who then bestowed its gifts on a neighbouring tribe with whom it might be, though not necessarily, on amicable terms, since at some stage the gifts eventually would be reimbursed.

For every few years the Moka retraced its steps. And it was this return of the villagers' wealth that provided the key to understanding tribal relations in the Keramuti, as well as to understanding the villagers' evaluation of their own prosperity, as the number of pigs acquired when the ceremony was on its way south was not always considered equal to the number dispensed when the Moka had been going north.

Being able to declare yourself better off than your neighbours, knowing it was they who had contributed to such a state of affairs, meant that you could consider yourself to be on worthy terms. On the other hand if, like the Bolgi, you pleaded poverty, then of course you need look no further for the cause of it than the Endai. Their numerous villages were overlooked by the Bolgi from their position high on the ridge, clearly a strategic position enabling them to conceal themselves among the enormous wind-scrubbed boulders strung together like some Brobdingnagian necklace around the throat of the western Keramuti.

It was the smoke from their fires that gave them away. Seeping through the thatched roofs it drifted across the skykine, a grey skirt from under which cassowary, pig, chicken and child loomed, ethereal, still; the air calm, the light a gentian violet.

In the steamy haze below, the vegetation of *kunai* grass and *pit pit*, *galip*, *yar* and pandanus seemed to fuse into a wall of solid green, from which the Bolgi men called out to one another on their bamboo flutes, while the women foraged, weeded, or washed the evening's *kaukau* in silver streams, surrounded by the screeching of parrots.

Small, secluded, almost invisible, it seemed at first glance the village of Gelmbolg had managed to evade the growing army of international researchers whose tiny planes could frequently be seen trying to map the plethora of settlements from the air. And yet no sooner had Richard arrived than he sensed among those who were there to greet him, a feeling of disappointment. As if in tumbling from the back of the truck with little more than numerous layers of dust as luggage he was somehow failing to take them seriously – arriving without a *kamera*, without rolls of *pepa bilong mekim poto*, or *teprikoda*, or *glas bilong lukim fa*, without a sketchpad, or notebook even. Indeed all they were able to find as they rummaged through his pack was a pocket diary, a packet of dry biscuits, fresh socks and a couple of empty water bottles which the children dutifully hurried away to refill.

It was left to Nathaniel to explain the purpose of his visit though with the returning *manki* being joyously carried off by their *wantoks* the crowd soon dwindled and he was led to the *manhaus* where he was warmly welcomed by Nathaniel's grandfather. The old man apologised for not being in the square to meet him but pointed out that with so many women and children about – the men were all elsewhere preparing for war – he preferred to spend the afternoons sleeping in the *manhaus*.

That evening, crouching beside an open fire in a bamboo hut belonging to Nathaniel's family, Richard felt grateful for the thick blanket of smoke which made his eyes water. It helped to obscure the uncertainty he felt, surrounded by village elders as well as members of the Kiakoa family whose reaction – or rather lack of it – to the news of his latest failure to win Nixon's reinstatement had left him mystified. For he had come fully prepared to face their anger. And yet all he saw in the circle of peat-brown faces resting with a timeless ambience in the glow of the fire was an inordinate calm.

Indeed so warm and still was the light in their eyes that were it not for the aching of his limbs as a result of the strenuous journey here he might have felt the whole thing was an illusion; his presence among them on the eve of an important battle, might, after all, be a dream induced by a whole afternoon of chewing betel-nut in the *manhaus* with Nathaniel's grandfather . . . a dream whose spell he grew suspicious of.

And so he tried to break free by turning to Nathaniel, who was sitting cross-legged on the floor beside him with his bootlaces undone, his leather belt loosely coiled in his lap.

'I don't understand. When you told me the Bolgi were going to fight, I expected to see the village in . . . well in some kind of uproar; people rushing about, armed, frightened. Not sitting calmly in the *manhaus*. Aren't the Bolgi afraid? Of going to war? Of dying?'

The elders, who listened with a quiet indulgence while Nathaniel translated, sucked their teeth and then, without breaking the dream-like spell, began to debate among themselves, leaving the handful of women gathered near the doorway quietly bemused as they awaited the outcome. Nathaniel informed him with little more than a stoical shrug that since the purpose of warfare was not to kill, the fear of dying played little part in the events leading up to it.

Wincing as the smoke continued to sting his eyes, Richard replied that the elders must have misunderstood. For death lay at the heart of all wars. Individuals always died.

Once more the men renewed their deliberations while the women calmly plucked fleas from each other's hair, split them between their thumbnails and tossed the broken shells on to the fire. After some hesitation, Nathaniel replied that the elders believed it was he, the *masta*, who had misunderstood.

Frowning at the thin figures whose white, shell collars swelled through his tears, Richard waited for them to explain. This time Nathaniel took a deep breath before pointing out that although it was true that death lay at the heart of all wars, it was only in the sense that the spirit of life was central to man – in the same way that the flickering flames were central to the fire. Of course this did not mean one actually had to place one's hand in the fire to feel its warmth. Because of the intensity of its heat, because of the natural intensity of the spirit of life – of death – one was obliged to remain upon the fringes. For as long as man remained a part of the earth this was his fate. The fringes were sufficient to meet his earth-bound needs. On the other hand, to venture towards the centre was ultimately to become part of the invisible – the eternal force of life. But this was not a course one undertook without long and arduous preparation. To be responsible therefore for the death of another person, even during the heat of a battle, was to run the risk of robbing him, and so also oneself, of the opportunity of such a preparation. As for the *purpose* of warfare which he insisted on knowing . . .

Here Nathaniel paused, the silence punctuated only by fitful hissing as the villagers spat into the fire. Richard pulled a crumpled handkerchief from his pocket and wiped the smoke-stained tears from his cheeks. A village pig snorted as it ambled past the door, its twisted tusks slashing the night's satin flesh. Conscious of the elders' scrutiny, Nathaniel continued.

The purpose of war was not to kill, and so challenge that balance which existed between the forces of good and evil, thus affecting the path man's development would take. To tamper with this balance was to risk consequences man would no longer have any control over. The purpose therefore of war conducted between the tribes was to instil in the enemy a minimum level of respect. It was not particularly concerned with winning or losing, since even in losing it was possible to command the respect of one's adversary. And in winning, well, one did not go about declaring a victory over the seasons once the harvest was gathered in. What one celebrated was a partnership, a commitment to *bung wan taim*, establishing a partnership of mutual stability in which both oneself and one's enemy were *olsem*.

'War?' Richard enquired, feeling himself carried inexorably upon their frictionless tide, 'is an act of *stability*? Of *co-existence*?'

Their faces tumbled forward like dominoes in the dancing light.

It was so.

Then why not just talk and avoid the bloodshed altogether? Sometimes that was possible, they replied. But not always, since if a form of aggression was committed by one who failed to understand the inviolable boundaries of man, then there was the danger they might try to claim for themselves that fire which they had previously spoken of, forcing people to live in its shadow – at least while they remained on the earth since they could never be forced to live in this way for ever.

Buoyed as much by the springiness of the *pit pit* floor as by the soothing effects of the betel nut, Richard began to feel less defensive. The dull aching of his limbs, the painful stinging of his eyes gave way to a light-headedness which left him open and vulnerable. And yet floating through the night he felt neither alone nor afraid, but protected by the villagers' willingness to weave patiently their *bilum*-like history, in which they gathered him up and carried him along on their backs as though he were a child.

His suggestion that it was hardly possible to avoid death in the middle of a war seemed childishly naive. And yet if this *was* the case, wasn't the whole business merely a self-perpetuating cycle, involving the deliberate teasing of one's enemy, in an effort to instil perhaps too high a level of fear, followed by the virtual certainty of attack? This then led them to seek redress, and make further efforts to find even finer levels of balance, which in the long run could only become even more insecure.

Through the whorls of smoke hanging over the fire he thought he detected the first signs of uncertainty dangling like a piece of torn *tapa* cloth between them. Flexing his fingers which felt strangely distant, at first he took the hand held up in the darkness in front of him to be his own. He then realised a finger was missing, and that it was really on the far side of the fire, and the voice behind it, as Nathaniel's sudden discomfort revealed, belonged to the youth's grandmother.

The hand with its amputated finger was all he could see for she made no attempt to enter into the inner circle. Instead she remained concealed among the rest of the women, from where she acknowledged that what the *masta* had said was true, only the men would never admit it. In so many things the men did they were afraid, but they put on masks of courage to hide their fear so others in turn would be afraid of them. Now it had gone on for so long they found it difficult to tell the difference between fear and courage. Even in themselves they could not tell the two apart. Instead they raced from one fight to the other, seeking the solution that was already in them. Of course they would not admit it, just as they could not bring themselves to admit that everything was changing. In the past a warrior could be respected, as much by the enemy as by his own family. For his actions were governed by rules which had been handed down through the generations. While today . . . ?

Richard could sense the discomfort beginning to spread among the former warriors, whose white hair frothed like foam round the shores of the crackling fire. He could see the grim shadows sketched upon Nathaniel's brow as the youth continued to translate.

. . . How was one to hand down rules today to those who no longer grew up in the village? To those living in the towns and cities, who made up their own rules as they went along, allowing them to use a truck to provoke one of their enemy – as the Endai had done, killing her son, Nathaniel's father, by running him down. The police had said it was an accident. They said the villagers would have to get used to the roads; that her son must have seen the truck coming but had failed to get out of the way. They accused him of behaving like a *kanaka*.

It was when Nixon had learnt of his father's death that he had attacked the Endai boy at school. The school had not understood and had expelled him. Now he was preparing with the rest of the men to take his revenge having travelled back from Biyufa especially to take part in the fight. Yet his mood was not a good one, she said. There was every chance he would fail to obey the leaders. Like so many of the younger ones who had attended school Nixon no longer believed the rules were made by the people but made by the government. The government made rules for driving on the roads and yet still people were killed. Nothing was being done to restore the balance. These things were simply called 'accidents'. The policeman had said it was a price that would have to be paid.

Richard could no longer see her hand. Her voice began to sound less pained and more matter-of-fact. Having rebuked Nathaniel earlier for his stuttering translation, she now allowed her grandson to convey not only the meaning but more importantly the tone of her soliloquy. The tone of the women, like the rules for battle, seemed just as much to have been handed down through the generations; a tone less quiet and uncomplaining in its sacrifice, yet without forcing or even pleading with them, more of a mirror subtly held up to the men so they could see themselves in it should they find the courage to look.

Not surprisingly Nathaniel's voice rose scarcely above a whisper as he conveyed his grandmother's concern over Nixon's readiness to fight in such an angry mood. In the past a warrior – yes even an old *meri* such as herself understood the principles of warfare – did not shoot out of anger. He waited until he was calm and the moment was right. Only in this way was death avoided. For one did not shoot to kill, only to wound; to make one's point as it were. The waiting might take one day or ten. It was of no consequence. What mattered was the preparation. One's state of mind. Regrettably Nixon's was not good. Hearing of his father's death, he and his cousins had sought revenge on the Endai in the town, not only far away from their enemy's territory, but far from their own home in the mountains. They had wanted to turn all of the world into a battlefield. They did not think of the next day, when the Endai would return, seeking their own revenge. In this way people would no longer be safe. They would always have to be on their guard wherever they went.

Was it good to live with such fear in one's soul having given one's enemy cause to retaliate because one had attacked in a way that showed a lack of respect; not only for oneself, but for the fact that people whoever they were, were *olsem*.

Naturally the younger ones – neither Bolgi or Endai – thought of these things. They referred to people from the village as *kanakas*, saying they did not understand. Even the officials called the villagers *kanakas* because they were constantly fighting among themselves and did not understand the ways of the government. But it was *they* who did not understand, they who had forgotten the past and the ways of the village. Like the young ones, once they had been to school they did not wish to return to their families. Only when there was trouble did they go back, knowing the village was the only place that was safe.

But now this also was beginning to change. For this reason Nathaniel's grandmother belived that the *masta* should return first thing in the morning to the station. He had chosen a bad time to visit them. Of course if the Endai were to attack the village it was unlikely they would harm him. But then there were these young ones, even amongst the Bolgi, who might do something foolish. Already some of Nixon's cousins were angry that he had come.

Nathaniel suddenly swung round, dropping the belt he'd been twisting in his hands on his steel-capped boots. Like an axe hurtling into the trunk of a tree, a piercing voice came from outside. The night's patience found itself flung like kindling on to the fire and the air blazed with a crackling passion.

Nathaniel's mother, a tall, surprisingly slender figure, burst into the centre of the hut. The smell of earth, of pig's fat followed her, drawing Richard's eyes to her large, dirt-stained feet, to her knees that were worn and grey, and the breasts that were already exhausted, hanging from her like the faded ribbons of battle.

Knotting a torn *lap lap* at her waist, she stared with blistering eyes around her, causing those near the fire to shuffle uneasily. She made it known through Nathaniel, who was by now severely embarrassed, that it had been her money, earned from growing coffee, which had paid for Nixon's schooling. It had been her decision and no one else's to send the boy to secondary school. In fact many, including her late husband, had been angry with her at the time saying it was a waste of the village's resources. But she had thought he would do well as he was intelligent and when she grew old he could look after her. Now she had lost everything. Yet it was not the boy's fault, though the school continued to deny that it was to blame. Whose responsibility then was it? Surely as the boy's mother she had a right to know.

Inevitably the word *kanaka* was propelled across the room, followed in its wake by a sharp cracking of bamboo and the sound of derisive laughter. Drawing herself up to her full height, the angry figure cast a shadow over the hut. The fury of Nathaniel's grandfather was in turn aroused, so that Richard felt he was spinning upon a roulette wheel of Bolgi fury and frustration. Glances fastened upon him as he hurriedly sought the reassurance of Nathaniel's translation.

But Nathaniel endeavoured to escape the task, tugging morosely at his bootlaces. Until the decision to send for one of the *manki* at last persuaded him to continue, though he did so reluctantly, with his head bowed, his eyes screwed tight, as though the smoke had pricked their jelly orbs; explaining that it was he, the *masta*, whom his mother held responsible, since it had been in his power to prevent Nixon from being expelled. Not that she was asking for Nixon to be taken back – it was too late for that. It was a question of the three hundred kina – the cost of his school fees. After all, it wasn't as though he, like herself, was an impoverished *kanaka*.

Immediately the men sprang to his defence. While the betel-juice they spat landed in violent blobs upon the stones around the fire, Nathaniel wrestled with the translation. What was there, they asked, confronting his mother, that made her think the *masta* should be the one to repay the three hundred kina? How could she be sure that her son wasn't the one to blame? After all, hadn't he acted recklessly in the first place by attacking the Endai boy at school? How could she tell Nixon hadn't deliberately sought expulsion so he could work in his uncle's garage? Was it not the wish of the young ones to escape to the towns?

Nathaniel's mother clapped her hands in defiance. She demanded to know whether they thought then that the responsibility was hers, when at the time her son had been at school, supposedly being looked after by the *masta*? How could she be the one responsible?

The men plucking at their beards became noticeably subdued. It was true the responsibility was not hers, they conceded. It lay with the government. And they agreed that he worked for the government. But how could one man, all by himself, be responsible for carrying out its duties?

Then what were they saying? No man at all? That the government was made up of a tribe of ghosts? Who grew fat without eating? Not even a whole tribe of *kanakas* hiding in the forest was so, without a face.

But then not even a whole tribe of *kanakas* was as foolish as she, they chorused. The wheel continued to gather momentum, spinning round and round – a whirling of crimson and black, of black and crimson, the one spilling into the other as their mouths burst open then shut and the air grew tense with the incessant hissing of betel-juice being spat into the flames of the fire.

It was not right that the *masta* should be spoken to in this way. Nor that she should involve herself in the business of the authorities which she, even they themselves, did not fully understand.

So should she forfeit the three hundred kina that was hers then?

Ah money!

The vehemence of their exclamation appeared to give the wheel yet a further boost. So this was the source of her anger? Her quarrel wasn't over what was right or wrong. She was concerned with money.

And they? came the stubborn reply. As Nathaniel's mother pressed the palms of her hands upon her smoky thighs, she leant towards them so that for the first time he was able to see the fine, even elegant mouth and pointed chin, thrust not at them, but towards the ground in a gesture of dismay.

And they? she repeated defiantly. Didn't they grow coffee? Didn't they try to find the best price for it when they sold it? It was only to people like the *masta* that such a sum of money was of no consequence. It was for this reason she'd decided to approach him. *He* could afford it. Not the school. Not the government. But the *masta*.

The men continued to rise to his defence. It was true the *masta* could afford it, but that was not the point. In any case such money represented the power of his learning. It was not to be squandered.

Power? She was not talking of power, but responsibility.

Not responsibility, but money.

Surely one could not separate the two?

Then was money not also power?

It was not power she sought.

Money without power?

Money to live.

Money from the *masta* – whose richness made him alone responsible for her unhappiness?

Should his richness excuse him from responsibility?

It was the good fortune of the powerful that they should be excused.

And would they excuse the Endai, she retorted, who were more powerful than they, for the death of her husband? Why were their very own sons even now preparing to challenge their neighbours – if not because they had exercised power without responsibility?

She would prefer it if the Bolgi did not defend themselves?

She would prefer it if the talk in the *manhaus* was not always only of war. All that talk of fighting, where had it got them? As her mother had earlier indicated, not until they had understood the value of life over lifeless things, would they be free of their slavery. Not until they had learnt that the balance of power, with all its rules, with all its fears and revenges, was nothing beside the balance of *life*. This was the real *masta*. Not man.

Nathaniel's hand came to rest reassuringly on his knee. Outside, figures whispered among themselves as they came and went, flitting across the stony ground in front of the hut.

All the same, the boy's grandfather was heard to say, it was no way to treat a guest of the Bolgi people, no matter the wrong which had been done to her. To which the old man's daughter defiantly replied that the *masta* was a guest of the Kiakoa family, and not of *all* the Bolgi people. There were many in the village who wished he hadn't come. Yet she herself remained, they snorted. But then she was a member of the Kiakoa family, wasn't she? Even so, that wasn't the reason she was there. She had only come to put her case before them. Now that she had done so, she would leave.

Retreating with an abruptness uncharacteristic of the Bolgi, Richard saw in her shadow upon the walls the measure of the pain she was being asked to bear, distorted by the light of the fire into a set of dark and terrible wings which threatened to burst the hut at its seams. Yet she managed to slip through the crowded doorway and was gone.

In the silence that followed the wheel lay still, though he sensed hands continuing to hover over it, the darkness taunting him upon his foggy, Pilate's throne . . .

The balance of life. This was the real masta. *Not man.*

20

Richard crawled out of the smoke-filled hut, shielding his eyes from the morning glare. Thrusting his arms above his head, he breathed in the crisp mountain air, sprinkled with the scent of eucalyptus. In front of him the village square lay silent and deserted, the cold earth carpeted in bluebells, bracken fern and foxgloves, softening the jagged outline of the rocks that lay like the props of an abandoned play behind the curtain of casuarina trees.

Gazing at the mounds of purple-black soil in the gardens below, his eyes slowly began to adjust to the light. As his gaze travelled over the lush slopes of coffee he tried to imagine what the Keramuti would look like in twenty years' time, with shops and government offices, telephone lines and metal roads. He promptly found himself squinting again, his vision of the future fading among the sombre shadows of the distant forests, refusing to leave the comfort of the dark, to pit its strength agains the grim wariness of Nathaniel's grandmother . . .

'How was one to hand down rules today to those who no longer grew up in the village? To those living in the towns and cities, who made up their own rules as they went along . . . allowing them to use a truck to provoke one of their enemy . . . as the Endai had done, killing her son, Nathaniel's father . . .'

But while he could understand her anguish, even her distrust, what he could not explain was her grandson's own reticence over the matter. Why hadn't Nathaniel told him? Why had he kept it a secret? Was it shame . . . ? *'they accused him of behaving like a* kanaka'; the realisation that by playing chicken with the Endai truck his father had needlessly thrown away his life, thereby jeopardising the future of the rest of the family?

Or was it the shame that came from seeing his father killed by the 'new force', of which he, the son, had become an unswerving advocate? In which case it was conceivable that in wishing to atone, Nathaniel might attempt to join Nixon and the others – indeed might at that very moment be preparing to go to war with the Endai. Why else had he tried to cover up his role in the destruction of the pipe at school? Why else had he attempted to silence the *manki*? Once again the past seemed to have caught up with the young Bolgi. Perhaps this time it would not let go . . .

In the past a warrior . . . did not shoot out of anger. He waited until he was calm and the moment was right . . . Only in the way . . . was death avoided . . . one did not shoot to kill . . . What mattered was the preparation . . . One's state of mind.

And yet, was it really the past catching up? Or was it the new force spinning out of control? As Rachel had always feared it might.

Recalling that the price of his own atonement had been set at just three hundred kina, Richard set off to look for Nathaniel's mother, only to find his path blocked by a large, fiesty pig bursting out of a nearby hut. Its ears flapping, it bounded into the sunlight where, momentarily blinded, it paused, sniffing at the air. Its body was still warm from the heat of the fire around which it had just been caught scavenging.

Behind it a young girl emerged, throwing around her waist the same torn *lap lap* which Nathaniel's mother had worn the night before. Dark-eyed and aloof, her shaven head added a hard implacability to her tiny breasts. She swung casually past him and proceeded to stalk the snorting animal whose indiscriminate appetite had led it to begin digging up the soil in the middle of a colony of ground orchids, its discoid snout shovelling aside the dawn-fresh stems while its legs, like its tusks, punched outwards. As the girl stole out beyond the line of early morning shadows, the animal glanced back over its shoulder. It reminded Richard of the broad-backed Tamworth squatting in the middle of the road outside Biyufa, its eyes sunken and slow, betraying not the slightest trace of suspicion as it watched him approach in the speeding Land Cruiser, waiting for him to swerve – *knowing* he would swerve – its front feet twinkling in the dust like copper rivets. It was not the sort of trust one broke. The balance of life, as Nathaniel's grandmother would have it, it alone was *masta*. Not man.

Just then the girl darted forward and grabbed the animal by its tail. As she dragged it away, its jaw sweeping the ground like some obsolescent mine detector, the whole of Gelmbolg erupted in an earth-shattering roar.

Armed warriors burst out of the forest, rushing past the girl, past the squealing pig and its fountain of steaming urine. They poured through the rocky labyrinths of the village, through the pockets of sun and mist, a torrent of polished limbs, feathers, spears, bows and *tamioks*; a tumultuous wave of flesh and steel that descended upon the *manhaus* where, oblivious to the presence of women and children emerging raw-eyed and bemused in the shadows, they began to argue among themselves, drumming their feet and chanting.

Rubbed with pig's fat and painted in hoops and flashes of purple and yellow dye, their bodies shimmered in the light, sweating like sticks of gelignite amidst the furious rattling of unfired arrows in whose ugly barbs their enmity lay sealed; their eyes lit up, arms extended fuse-like, their beaded lips spluttering incoherently.

Hardly the picture of Highland warfare he'd been drawn the night before, Richard reflected. Or was it the aftermath? The elders had never really got round to that. The aftermath of defeat?

But while the ground became hard and greasy beneath the warriors' feet, it was the calmness of the women that attracted his attention, followed by the bemused expression of Nathaniel's grandfather who emerged from beyond the volatile woodpile of bows in the company of his grandson.

Richard was surprised to see the old man wearing one of Nathaniel's safari jackets and wondered whether this was some sort of tribute, a sign that the old ways had come to an end, that his grandson's new force had finally triumphed.

Having abandoned his own fatigues in favour of an open-necked shirt, grey trousers and a pair of black leather shoes, Nathaniel stepped confidently once more into his role of translator, explaining against a background of relentless chanting that what they were witnessing was a warring party in its death throes. For the young men had set out before dawn to attack the Endai, only to be themselves attacked – and without an Endai arrow in sight, although some swore they had seen their neighbours hiding in the forest behind the ranks of uniformed policemen.

This was the first time the police had ever entered the forest. They had come not in their jeeps but on foot, unobserved. They had brought food and weapons with them; had spent an unknown number of days watching the comings and goings of the Bolgi, with the result that even though the warring party had set out much earlier than planned, the police had been ready, catching the men by surprise. It was a surprise that now shamed them, and rightly so, Nathaniel was at pains to point out.

For in their hot-headedness they had not bothered to go by the normal secret pathways but instead had chosen the shortest route over a footbridge at the Waramai where the police had been able to carry out the easiest of ambushes. Panicking, one of the men had leapt from the bridge and fallen on to the rocks below. His body had been swept away by the Waramai. This had led his *wantoks* to spear a policeman. The police then opened fire with their guns and hit a number of Bolgi who they rounded up and took as prisoners. This was something that had not happened before. It was not a custom of the tribes to take prisoners. Instead they allowed their enemies to return home – sometimes even helping to carry the wounded part of the way. With the police clearly everything was different. Nixon himself was among those captured and would be taken to jail. Also a heavy fine would be levied upon the village, which the people would find difficult to pay, especially now that the price of coffee was beginning to fall.

Having returned to the *manhaus* the men were presently arguing about what to do next. Some wished to attack the government station where those who had been captured would be held until either they were transported into Biyufa or a visiting magistrate arrived to hear their case.

However there was disagreement among them over this. Some said it would be wrong to fight beyond the village boundary, while others claimed that with the extension of the road the boundary was shrinking and that soon there would be nowhere left to fight.

Again, some said it was easy to blame the police when really the trouble lay with themselves. For they had been careless, allowing the Endai to outwit them. Against this, others argued that the Endai hadn't outwitted them. It was the government which had won, defeating not only the Bolgi but the Endai as well, since it was clear that by calling in the police their neighbours had given in to the government's rules forbidding payback, forbidding the tribes the right to defend their honour.

This led a number of men to argue that the only solution was for the Endai and Bolgi to join together to fight against outside interference. To which a small but experienced group replied that if the Bolgi wished to restore the balance of power between themselves and their neighbours then they too would have to learn the new ways, as the Endai had done, or else not fight at all. For to fight would make them all extinct. Yet *not* to fight, said others, would also make them extinct.

To which the elders, who like Nathaniel's grandfather had counselled against the morning's attack, replied that not to fight meant they would be forced to find peace among themselves.

It was this last thought, Nathaniel revealed, which was causing his grandfather to laugh. For the old warrior was wondering how it was possible for such hotheads who had failed to observe the traditional rules of battle ever to find peace among themselves. Even with the village's new wealth, the food they could buy from Biyufa, the houses they could build, they were still not happy. This was the lesson he had learnt from their discussion the night before when his daughter, Nathaniel's mother, had shown that she could be as angry as any of the warriors and all over three hundred kina.

Clearly the peace they were talking about was a pipe-dream. Indeed the truth was the Bolgi men were struggling to come to terms with the fact that it was themselves and not the Endai who were to blame for their defeat, a struggle they might yet try to sidestep by blaming the *masta*, as his mother had done for Nixon's expulsion. Which was why his grandfather had decided it was best that they leave the village at once and return to the school. Already there was a truck waiting to take them.

Once again feeling that he was spinning round on a roulette wheel of Bolgi rage and despair, Richard could only look on helplessly as Nathaniel's grandfather gave the order for his pack to be brought from the hut. Whereupon, still grinning broadly, the old man held out his hand.

Naturally he did not think it right, Nathaniel explained, that they should have to leave in such a manner. Perhaps one day, his grandfather suggested, things would be different. Gelmbolg would become a small town with its own council. Perhaps the *kanakas* would no more act like *kanakas* and they would welcome him back.

Behind the exploding nebula of warriors, the village's pandanus trees stood stark, stripped and still. In the glare of the morning sun the men seemed to add to the cascade of silvery leaves. Even the old man, with his hoary chest and spidery thighs, seemed momentarily caught up in the storm. For there was a new urgency about him as he led them down to the truck parked on the outskirts of the village.

As they clambered aboard they were surrounded by *pikininis*, startled as much, Richard sensed, by the spectacle of the *masta* fleeing their village, as by the sight of the armed men noisily remonstrating outside the *manhaus*. The presence of children might have made light of it all were it not for the deep awe with which they clutched each other by the arm, leaving prints like petals in one another's flesh.

As Nathaniel's grandfather stepped back and waved, the truck, itself a warrior of sorts, sprang to life. Soon they were hurtling down the dirt-track road leading back to the station.

21

He was wearing some kind of bullet-proof jacket. He could feel it weighing him down, while his feet, clamped in iron-shod boots, slewed like the broken caterpillar-tracks of a tank over the path of iron-red stones, throwing up sparks that set fire to the nearby bushes. The fire was spreading, its flames fanned by his broad, sail-braced shoulders. Within seconds it seemed the horizon was a glowing ring, discharging seething columns of smoke into the air. The smoke filled his throat and lungs as the raw-red ring, spurred on by the wind, smashed its festering fist into his face, the pale knuckles of white heat rocking him back on his feet. Until the pain in his chest from the smoke, from the barbed plumes of slick, black fumes sent him crashing to the ground, into the soft wet turf that squelched as he landed among ...

He looked up. The flames were melting into yellow gorse bushes. All around he could see green fields drenched in dandelions. Sycamores, elms and copper beeches towered over sun-warmed paddocks, over duck-filled ponds and winding, country lanes – the latter converging upon a busy dual-carriageway. Here he could see the traffic stalking the bristling columns of a nearby town; a steady stream of steel bearing down on the blond matador; he could feel the jar of flesh against the body of steel; the car's brakes burning a futile blister in the fog as the fists rained down on the window, the fists of the boy's mother, collapsing voiceless with grief on her knees beside her child in the gutter.

He tried to get to his feet but it was as though the pain in his chest had a voice of its own, ordering him to be still. In the vast, untended silence he began to hear all manner of sounds ... the swooning of pollen being carried off by the breeze; the baking of leaves in the hot sun; insects wheezing as they stretched in their sleep ... sounds that seemed to impregnate his skin, transforming his body into a living cacophony.

Observing a half-open gate nearby, he managed to drag himself over, startled to find a sad, lugubrious-looking animal lurking in the field behind it, watching him. It was old. Its coat was weathered. Its ponderous forehead and moribund flanks stank from purulent sores, while its eyes ballooned in a fevered mist. As it hobbled towards him, its hooves sinking into the soft earth, a plaintive sigh seemed to escape from its ragged nostrils.

He swung the gate shut to prevent the animal from escaping; then found himself reaching over the top of the rusty frame. He felt its warm breath tickle his fingers. Immediately his hand began to tremble, to shrink into a self-mocking fist.

'Richard!'

His arm fell to his side as she swept past him. Pausing to wrench up a handful of grass by its roots, she clambered up on to the gate. He saw the lilac lips curl back as she shoved the grass into the animal's face, its worn, cobbled-stone teeth chafing against her cold-reddened fingers. She swung round.

'I'm the only one who ever feeds him.'

A short, splintered-looking creature, with uncombed hair and a boyish swagger, she proceeded to climb further up the gate, her boots leaving dollops of mud on the sagging rungs.

'They all say he's too old; say he should be put down. Would you like to be put down when you get too old?'

He edged away nervously. With a sigh she began to stroke the animal's forehead. He continued to retreat.

'Richard!' Her voice sounded cynical. 'You forgot your satchel.'

He looked back over his shoulder at the slender figure crucified upon the iron gate. Though crusted with dirt, her skin seemed to glow with a silken transparency; her eyes buoyant as lily-pads. Her broad, flat nose ran with a white sap that lay trapped in the swell of sadness upon her upper lip; a sadness which slowly drip-dripped until, wiping her nose on the bottom of her filthy singlet that hung out over a pair of khaki shorts, she leapt recklessly to the ground.

'Never mind, I'll bring it.'

Alarmed, he began to stumble across the open countryside.

'Don't you want it?' she called out.

'N-No,' he managed to splutter. 'It . . . isn't mine.'

Undeterred, she scooped up the leather satchel and set off after him. He could smell the sour animal odour she gave off, hear the scudding of her boots and the sound of the heavy satchel which he refused to take brushing against her leg.

'Why do you say it isn't yours?'

'Because it isn't.'

'There's no need to pretend you know. No need to be afraid either.'
'I'm not afraid.'
'Then why are you wearing that bullet-proof jacket?'
'Actually it's . . . Well, it's because . . .'
'It doesn't really matter, I already know everything there is to know about you. It's all in this satchel.'
'What do you mean – everything?'
'Oh, you know.'

Biting her lip, it was as if she'd succeeded in draining the blood from the countryside, leaving it white and exhausted. The whiteness made his eyes water and gave him gooseflesh, before he realised they'd entered a bank of cloud. For they were climbing, his feet once more dragging, his breath coming in laboured bursts. He could still hear the satchel chafing against her leg though the sound grew increasingly faint. He stopped and waited for her to catch up; unable to explain his reluctance to go on without her.

'See. You are afraid,' she laughed, emerging pale and shivering beside him; 'and all you had to do was hold out your hand. It's only fear that stops us from reaching out; from opening the gate; feeling the hot breath of life – Ngai's hot breath steaming down our neck; feeling the heart of the universe beating in his bellows; the timeless energy. Unlike the Dervishes who, when they dance, tap into life's energy, there are people who are so frightened of life that they feel they must tie it down, control it, order it to do whatever they want. It's as though they've become so terrified by the vastness of the universe, that only by imprisoning all the species in it do they feel safe, feel that they have earned the right to live . . .'

Her voice began to fade. She was falling further and further behind. He realised she must be tiring and held out his hand. But . . . She was right. He was afraid. Not that she would reject it, but that it was already too late. Yet he felt sure she wouldn't abandon him. For some reason he trusted her. He sensed she knew where she wanted to go, though he was worried they would not be able to find their way back down the mountain again. And so, unable to hide his anxiety, he shouted out: 'You can't blame people for being afraid.'

'That depends,' she replied, startling him by her close – if invisible – proximity, 'on what they're afraid of. Take Ngai for instance. Just because he's old . . .'

'He's senile.'

'He's still alive!'

'Only just. And costing us money. More than the family can afford. It's all very well taking a moralistic view. The fact is it's finance that shapes our *lives as much as love or sentiment. As much even as your cosmic energy. Money is energy too, you know. You could say it's the blood of our time. It's money that . . .'*

He stopped. Something was wrong. His words appeared to be losing themselves in the bank of thick, white cloud; were failing to condense into something more solid or tangible. They were slipping away, like aborted foetuses, leaving him with the stain of defeat on his hands, with a cruel sense of betrayal.

He spun round but he knew she had gone. She had quietly melted away, saying nothing in her defence; refusing to listen to his excuses. Then he saw her, standing shrunken and dispirited in the distance, her body almost translucent.

Trembling, she dropped the heavy satchel at her feet. The gate she'd earlier climbed so triumphantly now loomed behind her like a gallows. Slowly she reached up for the latch.

'Janice!' he shouted.

She hesitated.

'Ngai?' he heard her call.

'Janice. Wait!' A sullen click answered him. 'Janice, I can explain.'

The gate swung open. 'Ngai?'

But Ngai, as he already knew, lay behind the hedge with a bullet through his brain.

22

HUNGRY KIWIS SAVAGE BIRD OF PARADISE

Today at the ANZAC Stadium in Fairfax a capacity crowd of twenty-five thousand spectators saw a ferocious New Zealand pack tear the national team apart in a display which owed more to a feast in some of the wilder parts of the Keramuti than an ordinary game of rugby league. The Kiwis gorged themselves on nine juicy tries and might have plundered even more but for a tropical storm late in the second half which seemed to dampen their appetites. But by then the hapless Bird of Paradise's feathers were so widely scattered about the field that the sharp clawed Kiwis would have been unlikely to find any meat left on the bones. In fact so brutal was the mauling that one is forced to ponder the wisdom of allowing the series to go ahead. For the truth is our playing standards do not match those of our neighbours Australia and New Zealand. And until they do it is surely best that we mix with birds of our own feather rather than allow ourselves to be savaged by bigger game.

Time the selectors were savaged, muttered Richard to himself, as a shadow fell across the back page of the *Fairfax Herald*. A team without a solitary player from the Keramuti in it. What did they expect? Not that it'd do the 'birds' any harm. It was just what they needed to toughen them up. A little less of paradise. Bit more of the real world.

The shadow was that of a child-hawker who stood peering in through the window of the Land Rover with large, tedium-filled eyes. Richard handed over a one kina coin in exchange for a 'spirit' butterfly and watched as the child turned away, glancing surreptitiously at the photograph in the paper of the 'sharp clawed Kiwis gorging themselves on one of their nine tries'. He tossed the crudely sculpted butterfly on to the seat beside him and looked at his watch. Oh, do hurry up, Rachel! It's almost twelve. We still have to call in at the garage on our way.

He glanced at the butterfly again, at the garishly painted wing studded with bright, vermilion seeds, which had just broken off, exposing bits of grass in the coarse, sunbaked mud. He leaned on the hooter. The child-hawker scampered away in the crowd of Saturday shoppers, with her string bag of 'spirit' artefacts swinging from her naked shoulder.

Inside the Biyufa General Meat Store, which was located at the back of a litter-strewn precinct just off the main road, the whine of the butcher's saw was setting Rachel's teeth on edge. She tried to shut out the noise by concentrating on the shopping that still had to be done in the short time that was left before closing. Her thoughts turned inevitably to Richard's match in the afternoon, dredging up the embarrassing spectacle of Richard arguing with the referee in the previous week's game and almost being sent off, saved only by Nathaniel's skilful intervention. Her mind sifted through the steady stream of arguments – with the staff over Nixon's future, with Meredith, the Ombudsman, the Minister . . . with the immigration officials at Nairobi airport who had claimed he was on their list of undesirables . . .

As the saw continued to tear through meat and bone she clutched her order in heat-swollen fingers, watching as scraps of sinew and gristle fell to the floor where they were kicked aside by the proprietor – Winston Sigulo, younger son of Malachy Davis. A stocky, curly headed figure wearing shorts and a sweat-stained vest, he had only moments before fired one of his staff, leaving the rest in a sulk. It seemed to Rachel that as a result they hacked at the fatty carcasses dangling from the rail overhead with a barely restrained brutality, their stainless steel knives splitting apart the joints of fly-covered meat which skidded and slapped against their plastic aprons, against the bouncing scales and blood-soaked counter.

The shop was full. While children played in the sawdust, customers dressed in *mals* and *bilas* jostled in the dank interior. Some lit long, newspaper-rolled cigarettes while they waited, others chewed betel-nut: tiny, leaf-wrapped parcels of powdered lime threaded their way from hand to hand like an army of umbrella ants marching through the undergrowth. At the counter a female bank clerk in a striped green uniform looked on as a small, wizened woman beside her handed over a pile of crumpled notes which seemed to slip like bits of skin through her cracked fingers. Collecting her blood-soaked parcel the woman, whose eyes were as yellow as the fat on the meat she had bought, turned and squeezed her way through the forest of feathers, fur and pointed tricorn hats.

Trapped at the far end of the counter, between an unplugged freezer smelling of stale offal, and a group of roadworkers in heavy overalls who were crushing her against the sticky glass, Rachel found herself struggling for air. She had not been well. A stomach bug, the result she suspected of drinking contaminated water, had kept her in bed for most of the week. Now the heat and flies and the incessant whine of the butcher's saw, along with the smell of blood and damp sawdust made her feel weak and unsteady on her feet once more, obliging her to lean on the arm of the young woman beside her who was breast-feeding her infant.

The woman smiled, milk trickling down the infant's chin as the nipple was dislodged from its lips. But then her expression changed as Rachel collapsed and fell to the floor.

Outside Richard continued to lean on the hooter, until it occurred to him that Rachel might have gone on to the chemist further down the street. He folded the week-old newspaper, headline: MINISTER OPENS NEW JAIL IN KERAMUTI and turned the key in the ignition. He drove slowly through the crowd of shoppers, rendered mute by the roar of passing trucks whose wheels threw up clouds of orange dust, trapping the heat in the heart of the busy town.

Rounding a tractor that was pumping out sewage from a narrow lane behind the courts, he pulled up outside the chemist, squeezing the vehicle into the shade of an inclining eucalyptus tree. Through its feathery leaves he could see in the distance the Mediterranean-style roof of the Flight Deck Hotel, or Flat Sponge, as Rachel had dubbed it, maintaining that its Sydney-based architects had got the mix of 'ingredients' all wrong.

It was a mix that consisted of Greek and Italian marble – courtyard, foyer and bathrooms; oak beams – dining room, breakfast room, bar, with chrome furnishings from Germany, bedroom fabrics and batiques from Indonesia, Oriental rugs, Australian wrought-iron sculpture and stuffed Sepik crocodiles; none of which, as one approached the hotel along the newly tarred road from the airport, prevented the building from bobbing up out of the heat as though it were simply yet another billboard, one of twenty or more, soaring above the hibiscus and bougainvillaea hedges, boasting: THE BEER OF TOMORROW. GET IT TODAY. GET PACIFIC LAGER!

It wasn't until one drove past the guards at the gate that the sun umbrellas punctuating the roof leapt into view, revealing the heads of the buffet bar patrons dotted like pigeon droppings along the reed balustrade. With their beers and their imported whiskies raised over the barbecue fires, the guests gave the building that live, above all international dimension so desperately sought by its creators. In Rachel's view, though, it was . . . 'the same old story: the bush tarted up; packaged along with the locals and the wildlife . . . life distilled through a camera lens, through the bottom of a glass. Never touched or smelled. Paradise from the balcony.'

Which was why on one frantic shopping trip, shortly after he'd left hospital, she'd surprised him by advocating they have lunch at the 'Sponge', followed by a swim in the hotel pool before they drove back to Keramuti.

'It's the heat. All this rushing about; trying to show the boys everything before the shops close.'

And although he'd been planning to pick up the *manki* on the way back and drive them out to the edge of the escarpment to show them the vast sugar plantations flourishing down on the coastal plain, Rachel had been adamant.

'I wasn't only thinking of myself, Richard. You heard what the doctor said. You have to give your body time to recover. Besides, the boys are exhausted.'

And so with his elbows sinking into the soft grass, he had found himself staring across the pool at the young first formers who squatted some distance from the edge, their legs folded beneath them like diminutive Buddhas. Only an hour before they'd been pulling him by the arm into Lee-Yang's for a game of pinball. This was followed by a visit to the open-air cinema where, with their hands hovering above their gun-slinger hips they'd stalked each other in front of the wide, cement screen, making enough noise to alarm the crippled guard. The guard, not seeing him in the shadows, had proceeded to chase them over the fence and into the bus station where Richard had lost sight of them among the noisy throng waiting to board the new fleet of air-conditioned coaches operating between the Highlands and the coast. He had had to request the station superintendent to page them over the tannoy; their pride at hearing their names announced in public bringing them strutting through the crowd, their naked bellies like balloons, their spirits soaring.

Even now he could still see the tawny figures with their shaven heads and eyes fixed on the hotel gate, waiting for Nathaniel who had promised them a tour of his uncle's garage. Having played a version of Blind Man's Buff with them in the shallows, Rachel slipped through the water towards them, her wary glance taking in the school of human lizards sunning themselves on the slatted beds scattered like confetti on the emerald lawn; the tall glasses and melting ice-cubes; the trail of smoke from the barbecue buffet . . . And the swivelling heads of the tiny Buddhas who, as she approached them, eyed her sombrely.

Moments later they were scooping up their belongings and bolting jubilantly down the drive, leaving Rachel to flick her way back across the pool. Her ankles caught the sun as she dived, disappearing beneath the rippled surface as he called out to her, demanding to know why she had allowed the *manki* to run off on their own like that.

For a while she circled lazily under the water, her hair drawn back off her face so that her eyes seemed to bulge, seemed to fill with an overwhelming sadness. It was as though the act of allowing the *manki* to run free had triggered in her some memory of her own childhood; of being forbidden to leave the yard of their Lancashire cottage in case her mother needed to send her on an errand; of being forbidden to run to school lest she fell and grazed her knees; of being told to stay away from the old mill where in the hot summer evenings the young Jezebels gathered.

Leaning over the side of the pool he dipped his hand into the water. Immediately she shot up beneath him, her hair fanning out over her shoulders, her mouth round and succulent as a coconut.

'Think they've overdone the chlorine,' she panted.

He pointed to a khaki shirt that had been left behind on the grass. 'I hope you told them to keep away from the bus station. Could find yourself on one of Janice's "round ups".'

Rachel nestled against the side of the pool, her chin resting in a puddle that had formed on the sun-warmed tiles. 'It seemed cruel to keep them waiting. After all, Nathaniel might have forgotten. Oh I know he gave you his word but then . . . you don't think he's trying to do too much, do you? He isn't even out of school yet and you've got him writing up his uncle's books.'

'Good practice I would have thought.'

'His school work is showing signs of deteriorating.'

'Yes, well, there's still plenty of time. It's another year before he takes his finals.'

'Suppose he doesn't make it?'

'Don't worry, I'll see to it. I'll make sure he keeps his work up to date.'

'The other teachers may not like you interfering.'

'I should have thought they'd appreciate all the help they can get. All the boy needs is a bit of extra tuition. I imagine his grades should at least be good enough to win a place at college.'

'Except that it isn't college he's talking about. I thought you knew. He's been asking about England. About studying at an English university.'

'Well I don't see why not. It's something we could look into.'

'What about the money? Or will you see to that as well? Do what your father did, open a secret account?'

'I think that's unfair. Besides he has *wantoks*. I expect they'll be only too willing to help.'

Rachel sighed as the water lapped over the edge of the pool, forcing her to untangle a string of saliva from her lips. 'The only people Nathaniel spends any time with these days, Richard, are you and his uncle, here in Biyufa. What makes you think the rest of them will be so keen . . . given he's written them off as a bunch of *kanakas*?'

'He's still their main source of hope.'

'He may let them down. What's more, they may blame you if he does.'

'Why should they?'

'Same reason the Kikuyu blamed your father for . . .'

Rachel gave a start as two young girls – one tanned and stringy, the other squat and fair – ran and launched themselves noisily through the air, landing only inches away in the water so that the waves burst over her head, swamping the side of the pool.

Watching the water trickle down Rachel's brow, following the magnetic curve of her cheeks, Richard saw her gulp and shiver. The shock had caused her to shut her eyes, but not before he'd seen a shadow flicker briefly through their chlorined brightness. It was the same dark and forbidding shadow which had found her greeting the news that he'd refused Meredith's offer of special leave with lachrymose silence.

'Teach yer to bring the *kanakas* to swim in our pool!' snapped the first girl, clambering out over the side.

'Yeah and they can't even swim,' pouted the second, holding on to the straps of her costume which had come undone.

Treading water, Rachel ignored them and they quickly ran off across the grass. Richard offered to help her out of the pool but she shook her head, surprising him by reaching out and contritely running her fingers along the scar slanted across his chest. The skin was still raw and inflamed as a result of the infection he'd suffered after the stitches had burst.

'Sorry,' she said. 'I didn't think . . .'

He took her hand. 'There's still time to collect the *manki* and drive out to the—'

'Richard!' she cried, sinking as she let go. Grabbing the side of the pool she swallowed, spluttered. 'We're not going anywhere. Not now. Not this afternoon. Not . . .'

'What do you mean?' he said.

'I mean it's ages since we had any time to ourselves. For instance, when did we last spend an evening alone together, without Nathaniel, or the *manki* hovering nearby? Without some committee or other to see you from the co-operative? When was the last time we got away? Had a meal together? Talked?'

'You mean about Janice? And "Chicken" Bell?'

Her long legs pumping, Rachel continued to tread water; her nostrils flared, her feet fractured by the light. 'I mean about *us*. About Janice as well, yes. And the Keramuti. But mostly about us. Now I know the plan was to drive back this afternoon . . . but I've been thinking. Why don't we stay overnight? It'll be the first time we've stayed at the "Sponge" since we arrived. Remember that first night? Tony banging on our door. Wouldn't leave us alone. What was it he kept shouting? "Plenty-a time for all that where you're going". Beginning to sound like a case for the Trades Description Act.'

'What about the boys? Where'll they stay?'

'Perhaps we could persuade Nathaniel's uncle to put them up for the night. I doubt whether they'd want to stay at the "Sponge".'

'Why not?'

'After this afternoon's fiasco when you tried to coax them up the stairs to the buffet?'

'I thought they'd enjoy it. New faces. Whole new world . . .'

'They were perfectly happy to eat at Lee-Yangs.'

'Bit dodgy on the stomach. Anyway I expect it was only the stuffed *puk puk* in the lobby that frightened them. That or the doorman shouting . . . something about not having a ticket.'

'He meant the buffet ticket.'

'I suppose they've made straight for the pinball machine. I do hope you told them to be back before dark, Rachel.'

Rachel shoved her arms out on either side of her, her elbows poised above the shimmering tiles. Her shoulders were brown, her breasts pale and buoyant in the water. 'Actually I asked them whether they'd like to go to the cinema tonight.'

'You *what*?'

She started to laugh and lurched out of the pool. 'My God! You saw them. They were ecstatic. Now will you stop worrying about the *manki* and start thinking about us for a change? A room on the top floor, don't you think? Away from the noise of the bar.'

Kneeling on the edge of the lawn, Rachel skilfully wrung the water out of her hair before throwing the long lambent strands back over her shoulder. Blocking out the sun her body gave off a refreshing coolness, quivering like a pink hibiscus heavy with dew, the soft, vibrant petals fanning their fragrance over him, her lips meeting his, only to dart away recklessly. The swiftness of her movements startled him. But while her knee dug carelessly into his wound, water already warmed by the air and the fecundity of longing ran from her breasts and belly, sliding over his skin. As she leaned across and lifted their clothes from the grass she brushed his lips with her finger, then deftly pulled him up after her.

Impervious to the stares of the recumbent onlookers, they crossed the lawn where the dampness of the sprinklers hung in a steamy haze over the front of the hotel. He felt the wet heaviness of her hair, and the heat of her fingers snagging his flesh. Reaching the drive they found the tarred surface melting and ran in their bare feet up the marble stairs into the lobby.

Rachel opened her eyes and saw the young woman whose arm she had been leaning on earlier bending over her, administering a damp handkerchief to her forehead. The woman now folded the handkerchief and began brushing the sawdust from Rachel's cheeks.

'I tink yu orait now, miss. Yu lie isi. Butcherman bring yu sum brandy.'

Rachel looked up into the warm face of the woman who continued to brush the foul-smelling sawdust from her skin. A glass of water stood on the ground beside her into which she dipped the white handkerchief. Rachel smelt the strong scent with which it was impregnated and noticed the woman's smooth skin glistening with perspiration. Her hands were broad yet light, her breasts unsupported and heavy, with drops of milk staining her blue cotton blouse. Rachel remembered the infant she had seen feeding and tried to look round to see what had become of it, but the faces of the crowd swayed drunkenly over her, as though dangling from the large butcher's hooks suspended from the metal rail behind the counter. She could hear the steel grating as the hooks were shoved to and fro, as the heads swung from side to side – dark, blood-filled heads, swaying in the damp, blood-filled light.

'Richard,' she heard herself calling out. 'Richard, no, please don't . . .'

'Sssh. Sssh. Yu close your eyes now miss. Butcherman come in jus a minute.'

'No, Richard, please don't argue. It'll only make things worse . . .'

'Sssh. Sssh.'

'But I'm only trying to help.' Her voice echoed in the distance, in the noisy, sultry cave that was the arrivals area of the airport terminal in Nairobi, where jet-lagged passengers clustered round Customs and Immigration waving their papers in the air, as though a swarm of locusts had just descended upon the ground.

'Please try to understand . . . No the man isn't being deliberately difficult. It's his job. He says your name's on the computer . . . I don't know . . . some kind of list . . . *undesirables*? What on earth possessed you to risk coming back? What do you mean you haven't done anything? He's just told you it's on the computer. Under what name? What name did you give? Richard Albert Green? Heavens! Rachel Victoria Tormey. Albert meets Victoria. My God, he says it's to do with the murder of a Kikuyu boy. No, it isn't because he's a Kikuyu himself. You were born here? Well why shouldn't they want you back? I wonder if it's possible they may be confusing you with someone else? Should be easy enough to check. All they need is your date of birth . . . Yes, he can see it's in your passport. Look, I know it's been a long flight but that's no reason . . . who me? Oh I'm a regular. Condition of father's will I visit his former parishioners . . . helped look after me just after I was born . . . shores of Lake Victoria — Rachel *Victoria*. No, I'm not on their list. Why should I . . . ? What on earth did you do? Must have been something . . . maybe you're right. Maybe the computer has got you muddled up with . . . here he is . . . Richard Albert Green. Date of birth — 31 May 1910. Good heavens! That makes you seventy-what? Ha ha, isn't that funny? Yes, of course he apologises. See, he's stamping your passport. It means they're letting you in. What? Your father? Also Richard Albert Green. You mean your father murdered the boy?'

'Rachel?' said Richard, clearing a path through the crowd in the butcher's and kneeling down in the sawdust beside her. 'Rachel, come on. It's only the heat.'

Rachel opened her eyes. But the faces overhead were blurred, spinning round and round like swarms of flies; like the yellow fans lazily humming in the airport terminal.

'Still waiting?' she asked as the long blades wobbled and hummed, until the noise of a Jumbo's engines burst through the plate glass windows, drowning out the sound of her voice, though she heard it faintly, as though from a distance. Or was it the sound of the butcher's saw?

'Sorry that was awfully callous of me. Look, why don't we share a taxi? An accident? Oh, you mean the boy. Time of the Mau Mau rebellion. Always reminds me of that phrase . . . father used to use it whenever he spoke about the fifties . . . "Everyone a little jumpy"; as though it could explain away all the bloodshed. A friend? Mwangi? Then how . . . ? At night? You mean he was coming to *warn* you . . . ?'

'Rachel?' said Richard gently but firmly, as the crowd began to press in on the *masta* and his *meri*; the swish of their net aprons and leafy skirts heightening the sighs, the sound of air being sucked in through their teeth. 'Rachel come on. You'll be all right once you get outside. Bit of fresh air . . .'

'Means Mau Mau would have burned you out anyway. Hardly needed an excuse. Their land after all. Still, can't imagine why your father . . . firing blind like that. Tried to make it up? By sending Mwangi's family money? Could have been you he was really making it up to, seeing as it was your friend he'd killed. Preposterous? You mean you think he did it out of love? I suppose you'll tell me next he loved Africa. Isn't that what they all say? Question is . . . Whose Africa? The Mzungus . . . ?'

'Rachel, here, drink this,' said Richard, taking the ice-filled tumbler of brandy from the proprietor who began brusquely shoving the crowd towards the door. Rachel felt the glass jammed up against her teeth. She felt the ice-cold fire swoop down the back of her throat and into her belly. She jerked her head away, coughed and spluttered.

Richard supported her head in his hands, while the young woman looked on sympathetically over his shoulder, stroking the infant she had tucked away in her *bilum*. The infant lay asleep, clutching in its tiny fist the corner of the handkerchief which the woman had used to cool Rachel's forehead. Against its dark, satin skin specks of sawdust glittered like gold. Rachel stretched out her hand towards it.

'That's it,' said Richard, pulling her gently to her feet. 'Think you can make it back to the Land Rover?'

PART FOUR

23

A convoy of dumper trucks swept past the Keramuti Highway Tavern and, like a field of daisies, the white metal caps on the bottles of Pacific lager arrayed behind the bar shivered on their long green stems. Buffeted by the wind, a clump of weeds sprouting inside the doorway disgorged a cloud of gnats. A turquoise butterfly floated over the heads of rusty nails protruding from the foot of the bar, brushing the edges of bent bottle caps scattered in the dirt and the jagged teeth of a bully-beef tin that lay stranded in a pool of urine, before finally sailing off into the trees crowded together like a Japanese screen on the slopes beyond the tavern wall. While flies circled in a frenzy above the mouths of discarded 'greenies', the dog responsible for the pool of urine, a sallow-faced mongrel lying sprawled in the shade outside, quietly opened its eyes and stared at the massive wheels passing within inches of its nose.

The trucks groaned beneath their towering loads of turmeric-coloured sand, which the mechanical diggers of the Victoria Engineering Company were excavating a mile and a half up the road, at the site of a new mountain pass. The pass led to the neighbouring province of Arua – reported recently to have granted drilling licences to two major oil companies whose explorations had indicated the presence of substantial deposits of oil and gas. The wooded shoulder of the mountain dividing the provinces was already reduced to a brittle honeycomb, out of which a steady stream of vehicles emerged, reeling round the heady bends like smoke-drugged bees.

As the drivers flashed their lights and pummelled their horns inside their tinted glass cabins, the trucks rumbled away through the forest. Clouds of dust kicked up by the vehicles swirled out far over the valley, dousing the flames of the villagers' land-clearing fires, obscuring the white-hot glare of the sun so that day turned to dark, brooding dusk, and the tongues of the two men at the bar to sandpaper.

The dust settling around them, they scooped up their drinks, the one tilting the bottle impatiently to his lips, the other concealing in it a long, thin hand which crackled like a brown paper bag. Beer was all they sold at the tavern and Meredith who, earlier in the day, had helped finish off a bottle of his favourite Glenfiddich in the prison commander's office, was showing a marked reluctance to tackle the popular 'greenie'.

'Stuff's enough to make yer . . . well it ought-a at least be enough to make a man think twice 'bout staying on.'

Richard pumped his cheeks furiously, allowing the warm beer to fizz in his mouth.

'Christ, haven't yer had enough, Richie?'

The beer soared and foamed at the back of his throat, seething forward over his tongue which knocked it back like a tidal wall, so that it spun round the inside of his bloated cheeks and then sank in a confusion of cross-currents, tasting of corned beef, sediment and salt water.

'Anyone else would-a thrown in the towel by now. You? You hitch yourself to another contract!'

Richard held the half-empty bottle aloft. 'It would seem Industry takes a rather different view from Education.'

'Board-a Governors,' Meredith growled. 'Was their decision to let you go.'

Richard gulped down another cross-current of foaming beer.

'Anyway means yer free to concentrate on the co-operative. Even bigger fight on your hands there, way coffee prices've been tumbling. No Ombudsman to appeal to either. Excommunicated – I'm talking nations never mind individuals. Sink or swim.'

'Oh, I shouldn't worry,' said Richard, swatting away a fly with the back of his hand. 'Coffee's pretty resilient. Bound to pick up again. It might take a while, but then the way to survive is to diversify. You've heard about the saw mill? The co-operative's also just signed a deal with . . .'

'I heard it was a cement factory,' said Meredith, frowning.

'That's what we're still negotiating.'

Meredith's eyes widened, bloodshot and ragged around the edges, like rusty bottle-caps.

'Bloody hell it'll take years! Way things are going. Best part-a decade, yer ask me.'

'It all depends,' replied Richard. 'If the authorities were to seal the highway between her and Biyufa I reckon we could be up and running in half the time.'

'Half?' exclaimed Meredith, as a fleet of trucks thundered past the tavern, this time carrying away tons of blasted rock, piled high like storm clouds. 'You'll be lucky. Haven't yer heard? Coffee isn't the only market on the slide. Copper's just bombed. Government's had to announce a whole round-a cut-backs. Only reason they're able to go ahead with the Arua pass is it's being funded by the oil companies. Buggers can't get their equipment in there fast enough.'

The dust brought further swarms of flies that settled upon the rubbish left earlier by the roadworkers during their lunch-break. Most of it had already been picked over by a pregnant Saddleback, now sauntering off, its hindquarters swaying truck-like as it followed the trail of crisp packets and empty bully-beef tins lining the side of the road.

'Personally,' said Meredith, picking the corner of the label on the bottle with his fingernail, 'I reckon it's more to do with ministers creaming off the profits from the Sina mine than the bottom falling out-a the market. All the same, it's bound to affect a lot-a contracts. My advice to you is to pull out now, Richie. You and Rachel've done yer bit. Ask me, bloody girl deserves—'

'We're not asking the government for any money. We're negotiating directly with the banks: Yokohama; Jakarta Commercial; New South Wales. Co-operative has offered to put up fifteen per cent.'

'Christ, I didn't know yer were making that kind of money.'

'We're not. At least not yet. We're having to borrow most of it.'

Meredith peeled away the remains of the label from the bottle, leaving behind a white underskirt, torn and soiled. 'You must be doing some pretty smooth talking. You sure the *kanakas* know what they're letting themselves in for? Profits in the year . . . ?'

'It isn't just about profits. It's about getting a seat on the board; becoming part of the decision-making process. It means the villagers can choose the sort of development *they* want. It also means they share the responsibility.'

Meredith crumpled the label in his fist. 'You can dress it up any way you like, Richie. Fact is, it's *all* about profits. Only thing interests the *kanakas* is how much money they can make.'

'In this case quite a lot I should've thought. Bearing in mind it isn't only the shareholders who'll benefit. Think of the jobs we'll be creating. The boost it'll give to the local economy. Chance even for the excommunicated to work their way back into the fold.'

'Sure, at some vague point in the future. Question is, will the *kanakas* wait that long? Any money the co-operative makes in the short term's going to have to pay off the loan. Last manager of a business I know tried to reinvest a share of the annual profits instead of paying off his shareholders got run out-a town. And that was after they ransacked his house. Thought he'd been stashing the money away under his mattress.'

'It's all a matter of vision,' said Richard angling the bottle between his fingers so that its long neck caught the sun's rays through a hole in the roof and he could see the tiny specks of dust floating in his beer. 'Getting them to see far enough ahead into the future; to realise that they can be masters of their own destiny.'

'*Masters?*'

'Why not?'

Meredith tossed the screwed up label on to the ground, crushing it under his foot.

'Look,' said Richard, 'it wasn't until we started throwing money at them – imposing our cash-based economy on theirs – that they lost control. Think of how they've managed to look after the land. Some of these terraces are hundreds of years old. They could only have survived with an eye to the future. For God's sake, the villagers have enjoyed thousands of years of sustainable agriculture! We should be able to draw on that knowledge, to join their skills to ours so that we can build something new between us, something visionary.'

Meredith stared at the angled shaft of light, at the bottle dancing with increasing agitation between Richard's hardened fingers. 'Vision,' he said; 'is that what's keeping yer out here?'

'No sense in saddling them with the past,' said Richard, jamming the bottle to his lips. 'It was the past that did for Malachy Davis's son, Wayne. Only a sense of vision, will save his brother, Sigulo.'

'And Rachel? She share this vision thing of yours?'

Richard grimaced as he swallowed the warm beer, feeling the grit it dislodged scraping against his teeth. 'She's agreed to stay on. I think that speaks for itself, don't you?'

Meredith shrugged. 'It won't get any easier. Unemployment rising. Kids are beginning to lose motivation.'

'A couple of months and I expect it'll all change. What with the saw mill, and the cement factory . . . things are bound to pick up.'

'Christ, yer wanna get your head out-a the clouds, Richie. Cost yer more than your girlfriend if yer not careful. Though I don't suppose yer can get a more down-to-earth vision – a more *concrete* vision – than a cement works, hey? Unless yer count the new prison. Your baby too from what I hear.'

Richard set the empty bottle down on the makeshift counter. 'You've obviously been talking to the ADC. I don't think you'll find anyone else making that connection.'

'Oh I don't know. ADC's a pretty modest sort-a bloke. Doesn't mind passing on the credit. Reckons it all came about as a result-a you and him exploring the idea of the cement factory.'

'What he means is he held a series of talks with the co-operative's management committee, of which I happen to be a member.'

'Well, whatever,' said Meredith, toying with the idea of a drink, 'I guess he must've tired-a rounding up the *kanakas* every time they smashed their way out-a that old bamboo affair. Particularly embarrassing that last break-out – torching the whole compound! By the way, that kid, the one you were trying to help . . . ?'

'Nixon.'

'One of them, wasn't he? Been arrested for . . . ?'

'Manslaughter.'

'Speared a policeman, I hear.'

'In the arm for God's sake!' The police put the story about he'd been killed. Seems they were trying to frighten the buggers. Exact a little revenge of their own I suppose. Did a damned good job. Bolgi thought they were about to be packed off to Fairfax Central. Under the impression they were facing ten, fifteen years behind bars. Apparently some of them were told they'd be lucky if they got out at all. So, rather than wait for the trial they . . .'

'Yea, well, I'd like to see them burn their way out-a that monstrosity,' said Meredith, pointing to a gap in the trees, where on the far side of the river, in the grounds of the abandoned New Tribes Mission, the Provincial flag fluttered above the red brick walls of the Keramuti Detention Centre. 'Prison commander gave me a guided tour of the place. Iron bars, cement floors, concrete bunks . . .'

'Iron roof, no ceiling – hot as hell,' Richard pointed out, ordering another beer from the young barman who, looking up from his seat on an empty beer crate at the far end of the bar, carefully folded the yellowed pages of an old *Fairfax Herald*, counted out the change for the five kina note that Richard held up, and then carefully slid the dusted-down bottle across the counter. Tucking his faded Pacific lager T-shirt into his shorts, he wandered off to collect the empties lying among the deserted 'benches'.

There were no tables at the Keramuti Highway Tavern, the 'benches' little more than crumbling breeze-blocks pilfered during the construction of the jail. These were lined up along the low *pit pit* walls over which customers spat their betel-juice. The floor was earthen, the bar an old tree trunk split in two and covered with a strip of lino; while the roof consisted of blackened sheets of iron rescued from the ruins of its government-funded predecessor – set alight at the same time as the old jail by the escaping Bolgi.

Brazen though their break-out had been, Richard couldn't help recalling the fears expressed by Nathaniel's mother. The men had made off in a police

Land Rover, taking their guards with them as hostages, only to be recaptured a week later by the riot squad after numerous houses had been burned and animals slaughtered. The appearance of the riot squad under the hastily enacted Highlands Protection Bill, together with the ever-increasing numbers of excommunicated who regularly gathered up at the tavern to fling empty bottles at the government troops as they raced past in their Jeeps, meant that things were turning out just as the embattled figure had predicted . . .

'These young ones . . . do not think of the next day . . . Endai return . . . seeking their own revenge . . . people . . . no longer safe . . . always be on their guard wherever they went . . . to live with such fear in one's soul . . . ? having given one's enemy cause to retaliate because one had attacked in a way that showed lack of respect . . . not only for oneself but for the fact people . . . olsem!'

'So the prison commander's shown yer around too then?' said Meredith, glancing at his watch. 'Reckon the place could become a regular tourist attraction. Just what yer want up here. Think-a the income you'd generate if yer ran up a safari lodge with a couple-a thatched-roof bungalows overlooking the valley . . . guided tours . . . climbing expeditions, white-water rafting . . . Hell, it'd certainly put an end to the *kanakas* whingeing. Give 'em a chance to earn some easy bucks.'

Richard watched the young, barefooted barman gathering up the empty bottles lying scattered like insects about the floor. He'd been about to explain to Meredith that he hadn't been shown around the prison but had gone there to visit Nixon, who he knew blamed Meredith for failing to stand up to the Board of Governors. With the help of his *wantoks* Nixon had sworn to get even. But now that Meredith had accepted early retirement and was currently embarking on a final tour of the Keramuti before returning home to Queensland, there seemed little point. In any event, Richard felt a certain amount of sympathy for the former chief officer. Stumbling off for a pee round the back of the tavern, Meredith managed to scrape his head on a strand of wire hanging down from the roof, drawing a trickle of blood across his bare scalp which he seemed unaware of, allowing the flies to settle upon the broken skin.

There was something about Meredith that reminded him of his father, arriving back in England after having been cleared of Mwangi's murder. There was the same air of defeat. Rumours of behind the scenes efforts to get the charges dropped had merely served to increase publicity surrounding the case, resulting in a large number of journalists being present at the airport to greet him, firing their questions over the heads of the representatives from the colonial office. 'How's it feel to be home, Mr Green?' 'Any views on the trial? Some say it was held to placate the wogs.' 'D'you believe you've been made a scapegoat?' 'How would you describe the atmosphere in the colony at the moment?' 'Is it true you panicked – a man of your experience? A war hero?' 'What effect would you say the trial's had on your family? Is it true your son was friendly with the deceased?' 'What'll you do now? It's been more than twenty years – d'you think you'll be able to adjust?' 'Planning on chucking any more medals into the Avon, Mr Green?'

There was the same characteristic stoop, the dry, cracked lips and sleepless eyes that stared with a defiance that was in truth despair; a despair which had driven his father to sell off the farm at a loss. To his and Janice's horror he had bought a cottage in an isolated West Country village where, although he chatted with friends and neighbours, he would never visit or invite them over, preferring instead to lock himself away in the garden shed and pretend to be writing busily. One day it was a treatise on Coffee and the Kenyan economy, the next customs of the Kikuyu; whilst in his blackest mood, he claimed to be embarking on a biography of Rommel. It was a pretence that helped to smooth things over but also allowed a certain seediness to set in, though not in standards of appearance. For just as with Meredith who was brushing the dust from his shoes outside, they had always remained high. Meticulous to the last, his father had died lying curled up on the old camp-bed in a corner of the shed, still wearing his tie, his shoes polished, his belt folded under the lamp on the desk, beside the bottle of pills. Having left his will in a sealed envelope on top of the typewriter, he had saved them the trouble of sorting through all his papers. It had not taken them long to solve the mystery of where all the money had been going over the years: the family solicitor revealing the existence of a secret bank account, of which the balance – a third of the value of the estate – had been left to Mwangi's family.

No, the seediness as Richard saw it, lay in his father's shame. In his meek surrender to the transient forces of History. To the feelings of anger and bitterness sweeping through the country prior to the ending of the state of emergency – 'RIOT AS SETTLER SHOOTS FARMBOY'; 'WHITE FARMER MURDERS KIKUYU'.

These feelings had continued to haunt him long after he'd been freed so that it seemed as if he had come to believe in his guilt. He became a feeble and solitary figure lacking in courage; lacking the will to fight back. Richard had wanted him to fight back, begging, pleading with him – not in words in those clumsy schoolboy letters boasting of his success at rugby and cricket, but with his eyes, with shameful stolen looks which were unable to break the silence or the distance growing between them. Fighting back only when it was too late and he could no longer be hurt. When the truth behind the supposed Kikuyu raid on the farm and the shooting of Mwangi – not only kept from Richard's mother but still to the present day kept from Janice – when this small and tragic truth no longer mattered, having been absorbed by the larger, unfolding pattern of History.

Would Meredith, too, he wondered, noticing the sun-shrivelled figure once more glance at his watch as he re-entered the tavern, suffer the same lingering remorse in retirement, having spent so many years insisting: *'it's like taking part in a mannequin parade . . . strutting your stuff on the stage . . . the audience . . . kanakas . . . watch . . . imitate . . . last thing the Department wants is you imitating them'*? Wasn't that furtive glance at the watch the sign of a man who had given up the fight? Of someone who could see no hope for the *kanaka* because he could see none for himself?

And yet staring out over the *pit pit* wall, seeing the valley soaking up the sun, the white clouds piling up against the limestone cliffs; listening to the distant tattoo of the Waragoi, to the babble of bamboo flutes in the forest . . . how could one feel anything other than a sense of hope?

Despite the presence of the riot squad, it was hope that continued to drive the villagers on in their pusuit of wealth and a better standard of living. It had become an unstoppable force, epitomised by the sound of the heavy-duty lorries thundering up and down the highway, spraying the tavern walls with sand and gravel. Even Meredith, who was warily eyeing an approaching pick-up, would surely take away with him a sense of that speed of progress, a sense of that liberating energy?

'Christ! What the hell are they up to?'

Richard frowned as the dusty pick-up skidded to a halt in the dirt outside and a party of armed villagers sprang out, the sun shining on their feathered head-dresses, on the cropped plumes of their pointed arrows.

'Not sure I like the look of this lot, Ritchie.'

24

Their bodies were coated in a white, glutinous paste, flaking like skin as it dried in the hot sun. Their eyes were hollowed, their voices muted, giving rise to a sinister silence as they began to circle the tavern, tense and naked, rolling on the balls of their feet.

'*Hey, baman!*' Meredith yelled. '*Yu kisim i kam long plis. Kwik!*'

The young barman's eyes were clear and strong and the sweat that glistened on his cheeks gave his face a bright, self-confident glow. He dropped a clutch of empty bottles into an old *bilum* and shook his head.

'There is no need for the police. These men are not dangerous.'

'*Yu no givim maus long mi!*' Meredith barked. '*Yu kisim i kam long plis!*'

The barman shrugged and lifted the bulging *bilum* over his shoulder.

'*Hariup!*'

The glass bottles collided in the raw-stringed *bilum*. 'It is not necessary. They are not meaning any harm.'

'You know them?' asked Richard, keeping one eye on the intrepid yet slightly-built figure as he hauled the bottles round the back of the bar, the other on the villagers who continued to encircle the tavern, their silence broken only by the ominous rattling of their bows.

'I know them,' said the barman pausing beside a pile of empty crates. 'They are from the village next to mine.'

'Endai?'

'Yes. They are *wantoks*.'

'What do they want?'

The young barman grinned. Meredith, whose eyes were as red as the barman's gums, rapped the counter with his knuckles. 'Christ, what do yer think they want, Richie? Same idea as the mudmen of the Kagamuga. Prancing about in their *bilas* so they can—'

'Perhaps we ought to find out.'

'Must reckon we're bloody stupid. Shotgun's the only thing these *kanakas* understand.'

The bottles shattered as the *bilum* was flung to the floor. The barman leapt forward, the sweat from his cheeks scattering like shards of broken glass.

'No, please! No shotgun. These men are harmless. They are not coming to fight you.'

'Yer reckon?' Meredith snarled. 'What about the war paint?'

The barman wiped his hands on his shorts. 'When we have initiation we smear the bodies of the young boys with clay. We obtain it from a sacred site near Mount Elimbari which is used by all the tribes and which is blessed by the *tambaran* – the spirits of our ancestors. Usually the clay is kept on the body for two weks before it is washed off by the elders in the river. For us it represents the old skin that we must shed in order to become men. No one who has not been through this stage is allowed to—'

'Fight? Exactly. These aren't boys. What's more they're armed!'

'No,' said the barman, pointing to one of the men who had detached himself from the rest. 'Look. His weapon is useless.'

As the spectral-white figure advanced towards them, he stuck out a hand and began cautiously sliding his thick fingers inside Richard's shirt, spreading the sticky paste over his ribs, his belly, over the thickly knotted scar upon his chest. The bow he carried was rough, its string hanging loose. Richard thought he detected a flicker of amusement in the large turbid eyes.

'You see?' said the barman, taking the bow and handing it to Richard. 'It is not ready for shooting. Now it is yours. He is giving it to you. The other men will give you one of their arrows. You must take one from each of them.'

The men crept noiselessly into the tavern, crouching low as they gathered round him. They made no attempt to break their silence, merely grinning foolishly, revealing bright, purple gashes in their eerie masks – rent with tarnished teeth. The orange-tinted dust encasing their ankles, their bleached hair, frizzed like old-fashioned pipe cleaners, and satanic eyes, all exuded an air of buffoonery, that was rendered hauntingly ambiguous by the display of their boars' tusks.

Each having presented him with a single arrow, they began to nudge him towards the entrance. Their hands were gentle and cajoling, pawing at him so that he felt their hot breath on his face, smelt the warm rancidity of banana and betel-nut. Emerging in the bright sun he glanced back over his shoulder but could see no sign of Meredith. Perhaps he had gone to alert the police, though given the present state of affairs, with Nixon and his *wantoks* still awaiting trial, it would've been an act of the utmost folly. An act surely not even Meredith . . . ?

And yet, what if these white daemonic figures did have more sinister designs, more insidious motives? What if Rachel on her visit to Nimile Orapi's village had got it wrong, and the Endai did indeed hold him responsible for Nimile's death? Could they have deceived her, just as they might be trying to deceive him? Could she have allowed her distrust of Nathaniel and the Bolgi to blind her to the Endai's real concern?

'Did not think of the next day . . . month . . . Endai return . . . seeking their own revenge.'

Stabbing the point of the bow they'd presented him with into the ground, so that they could not steer him any further away from the tavern, he turned to the barman. 'Who are these men? What do they want?'

'Please,' said the barefooted figure, pointing to the battered vehicle. 'You go with them. You will come to no harm.'

'I'm not going anywhere until they've explained what it is they want from me. They haven't said anything up to now. Not a word.'

'It is the tradition. The uninitiated may not speak.'

'I don't understand.'

'It is as if they had not yet learned to talk. They may show you only by acting.'

With an exaggerated firmness, the villagers tugged and pulled at his arm. They took it in turns, each flexing their muscles, puffing out their cheeks, repeating the same melodramatic gestures – devious glances, silent snarls. Each played their part in a string of minor contests, threatening to win without ever quite pulling it off; allowing him to play the hero's role, to beat back their clumsy advances.

Eventually their masked expressions gave way to open embarrassment and they began to withdraw, a wounded cry rising among them, drowning out the screech of the cicadas in the nearby trees. Raising their loosened bows, they went through the motions of firing off their arrows into the air. They stamped their feet and chanted, before bounding across the stony ground into their vehicle which sagged and rocked as they continued their elegiac mime in the confined space at the back. Finally one of the men leapt over the tailboard, holding up a scrap of paper which he presented to Richard.

Richard flicked away bits of clay and unfolded the paper which had been torn from a child's exercise book. The shock at seeing Rachel's handwriting caused him to stagger in the hot sun, scattering the bow and arrows around him like the branches of a felled tree. Immediately the warm beer welled in the pit of his stomach, its sour foam biting against the constrictions of his throat, scraping away the dryness like shingle, sweeping up into the back of his mouth where it burned with a rawness intensified by the salt of its sour after-taste, and of his sweat.

He looked round anxiously, wondering where on earth Meredith had gone to, wondering whether he was going to raise the alarm. He could just see the back of Meredith's car on the far side of the tavern. But then even if he did alert the police it was Rachel the Endai held, *her* life, not his that was in danger. They had set out merely to distract him, giving their *wantoks* time to spirit Rachel out of the valley. Yet the whole idea seemed absurd . . . preposterous. In broad daylight? At a time of emergency? Surely someone would have seen; would have been able to sound the alarm.

'Please, Mr Green,' he heard the Endai barman quietly urging him in the background, 'you read this letter. It will explain everything.'

He glanced across at the inoffensive-looking group huddled together in the back of the pick-up. They smiled, their white faces macabre, yet anxious that he should return to the piece of paper. It felt clammy and was in danger of coming apart in his hands.

'*Richard,*' he read, '*I realise this may come as something of a shock to you. Certainly I was taken aback when emerging from the last lesson before lunch I found myself surrounded by armed men outside the classroom, though as soon as the children saw them they began to laugh, explaining that the villagers were acting out some sort of ritual – the purpose of which was eventually made clear to me, and I must admit I too found it rather amusing . . .*'

'Richie?' It was Meredith, winding down the window of his car. 'What do they want?'

'Actually, I'm not quite sure.'

'Well if it's money tell 'em . . .'

'No. It's not that. At least . . .'

Richard ignored the sweat trickling into his eyes and read on.

'*. . . Using one of the pupils as a translator, the men asked if I'd write a note to you on their behalf. You see the Endai are worried by the way your Bolgi progidy, Nathaniel, has been bullying one of their* wantoks *in Biyufa. I believe it's the same "rascal" that Nathaniel once tried to beat up outside Meredith's office, and who, as it turns out, happens to be a cousin-brother to Tapie, Nixon's old bête noir.*

The men are unable to deal with this matter themselves because they feel the old approaches – that is through Nathaniel's wantoks *in the village – no longer work. He no longer listens to the* kanakas. *Having become a major influence in the boy's life therefore, they feel it only right and proper that you should accept a* wantok's *share of responsibility for him. In other words by accepting this traditional role you too are being accepted into Keramuti society. You are if you like being made an honorary kanaka.*

It's in this regard that the Endai have asked me to warn you about Nathaniel, since if Tapie's cousin should come to any harm, it's to you, Richard, they'll look for compensation. They've already lost one child and not been compensated. They're determined not to lose another, even if he is only one of the many thousands of 'excommunicated'.

Sorry if this sounds rather callous, but the role I'm expected to play is one of dispassionate messenger, which might be no bad thing as the note will almost certainly be public knowledge by the time you read it. (Already half the school seems to be peering over my shoulder.) I did warn you. Nothing can ever remain secret for long in the Keramuti. Rachel.'

Shoving the note into his pocket he looked up. At once the villagers leaped joyfully out of the truck, arms waving, their white, shaggy heads flung back like raw cotton in the wind. Loudly trumpeting their victory, they dragged him back into the tavern, where the barman had already hoisted a crate of Pacific lager on to the counter and was busy flipping the metal caps on to the floor like broken fingernails.

'Richie,' he heard Meredith shouting from the car. 'Don't say I didn't warn you!'

The villagers paused and then began to laugh. Moments later there was a loud explosion and their laughter suddenly shrivelled and died, blossoming once more as they realised it was the sound of Meredith's car backfiring as it slid out on to the highway.

25

Given the mysterious silence, it might have been an ancient tomb or burial chamber were it not for the collection of flags hanging from the ceiling, their purpose clearly not to honour the dead but rather to trumpet the law of the land; to announce the fact that he, Richard Green was about to go on trial.

And yet even as he stepped into the dock, relieved that at last the truth would be revealed, he found himself facing an empty courtroom. A courtroom bedecked with flags but without . . . Where were they all? The judge and jury? The barristers, the noble silks? Where were the crowds, hungry for justice? The press to record their outrage? He had a right to know; indeed a duty, to free them of their shame.

All at once the doors burst open and the benches filled. Soon the courtroom was buzzing. But there was no indignation. No fury. Along with those seated in the public gallery, the jurors chatted idly amongst themselves, laughing out loud as if the court held no special significance, as if it – and if he – barely existed.

However, noticing his distress they quickly reached out towards him, their ministrations ceasing only briefly as the black-robed figure of the Public Prosecutor appeared in front of the Bench. Their hands caressed and guided him towards his seat, urging him with the intuitive skill of a mother putting her child to bed, to relax, not to be afraid.

But he was afraid. Afraid of the kindness they were using to confuse him. For they knew he was guilty. Everyone knew. He had been neither wrongfully arrested nor beaten up and forced to sign a false confession. As for political dissent? Or conscientious objection? Why, his crime was self-confessed, his trial a matter of form.

Ignoring his protestations, the Prosecutor bowed before the Bench. 'My lord . . .'

'Mrs Chamberlain!' he gasped.

'. . . the Prosecution withdraws its case.'

Immediately the flags overhead began to wave. A hand tugging at his elbow urged him forward to where the public were waiting to congratulate him. Instead he drew back. Their jubilation struck him as cruel and unjustified. They were teasing him. Not only teasing but hiding something from him, from themselves too as they soared upward in their noisy, flag-waving celebrations, ever up, up up . . . Until they saw the depth of his fear and their euphoria like the wax on Icarus' wings began to melt, to evaporate in the distraught, spinning silence. The euphoria of all but one.

His sister hurried to the front of the court. She laughed as she stood up on her toes, plucked a flag from the ceiling and threw it playfully at him. Her wig slipped from a mountain of greying curls and landed on the floor. Shoving it aside with her foot, she dug out her brief from among the folds of her gown and held it up to the crowd as though to encourage them, at the same time, like a nanny, she quietly chided him for sulking.

Bowing to the bench, she announced: 'As Attorney for the Defence I would like to place before the court as evidence, a record of my client's own words, written not long ago and testifying to a change of heart; that change nowhere else recorded except in this single page salvaged from a letter destined never to be sent.'

And then in a loud voice she began to read from the crumpled sheet of blue air-mail paper . . .

> *'. . . by planting himself in the middle of the road you could say he became the Keramuti's answer to 'Chicken' Bell. Except that as a beggar, rather than a matador, he would have had his hands patiently cupped while he waited, watching the trucks charge at him out of the dust. I never once saw him flinch, nor shake his fist in anger at those who raced by. Certainly he was never armed. Nor do I believe he was a decoy for the rascals hiding in the bushes – an opinion Nathaniel himself came to revise, never missing an opportunity to stop and ply the bewildered figure with boiled* kaukau *and cigarettes, specially purchased in Biyufa.*
>
> *'Like 'Chicken' Bell, however, his luck was destined to run out. The victim of a hit-and-run, his body was recovered a short while ago by the police. They say there is little they can do as they lack the resources to investigate. Incidents of this nature are almost a daily occurrence now as the Highway reaches deeper than ever before into the Highlands, like the claws of an ant-eater tearing down the mountain walls, flushing yet more tribes out into the open. Tribes whose prospects, one has to say,*

look somewhat uncertain. For while it's true coffee has made everyone financially better off, it has become increasingly clear that there is a price to be paid.

'You write of a "black hole" in modern education, of youngsters' vanishing aspirations. Here the danger, at least as some see it, is that the Keramuti – its traditions, folklore and ancestry – may soon find itself being sucked into the black hole of the international markets. A fate which has led Rachel to propose the Keramuti send volunteers to work among us at home so that they can determine for themselves the "progress" we have made.

'She, herself, nurses the desire to return home, although no doubt she would deny it. Her mood these days is mostly sombre and she seldom ventures out of the house, preferring the company of her books or else the tranquillity of her modest market garden, established with the help of a handful of women from Kerenga. Her unhappiness isn't altogether new. Rather, I suspect it dates back to Nimile Orapi drowning in the Waragoi, though why she should have taken the boy's death quite so badly, I'll never know. It's almost as though she blames herself. In fact it's as though history were repeating itself; not quite the history either you or mother took for granted, so the truth may come as something of a shock, Janice. Father – that bold, swarthy, khaki-clad figure – alive again and rushing into the room, seeing the shattered glass and me frozen with terror beside the bed; quickly prizing the gun from my hands, taking responsibility upon himself for Mwangi's death . . . "Saw the beggar trying to break in through the window. Thought it was the Mau Mau, start of a raid. You know what it's like these days, Sergeant. State of emergency. Everyone a little jumpy. Rather you didn't question the boy. Fast asleep at the time."

'Could it be that Rachel senses the truth? That like Father she'll return to England bearing a cross that isn't her own? Or is it simply that she knows I cannot stand the thought of leaving, of having to give up everything, all that I've worked for, struggled to . . .'

Her voice faltering, the page slipped through Janice's fingers and tumbled to the floor. Slowly the jury began to stir, rising sluggishly from their seats.

He could detect no sign of anger or pity on their faces, only an immense weariness. Yawning, rubbing their eyes, it was as though, having served on countless juries and engaged in endless debate, they had seen it all before. Having delivered a thousand verdicts, they delivered this, their latest, with the perfunctory air of an animal clearing its bowels: 'Not guilty on all counts'. Adding, almost as an afterthought, that they felt he harboured an exaggerated and misplaced sense of guilt; a guilt that had crippled his father and now was in danger of also crippling him; threatening to erode his natural enthusiasm with a debilitating angst.

Yet it lay within his power, they suggested, to fight back. All it took was a little courage. Fear of the past was all that his crime consisted of; and that wasn't really a matter of any jury. He was free to go. Free to return to the Keramuti, to the scene of his triumphant idealism . . .

'Free?' he cried. 'Triumphant?'

Only to be silenced by the judge, sailing past him into the courtroom. Tall and elegant, her long strides and pursed lips revealed a decisiveness about her role though she wore no wig, merely nodding politely to the court as she assumed her position on the Bench. All of a sudden the jury became agitated, began shouting at her, demanding she hear them out.

Frowning, she turned towards them, her gown transformed into a sweeping sea from whose foaming silk they scampered away, like crabs before the tide, fearful of the tumultuous waves of ribbon seething around her; a saffron, rose and purple spray billowing up against the walls of the court.

'Ladies and gentlemen of the jury,' she announced.

They crouched, shivering in their grey shells.

'It seems to me unfortunate that you should have confused your role with mine; that in mistaking your position you should have failed to grasp what it is the court requires of you. For by asking that you deliver a just verdict we, in effect, demand that your examination of the evidence be as unsparing of yourselves as of the accused. Thus we, that is society, require you put aside all prejudice, banish all thoughts of reprisal, any notion of revenge. In short we demand self-awareness; demand both the openness of self-knowledge and dignity in the service of one's fellow man.'

Imprisoned in the dock, he watched as the spray of multi-coloured light kept bursting around him, throwing into sharp relief the faces of the jury, frightened and pale.

'Now given,' she continued, her voice managing to sound both dispassionate and warm, 'that you have found the defendant innocent, does the evidence – the unsparing examination of ourselves – truly bear out such a

verdict? How for example, do we view the fate of "Chicken" Bell? One surely cannot lay the blame upon Fielding's Garage, upon one, Lewis Chamberlain, a mere apprentice in the trade, whose failure to detect the fault in the car's braking mechanism led to young Adam Bell being so cruelly struck down while on his way to school. How do we view the fate of Nimile Orapi, drowned in the Waragoi? Or the beggar, run down on the Keramuti Highway? Seven-year-old Mwangi, shot in an atmosphere of terror? Are they all to be seen merely as the victims of mischance? Each just happening to be in the wrong place at the wrong time?

Is this not to deny their deaths the sanctity they deserve? To deny ourselves the chance to doubt? Indeed it would seem that we, yes we, ladies and gentlemen, for the defendant does not stand alone in the dock, have grown used to feeding not only upon the suffering of hapless individuals, but upon the lie that such suffering is necessarily inevitable. A price worth paying. Thereby sparing both ourselves and our heirs the pain of self-examination.'

He noticed for the first time under the collar of her gown a tambu necklace. Each tiny, smoke-stained shell fitted snugly into the next, like an infant with its knees tucked under its chin, or lovers curled up beside each other in the dark, forming a delicate chain that sealed and protected an incorruptible love, a natural, unforced integrity. Yet the necklace also contained a number of common giri giri shells. She made no effort to hide this mark of frailty from the court so that slowly the jury began to rise up from their seats, to advance upon the gown of radiant ribbon.

All at once she appeared dwarfed by the Bench, by the coloured flags that began to stir overhead; her long plaits, like staves, pinned her down, enslaving her to a task that was rapidly growing beyond her.

'Yet I put it to you,' she pressed on with determination, *'that by seeking to avoid the pain of self-examination we have achieved the dubious distinction of immunising ourselves against understanding; understanding that may not only save future "victims of misadventure" but also save us from that which makes victims of us all: an environment reeling from the harsh blows which our burgeoning prosperity has delivered.*

What have we, who are immunised against understanding and enquiry, actually learned from our experience of the world? Of the rain-forests, for instance, other than that they are a source of raw materials; of the sea, other than that it is a vast hunting ground? For while the forests breathe on our behalf, we strangle them; while the oceans seek to replenish themselves, we use them as refuse bins; while the hungry starve . . .'

The rustle of flags grew louder, drowning out her urgent delivery. Taking *its cue from the jury, the crowd in the gallery began to chant obscenities at her. Pointing to the dock, they demanded his release, that the charges be struck from the record. The trial, they declared, was a charade with no place in a democracy.*

Fixing her eyes on the floor where the coloured ribbon now lay at her feet, she continued in a firm and defiant voice:

'Life, however often we mutilate it, shall always replenish itself, albeit on a time-scale far different from ours. So it is without despair that I must proceed to the end with a judgement which so many of you clearly find distasteful; a judgement we cannot escape, dare not set aside. For how much longer can we run away? How much further can our empires expand? Indeed is our existence in this world not proof enough of life that we must use our power to deny it? Need we continue following forever in the path of the defendant, banishing the inner voice to the archives, to a cold and barren silence?'

She stood up, a proud yet lonely figure trapped beneath the billowing flags. 'I believe not, ladies and gentlemen. Which is why I find your dismissal of the case on the grounds of mitigating circumstances to be a grave error.'

'Rachel?' *he heard himself cry out.*

'And for which reason I am obliged . . .'

He watched the jury closing in around her. Brandishing bows and steel axes, they stamped their feet and chanted, building themselves up into a frenzy so that the pig gris covering their bodies shimmered like tinfoil in the gloom.

'Rather, it is my duty to deliver—'

'Rachel!'

'—a verdict of—'

'Rachel!' *he screamed.*

26

Dawn, and a cold mist cradled in the valley. At the precast sink below the house Richard stood doing his washing, breaking off now and then to gaze at the ruins of Rachel's market garden where a village pig, its breath steaming, was foraging in the crumbly soil. The day before, the last day of term, pupils from Nimile Orapi's village had come to pull up the remains of the French beans, melons and zucchini to take back to the boy's family. Over the seasons, Rachel had regularly exchanged gifts with the Orapis, learning from them not only the art of market gardening but a little of the science of taxonomy. She had discovered how to identify indigenous plants, how to recognise tubers with toxic properties, how to pick, store and prepare local herbs, to treat infections; how to avoid *pikbel*, dizziness and period pains; she had been taught how to tell which bark was suitable for alleviating coughs and colds, which for easing rheumatism . . . all the while mastering the difficult *ples tok* of the Endai, quietly, surreptitiously. For until recently no one but the women of Kerenga had known about it, nurturing their secret like an illegitimate child.

He wondered what they would make of her abrupt departure. Whether they'd understand the suddenness or feel the same sense of betrayal. Or was this yet another secret shared between them? He knew, already, that there were Endai who blamed him for the beggar's death on the highway; they were said to be talking about revenge. Perhaps the women had confided in Rachel, advised her to leave, reasoning that, 'Where the honey went, there went the honey bird also'. Only surely Rachel would have warned him? Unless she had indeed made a decision . . .

But he was talking round the central question that kept raising itself, like the muddy rugby jersey he was trying to force into the water, billowing up in a bubble of air. He plunged his fist into the middle of it, but it persistently ballooned out on either side. The crux of it was whether he should stay on alone, or return with Rachel to England.

Returning to England would mean following in his father's footsteps . . . being bound by an almost crippling sense of loyalty. It would mean History repeating itself, without hope, or vision; without faith or aspiration, offering only recurring images of the past.

And yet were he to decide to stay it could be argued that that too showed a lack of vision. A readiness to abandon the staunchest expression of man's faith in the future, namely marriage. Recently he had proposed to Rachel, hoping to lift her out of the doldrums, hoping to carve a common destiny out of the lingering uncertainty that would withstand threats such as Meredith's . . . *'Cost yer more than your girlfriend yer not careful, Richie.'*

'Of course it's all very well,' he could almost hear Rachel's voice seeping through the dawn, through the bubbling of hot foam in the sink, 'claiming to be on the side of the villagers, but then have you ever stopped to ask yourself . . . ?'

He shoved his arms deep into the sink. The dye-stained water spilled over the edge, leaving his soiled clothes bobbing near the surface, partially submerged, partially visible in the dawn-lit foam. It occurred to him that one ought to view life in the same sort of way. One had to avoid trying to uncover every little detail, trying to examine every single aspect. Surely it was better to get on with things rather than be constantly dogged by analysis? Like riding a bicycle, the more you thought about it, the more you wobbled.

But there it was again. The question that wouldn't go away, trapped beneath the water in a bubble of air. Not whether he owed it to Rachel but did he have the courage to return to England with her? To accept that one's life belonged not only to oneself but to others with whom one was *olsem*. Did he have the courage to acknowledge these ties – between himself and Rachel, between himself and Janice, above all between himself and the past; to accept that they couldn't be ignored or wished away, that they couldn't be allowed to wither without lasting damage. Well did he?

He could remember staring at the brown suitcase with its dented corners and rusty locks, which the evening before Rachel had dragged out from under the bed. He could remember thinking that the dried insects lying crushed in the bottom were like pieces of confetti and that for the two of them their 'honeymoon' in the Keramuti had come to an undignified end. The smell of death and decay – the musty smell of England – had caused him to slam the lid down on the suitcase, though by then he'd known it was too late. As he tried to parry her criticism of him, even his argument had seemed brittle and lifeless, little more than a desultory skeleton to be picked and scavenged over.

'Of course it's all very well claiming to be on the side of the villagers, but then have you ever stopped to ask yourself whether it's what they want? Jobs, yes; only no longer as farmers, but hired hands; no longer as natural custodians of the forest, but lumberjacks. They see the *wantok* system collapse all round them, to be replaced by stocks, shares and . . . *rugby league*? Is this really what they want? Or is it what the West wants? What *you* want.'

'Which would you rather have, Rachel – the Kumuls versus the Taragau or the Bolgi versus the Endai? Rugby field or tribal battle ground? It's a simple choice. Between the past and the future.'

Rachel proceeded to scoop out the dead insects from the bottom of the suitcase, depositing them among the charred corpses of house moths and mosquitoes in the candle-holder sitting on the chest of drawers.

'You seem to think, Richard, the past is . . . some derelict building just waiting to be pulled down. You should be in property not community development. You could do all the pulling down you liked. And then start again with your "new force", before anyone had time to ask where this new vision of the future came from. This relentless altruism', she added testily, 'where does it come from? Have you ever wondered?'

Their bedroom wasn't much bigger than a boxroom. In it their iron-framed beds stood jammed together, leaving just enough space down the side for the chest of drawers, with a tiny mirror propped up against the inner wall. At the foot of the beds was a small alcove with a clothes rail. She sighed as she reached up and like an exhausted coffee-picker gathered her frayed skirts and faded blouses, her slender fingers wavering among the wire hangers. Outside, a mimosa tree thrust itself against the mosquito mesh, shutting out the sun's dying rays.

He leaned over and in the waning light grasped her hand upon the rail. It felt cold and fragile as it slid away. Rachel immediately withdrew, going down on her knees beside the chest of drawers, emptying each drawer over her shoulder, like a miner wielding a shovel at the coalface. When the last one jammed she swore. Rather than wrestle with it, she abandoned it and proceeded to sort through the rest of her things, her face angled away from him, submerged in an uncompromising darkness that reminded him of Mount Elimbari.

He swooped down over the beds, cracking the jammed drawer open from below with his fist, shattering its flimsy wood. Warily Rachel bent to retrieve the scattered fragments.

'You know,' she remarked, patiently stacking the pieces beside the mirror, 'I read somewhere that most rain-forest soil is actually sterile. It's the leaf-mould the trees feed on. It makes you wonder what the Bolgi would find if they were to clear away some of that fertile mulch that lies strewn about the floor of your own personal forest. That teeming, thriving jungle of concern.'

Leaning on his fists which were buried among the things she had thrown into the suitcase, he saw her eyes reflected in the mirror – the eyes of a child who had just thrown her toy into the fire and now stood watching, tearful and ashamed, as it slowly melted; refusing to make any attempt to rescue it or ask for it to be saved.

Yet he could detect no sign of anger or resentment in the stoic reflection. Her retreat was a bold attempt to conceal her pain, to fold it and pack it away along with the rest of her things, something he thought she'd tried for months on end to do in an effort to protect him. Much as the Bolgi had done that night in Gelmbolg; having woven their *bilum*-like history around him and hoisted him onto their backs, they had sought to prevent him from seeing the extent of their own suffering.

'I'm not suggesting the villagers don't need, or want any help, Richard. It's a question of motives. It's like the oil companies with those adverts for environmental protection and so on. You said they weren't being honest; just driven by the state of their balance sheets.'

'And you?' he cried, tearing his fists like bulging tubers out of the cold layers of her piled-up clothes. 'Just how honest are you being? What's driving you? What's made you suddenly decide you want to return to England? I thought we'd agreed . . .'

'You think I haven't tried to explain and get you to look closer at what we were doing; to examine whether really we had any right . . .' She broke off; even in the mounting darkness her eyes were unable to conceal her distress.

'What do you mean, any *right*? It was the remoteness, the solitude that attracted you to the Keramuti in the first place. There was no mention of right or wrong then. Only the fact that you had a manuscript to prepare and hadn't done the reading. All those books. It's cost a small fortune having them sent out. Haven't been near them in the last month, have you?'

'My work hasn't anything to do with this. It's *us* I'm talking about.'

'It's finished, isn't it?'

'Finished?'

'The manuscript. That's what this is all about, isn't it? Covering up your own selfish motives . . . the fact that the Keramuti's outlived its usefulness.'

'I'm not trying to cover up anything. The Keramuti, us . . . it's all the same. It's all unravelling. We're no longer helping the villagers. We're uprooting them. We're no longer helping ourselves. For heaven's sake, don't you think it's time we – people in the West – started asking why all these Third World societies keep coming unstuck in our embrace? Even you've had to admit you were disappointed; what with the prison break-out, the riot squad, the government's futile attempt to disarm the villagers . . .'

'Hardly the moment I would have thought to jump ship.'

'I'm not suggesting that. All I'm saying is it's time you accepted some of the responsibility.'

'By which you no doubt mean I should throw up everything. The co-operative. The sawmill. Everything I've struggled to achieve. And crawl back to England, like Father; regularly sending out sums of money to atone for my . . . It's only because you still think I'm responsible for . . . Because you, Rachel, no one else, happen to think I killed . . .'

But with the remains of the shattered drawer evoking a clumsy declaration of emptiness between them, he turned and stared fiercely out of the window. Confronted by the wretched tree blocking his view of the valley, its lubricious slopes streaked with purple and gold, he tore at the leaves lying trapped in the wire mesh. Their dry seeds scattered noisily over the floor so that her voice sounded distant like the vague scratchings of a cockroach on the other side of the wall.

'I never said I thought you killed Nimile Orapi. All I said was you – we all – had to share the blame. That's what the Endai were driving at when they staged the "initiation" ceremony at the tavern. They were trying to point out that in the end we are all *wantoks*. We all have a duty to each other, no matter where, or how we live. *Wantok* isn't only the "talk" of one one language, but a one-ness of heart. To claim as you do that you are not in any way responsible for Nimile Orapi's death . . . for the beggars, or even "Chicken" Bell, is to deny . . .'

'Look, here,' he blurted out, 'it was Janice who knocked the boy down, who failed to take the car back to Archie Fielding as soon as she noticed the brakes weren't working properly. I don't see how it has anything at all to do with me.'

'Perhaps if you'd taken the trouble to read her letters – those bleak descriptions of Kingsleigh, with its black holes and immunised youth – you might have understood. Knocking down the child at the bus stop . . . It was more than just an accident. Going to court and pleading guilty when all the witnesses testified to the boy's penchant for playing "chicken". It was a cry for help.'

He pressed his hands against the wire mesh, feeling the wire give, and then begin to bite, biting into the skin, into the hard, dirt-cracked flesh, creating its own fierce patterns, its own harsh map; 'You forget,' he insisted, 'Janice has a penchant of her own for amateur dramatics: throwing lemonade over the Kikuyu children; using the raid on the Edwards' farm as an excuse to follow Margaret Harding to England; spurring Ngai into Father's path in the feeble hope he would change his mind about having him put down. I could go on . . . stumbling through the minefield of the past. Only the old can afford the luxury.'

'It's no luxury,' sighed Rachel, sliding back the empty drawers behind him. 'It's a part of what we do every day. Otherwise we'd lose our sense of direction, lose what little control we have. Altruism isn't enough. It's only the forest canopy, the dazzling green that everyone notices.'

'Everyone except Janice,' he retorted, as the light outside continued to fade; the valley's gilded slopes turning cold and bloodless. 'As far as she's concerned there isn't any canopy. There's only the floor, the sterile soil where she roots about; never lifting her head up through the leaves. I mean, is it my fault Margaret Harding dumped her? That we couldn't afford to keep Ngai alive? That she felt betrayed?'

'I think you'll find your sister's letters say as much about the present as the past Richard; as much about the Keramuti as Kingsleigh. I've left them in the drawer, by the way. You might care to take the trouble to read them . . .'

He swung away from the window and saw those darkened eyes, like pieces of coal, turn to ash as she reached out to close the lid of the suitcase.

'This discussion isn't about Janice,' he said, angrily. 'It's supposed to be about *us* – remember?'

Rachel withdrew her hand, her fingers stealing toward the tambu shell necklace at her throat. Midway she paused and said abruptly: 'In that case, if I'm to commit myself to someone for the rest of my life, it would have to be a person who isn't driven to working for a world that exists somewhere "out there". The Third World exists alright – as much in here between us as outside.' And she shut the lid of the suitcase.

In the end she had gone, driving the Land Rover by herself to Biyufa. He hadn't seen her off. She had slipped away beneath the dawn mist; not starting the engine till she was halfway down the mountain.

He'd lain staring at the wire mesh stretched over the window. It was like the compound eye of a fly, through which one saw the same thing over and over again. Saw only the vast emptiness. The grey dawn. A thin grey light.

It was the way she had left, knowing how much he had wanted her to stay; sad, bruised and yet defiant, his stubbornness wounding her. Slipping silently out of bed, she had pushed open the rusty screen door, pausing before bumping her suitcase like a club-foot down the landing stairs. Left alone, he had just over twenty-four hours to decide: the scheduled flight to Sydney left Fairfax at noon the following day.

He removed his arms with their sleeves of green dye from the water, unbuttoned the oil-stained shirt he was wearing and was about to throw it into the sink when he heard a truck swing off the road and come speeding up the pathway to the house. He turned to see it pull up at the bottom of the landing, its bumper coming to rest against the lower step. Nathaniel jumped out to greet him.

Richard offered a green hand. Failing to see the humour of it, Nathaniel immediately dug out a sheet of paper from his shirt pocket. As he stepped over the pool of water which had formed round the base of the sink, Richard noticed the Bolgi's socks concertinaed about his ankles and his bootlaces were trailing through the dirt. His clothes were creased; his eyes crusty and swollen.

'I left the village while it was still dark,' he said quickly, handing over the piece of paper. Richard unfolded it. 'It is from my mother. But you will recognise my handwriting.'

A handwriting that had always struggled for consistency; those sturdy fingers bent on exploring every conceivable style so that no two paragraphs were ever alike.

' "Dear *masta*," ' he read out aloud. ' "*Masta* must leave the Keramuti today. *Kanakas* come. Young men from the village. They ask compensation of three thousand kina. Same as government fine for Gelmbolg. Young men decide *masta* should pay this fine or they burn his house. Burn down all school. Better *masta* leave. Last chance. *Ol meri sori tumus*. Nathaniel explain all things I not understand before. *Masta* not to blame. *Kanakas* no want to pay government fine." '

At the sound of water overflowing behind him, Richard returned to the sink and shut off the tap. The water was cold. The gas had gone out.

'The Kumul Air flight,' said Nathaniel, staring down at his soggy laces, 'it will arrive within the hour. Or if you like we can go by truck, though I do not think it is roadworthy. It may break down before we reach Biyufa.'

Richard felt the cold creeping up through his bare feet. 'Three thousand kina. What makes them think I have that kind of money?'

'It is too much for one man to pay by himself.'

'They threaten to burn down the school if I don't.'

'My mother is right. It is better you leave.'

'It would show the *kanakas* have beaten us.'

Nathaniel sought to rescue his laces from the expanding fringes of scum.

'Your mother says you explained things to her she previously didn't understand. Perhaps we can explain to the *kanakas*.'

'It is too late for that. All night my mother, grandmother and grandfather, they talked to Nixon. But he is no longer the cause of this problem. It is the young men who have been to Biyufa and to Fairfax to look for jobs but have been unsuccessful. They are saying that the village cannot afford to pay the government fine. Some of the elders have agreed with them. They believe Mrs Green . . . Miss Tormey is fighting on the side of the Endai against our people. So now they are thinking that you too are fighting against them.'

'That's absurd. After everything I've done to help your brother!' Richard replied angrily.

'It's because of your initiation by the Endai.'

'All we did was get drunk together.'

'Some say it was arranged by Miss Tormey.'

'Nonsense. She merely wrote down what they asked her to, same as you have done for your mother.'

'They say she is afraid of losing you. The villagers have seen that all has not been as it should between you and Miss Tormey. Now those elders are saying that she is using the power of Endai witchcraft to help win you back for herself.'

'But she's gone!' he cried. And heard the hopelessness of it ring through the empty house above their heads.

Nathaniel ruefully drew a line across the fringes of spilled water with his boot. 'I am sorry to hear it. Perhaps you will be able to meet up with her at the airport.'

'Doubtless confirming the elders' suspicions.'

'They are old men, Mr Green. For them it is easier to look back than to look forward. You and Miss Tormey agreed to come and live together in the Keramuti. It is right that you should also leave together. If there is any witchcraft in that, it is not what the elders are thinking of.'

'What if I was to raise enough money to pay the fine? Would that satisfy them and convince them neither Rachel nor I have ever deliberately lied or tried to mislead them?'

Nathaniel glanced anxiously over his shoulder at the truck. Richard noticed he had left the engine running. 'Please, Mr Green . . . My mother has sent me to warn you. She says it is the duty of a person who sees the danger coming to warn those who cannot see it. If you were to pay such a large fine then the villagers will think that you are much richer than they thought before and will return again another time. One man cannot be responsible by himself for all their mistakes. It is they, the hotheads, who shot the policeman in the forest; who burned down the tavern, stole the jeep and escaped from jail. It's not you who did any of these things. Whatever they may say, they know in their hearts that they are the guilty ones.'

The mist had cleared. The valley gleamed beneath a creaseless sky, as though it were a piece of coral lit up by the sun. With barely a wisp of smoke, or any sign of movement on the terraces above the Waragoi, it was as if, during the night, the villagers had gathered together all their belongings and trekked across the mountains to Biyufa; abandoning not only their huts but the thatched courthouse with its golden *pit pit* walls and crisp new flag, the hated prison, and lean-to tavern . . . abandoning the dazzling white buildings of the empty school.

It was a relieved yet broodingly silent Nathaniel who followed him out of the house half an hour later. Richard had rinsed the dye from his arms and found a fresh shirt. Driving down the side of the moutain, they saw the latest addition to Kumul Air's fleet of short-haul planes touch down at the far end of the landing strip – a de-Havilland Twin Otter with a Bird of Paradise insignia freshly painted on the tail.

Outside the ticket office Nathaniel finally broke his silence. 'I have a little bit of money, but not enough. Perhaps if you are able to lend me some, you will also buy a ticket for me to . . .'

The whine of the plane's propellers as it taxied to the end of the runway, caused Richard to flinch, while Nathaniel's jaw continued to pump, mouthing words, like a fish that had just been pulled out of the sea. '. . . not an easy thing for me to decide, but if I am to succeed in my future plans . . .'

The plane's engines exploded in a final roar, before cutting back. As the hatch was flung open the first of the arriving passengers, a soldier in crisp new fatigues, stepped out, slinging his rifle over his shoulder.

'. . . it's a chance that I must take. To see things for myself. Up to now I have been unable to escape the . . .' The noise of the plane's engines seemed to linger, drowning out the Bolgi's voice. But in truth Richard's thoughts were focused on an altogether different sound. He was remembering the sound of the Land Rover starting half-way down the mountain – the sudden emptiness stabbing him in the stomach, that had driven him out of bed, out of the deserted house, though it was barely light outside, where with nothing to distract him from the pain, he had started to do his washing. He had plunged his hands into the scalding water in an effort to restore the blood's circulation, to melt the numbness caused by her leaving . . . '. . . *if I'm to commit myself to someone for the rest of my life . . . isn't driven to working for a world . . . "out there". The Third World exists all right . . . as much in here between us as out there.'*

The first soldier was joined by five others. Together they climbed into a waiting jeep which then sped towards the bridge over the Waragoi. There were no other passengers apart from those waiting to board the return flight to Biyufa: a government land surveyor, who had flown in a few days before, with his Chinese assistant, and the postmaster whose wife ran a curio shop in the capital.

Observing a pall of black smoke rising from a heap of burning tyres near the end of the runway, Richard turned once more to Nathaniel.

'What about your uncle's garage? Who's going to keep the books, look after the business side of things now that he's been reinstated in the police? Does your mother know about this? Your grandfather? I don't imagine they'd be all that pleased if they found out I—'

'Please, Mr Green, they understand. It is my decision. I have discussed it with them.'

'It may be a decision you . . . what I mean is now that the state of emergency has put an end to the fighting between your people and the Endai, things in the Keramuti are beginning to look more hopeful. There's talk once more of peace and prosperity, of the need to attract new jobs into the area, new investment; the need to catch up with your *wantoks* on the coast. It won't be long before the Keramuti benefits from the oil next door in Arua, before it, too, becomes rich and prosperous.'

Nathaniel's head dropped, as though for the first time he had noticed his crumpled shirt and scuffed boots with their wet laces trailing behind in the grass.

Smoke from the burning tyres was now drifting across the landing strip and the pilot in the Twin Otter could be heard shouting over the cockpit radio 'Doesn't look too good, Marty; going to make a run for it, mate.' Richard dived hastily into the back of the truck, unlocked his briefcase and pulled out a bundle of letters.

'Look,' he said, pressing Nathaniel to take them, 'we could argue over this for hours, but there isn't time. No doubt there are people in Gelmbolg who'll say, well, that you've fallen for the siren voice of the West; even that I have been that voice, though of course there've been many others, not least your uncle, the people of Malato, Meredith. However, I feel my sister's letters should at least help to redress the balance, especially as there was a time when her situation wasn't all that different from yours. You see, she also wanted to get away. She hated the farm; hated visiting the Kikuyu villages around it, as Father used to do, insisting that we went with him and learnt to appreciate how fortunate we were compared to the children we saw playing in the dust with their wire cars. It wasn't until she'd left, until she'd arrrived in England that she realised she'd made a mistake. Even after all these years. Granted, England may have become her home, but then it's also become . . . Well, I'll let you read the letters and you can decide for yourself.'

While Nathaniel turned over the bundle of airmail letters thoughtfully in his hands, Richard glanced up at the smoke spewing into the sky. The black silken clouds screened out the sun, so that the light in the valley became sombre, almost funereal. Officials scurried down the side of the runway waving their arms and yelling; tiny, shadowy figures, like moths trapped behind a frayed curtain. Once more the cockpit radio crackled. 'Fire's spreading, Marty. Ready for take-off.'

Richard caught the attention of the baggage handler, who darted over to the plane with his suitcase just as the door was being shut. Immediately the de Havilland's engines burst into life and the smoke-scorched valley began to swarm with villagers trying to beat back the fire as it encroached upon the landing strip. The valley appeared to fade, to shrink like a burning photograph — like the compact bundle of letters in the Bolgi's broad hands, containing the lives Janice had managed to condense into them.

'Won't be a moment,' Richard shouted, and hastened into the ticket office. He emerged with two tickets, handing one to Nathaniel. It was a return made out to the capital. 'You can read the letters on the plane and then make up your mind.'

Nathaniel's eyes lit up. 'Fairfax! Why that it is all I'm asking Mr—'

'On my way, Marty,' came the voice from the cockpit.

'Hurry,' said Richard. 'Get your things out of the truck.'

The Bolgi dashed back to the pick-up. Moments later he reappeared, having changed his shirt and combed his hair, though his laces still trailed in the grass. Overhead the clouds of black smoke boiled like tar; the face of Mount Elimbari rising, twisted in eternal pain. Together they ran towards the plane.

Glossary of Pidgin terms

apinun good afternoon
banara bow and arrow(s)
Bambai yumi mekim wanem samting? What shall we do?
bikman an important person
bilas finery; ornaments; personal decoration
bilum all purpose net or string bag
brasbel pouch
brus native tobacco
buai betel-nut
bung wan taim to join and/or work together
fopela ten forty
galip tropical almond
glas belong lukim fa binoculars
gris oil; also pig's fat for smearing
Hayi, yumi yet nogat taim long tok. Yumi wokim strong. We haven't got time to talk. We have to hurry up.
jisas Jesus
kanakas savages
kapok silk-cotton
kapul opossum
kaukau sweet potato
kiap government official
kumul Bird of paradise
kunai sword grass
kwila ironwood
longlong slow; dull-witted
mal g-string
manhaus village meeting house – used only by men
manki young boy (usually uninitiated)
maski forget it

masta white man (also 'waitman')
meri woman
mon walnut
mumu food cooked in earthen ovens; a feast
numba tu kiap Assistant District Commissioner
olgeta everyone
oslem all one
pait fight
pikbel dysentery
pikinini small child
pit pit wild sugar cane, or reeds, used to weave mats and hut walls
pius fuse
plang wooden; of wood
ples tok mother tongue; language of a particular tribe or area
plis police
PMV public motor vehicle: ie licensed to carry passengers
pren friend
puk puk crocodile
pur pur grass skirt
pus pus sex
rabisman rascal
sampela some
sing sing traditional festival involving singing, dancing, feasting
sori tumus very sorry
stesin government post
swetim to sweat
tamiok axe; tomahawk
taragau eagle
teprikoda tape recorder
tisa teacher
tude today
tumbuna grandparents; great-grandparents; ancestors
wara water; river
wok walk
yar casuarina tree
yati teak
Yu no givim maus long mi! Don't give me any backchat!

FIC BOT
Botha, W.P.B.   1665
Wantok   9097

Crossroads School Library
500 DeBaliviere Ave
St Louis MO 63112